THE SMOKE IS RISING

THE SMOKE
IS RISING

MAHESH RAO

This comes with all my best wishes,

Mahesh Rao

DAUNT BOOKS

First published in Great Britain in 2014 by Daunt Books
83 Marylebone High Street
London W1U 4QW

1

Copyright © Mahesh Rao 2014

A CIP catalogue record for this title is available
from the British Library.

ISBN 978 1 907970 31 3

Typeset by Antony Gray
Printed and bound by T J International Ltd,
Padstow, Cornwall

www.dauntbooks.co.uk

TO MY FAMILY

THE SMOKE IS RISING

PROLOGUE

Dusk was stealing into the city. The pitiless heat of the day was now only a memory as a light wind picked up, bringing with it grit and dust from the Bangalore–Mysore highway. The furrows in the sky turned an inky violet and the coconut trees loomed solid and grey. At the northern approach to Mysore, the acrid smell of burning firewood drifted across tin rooftops. By six o'clock, the constant commotion of car horns, autorickshaw engines and accelerating scooters had risen up a register. Trays of freshly baked buns and puffs were being laid out in the Iyengar bakeries, their smell disorienting school children in the streets.

In the centre of the city, the crumbling houses seemed to breathe a sigh as they released residents on to porches and pavements. Office workers stood around food carts, hungrily watching expert hands slicing, seasoning and ladling. A stream of anxious out-of-towners took a wrong turning and headed away from Mysore Junction, their holdalls swinging recklessly. On the corner of Lansdowne Building and Sayyaji Rao Road, several neon signs sparked into action.

Girish paused as he made his way down Staircase B of Jyothi House. Procrastination after work had become something of a habit. He decided against continuing on into the basement to pick up his motorbike and emerged into the smog of Irwin Road. One of his junior colleagues was smoking in front of the building.

'What, sir, had your coffee?' he asked, hurriedly stubbing out his cigarette on the ground.

'Not yet,' replied Girish.

He glanced down at the butt, mashed into the mud. His colleague caught the look.

Shrugging, he said: 'Very dirty habit, sir. What to do?'

Girish did not respond. There was a moment's silence before the young man tried again.

'Going to have your coffee now, sir?'

'I don't know. Maybe. See you tomorrow.'

'Definitely, sir. I will definitely see you tomorrow.'

Girish walked slowly past the vegetable vendors, their gas lanterns emitting a pale, ghostly light. Trade at the novelty shops and fancy stores was picking up, their windows crammed full of *bindis*, bangles and piles of furry toys. At the Central Post Office junction, a boy selling dishcloths and almanacs had stationed himself in a prime position, anticipating the evening rush. In a shop doorway on Kali Temple Road, a tailor raised his voice as he defended his expertise.

As Girish cut through a side street, he glanced into the houses crammed into the block. Artless curiosity still enjoyed full respectability in this part of Mysore. Some windows were shut against the unexpected wind but a number had stayed open, revealing the yellow-blue haze of television sets. In one room a mother fed her baby little scoops of rice while he banged on the floor with a spoon. Next door, a card game was in progress, bowls of roasted peanuts and raw onion scattered across the table, the television's sound turned low to a manageable hum. Further along, an elderly woman was laboriously trying to bring some order to the chaos of newspapers and magazines on the sofa in her sitting room. In the house at the corner, a boy and a girl lay sprawled on the floor, their neglected homework pinned under their elbows as they stared up at the screen.

All the English, Hindi and Kannada news channels were reporting the successful launch earlier in the day of Chandrayaan-1, the first

Indian unmanned mission to the moon. The media had seized the historic moment. One television studio had transformed itself into a mini-planetarium, with a backdrop of shooting stars in front of which a giant silver moon revolved seductively.

'This is the future,' panted a reporter. 'This mission will ignite the imagination of all youngsters. It will give hope to every struggling child in this country. Won't we all remember where we were on this day?'

Girish turned into Sawday Road and stepped into the Vishram Coffee House, smoothing down his hair. He walked to a small table at the back of the restaurant and ordered a sugarless coffee. Service would be slow: the place was almost full.

A television was mounted on a precarious bracket in one corner of the restaurant. Images of the satellite flashed on the screen. There were sound bites from space experts, politicians and, inexplicably, a well-known wrestler. A number of white-coated, venerable-looking scientists sat in a row, their faces fuzzy with anxiety. Archive footage of the first moon landings was spliced with shots of the Deep Space Network centre at Byalalu, an unremarkable village outside Bangalore, stunned by its sudden fame. The camera swooped in to capture the scene it was seeking: cows grazing in the scrubland under the giant antenna that would enable the communication of pictures and scientific data from the satellite.

Next to Girish, the chat at the large corner table of the Vishram Coffee House was becoming animated.

'Seriously Kumar, just suppose you are a politician and you want to take a bribe. Some fellow turns up to your hotel room with crisp notes in a nice briefcase. Will you just count them in front of all and sundry, rub your belly and go home? There have been so many of these sting operations that you would at least be having a few doubts, no?'

'What I am saying is that their greed is too much.'

'But how can they not know about secret cameras? How? Even street sweepers are using them to catch their cheating wives.'

'Look at our poor Kumar. If he was a politician, with a face like that, no one would try and film him, even for some sting-ping operation.'

'And now see this nonsense. Sending spaceships to the moon.'

'You don't know? The government is looking for new areas for housing plots. We have run out here so it is exceptionally vital that we get to the moon before anyone else.'

'But I say, there is no reputable water source there.'

'No matter. There has been no water in Vidyaranyapuram for the last two and a half days. People from here will not notice any difference.'

On the pavement outside the restaurant a flower seller continued to string together jasmine blossoms at top speed. Her head was covered in a maroon knitted scarf and her eyes darted into the crowd, seeking any passing regulars. A novice priest clutching two overfilled plastic bags hurried past a throng of worshippers and walked into the Ganesh temple's side entrance, late for the evening *aarthi*. Charcoal clouds had pushed their way across to settle high above the spires of St Philomena's Church on Ashoka Road and, further away, dark rents had appeared in the sky over the horizon. A minibus stopped abruptly on the corner and disgorged its cargo of student nurses before nosing its way towards Nazarbad.

A sudden flash lit up the television screen in the coffee house, followed by an assault of reds and oranges as enormous globes of smoke moved in. Seconds of dull, lifeless sky later, the space vehicle's tail flared into sight. It pierced through the pale clouds and streaked upwards for a moment before being shrouded by a heavy mist. The white-coated scientists began to clap and cheer, hugging each other and making the thumbs-up sign at the cameras. It had been a perfect launch.

Girish had allowed his coffee to grow cold. He sighed, drained the glass and motioned to the waiter for the bill. It was getting late and he was expected at home. In a short while he would push open the front door to hear his wife turn the television off and scramble to her feet. He would hang his keys on the hook above the metal folding chair. The room would smell of food now cold in its pans.

The waiter finally brought the bill, slapping it down on the table.

'So long to bring one small bill?' asked Girish.

'So long to drink one small coffee?' asked the waiter, his face expressionless.

Girish dropped a few coins on the table and left the restaurant. As he reached Ashoka Road, there was a bang as a tyre burst. The darkness had completed its descent through the branches of the tamarind trees and over the drizzle-spattered shop fronts. Most of the crowds had thinned out but small groups remained outside KR Hospital and in front of the main entrance to Devaraja Market. Girish stepped into the road to avoid a glossy slick on the pavement. A steady stream of autorickshaws still honked their way down Irwin Road, leaving clouds of ugly fumes in their wake. Opposite Jyothi House a ragged figure was dragging a small Godrej wardrobe down a narrow alley that stank of urine.

Girish disappeared down Staircase B. A few minutes later he rode up the ramp from the basement, paused to nod at the watchman and then headed in the direction of Sitanagar. As he passed the approach road to Mysore Junction, he could hear the sound of an express train pulling in to Platform 2. In the distance, looming above his head, the clock on the tower near Sangam Talkies showed a quarter to two, a time it had proclaimed for at least three years.

PART ONE

Summer

CHAPTER ONE

SUSHEELA moved the Leaning Tower of Pisa so that it formed a straight line with the Eiffel Tower and the Taj Mahal. She noticed that the Pyramid of Giza seemed to have slid of its own accord below St Paul's Cathedral. The thought crossed her mind that Uma kept rearranging the formation simply to annoy her. Each fridge magnet secured a vital piece of information and was positioned for ease of reference. Susheela detached a crumpled card advertising a furniture showroom. She ripped it into little shreds and clasped them in her hand. The manager of the showroom had turned out to be a complete buffoon. He had shown no understanding of his trade or her requirements. She would not be repeating that mistake.

She opened the fridge door. Mini cartons of juice were lined neatly along one shelf: apple, orange, grape and guava. Next to them a jug contained about a litre of freshly made lemonade, condensation flecking its rim. If anyone wanted *badaam* milk, the morning's delivery would be boiled and cooled, the ground almonds stirred in, before being chilled in the freezer. As an emergency option there would always be yoghurt, thinned out and churned into a cold *lassi*, spiked with a dash of cumin.

Susheela remembered why she had come downstairs. It was this business with the missing sack of manure. She shut the fridge door; the manure was hardly likely to be there. The bag had invaded her thoughts just as she was beginning her morning exercises and the urge to carry out some form of investigation had been overwhelming. She had abandoned her stretches and come to the kitchen to see if the *mali* had arrived. In spite of his lengthy

17

protestations, she was convinced that he knew something about its disappearance. The nursery owner had been quite clear that he had sent over the sack and she had no reason to suspect his motives.

She walked across to the dining room windows to see if the *mali* was anywhere on the front lawn. Currents of dry heat were already beginning to claw their way up through the room, even at this time of morning. She turned on the air-conditioning unit and it let out a sinister growl. It had not been serviced for a while and a reminder needed to be slipped under the Eiffel Tower. There was no sign of the *mali*. Whether or not he had pilfered the manure, he was definitely late. She wondered for a moment whether he and Uma could have planned something together. Susheela had not spotted any signs of collusion and she had a fine instinct for intrigue being conducted under her roof. Uma was too aloof and reserved to indulge in such treacherous behaviour. Even if the *mali* dropped dead, she would probably just carry on with her work, silently mopping the floor around him.

Susheela knew she should return to her room and complete those exercises but her irritation made her immobile. Behind her, squares of sunlight shimmered on the rosewood table, polished through its nineteen-year life with great dedication. She noticed that the cracks in the plasterwork above the mirror had lengthened, forming a long and lopsided arrow. In the garden there was no movement at all; only a shocking white glare that would become even more ferocious as the day progressed.

Susheela shook her head and disposed of the tattered card. She supposed there was little point in compromising her health over what was essentially a bag of goat waste. The *mali* would be here sooner or later and there would be ample opportunity to uncover the truth. She switched off the air-conditioning unit and went back upstairs.

❖   ❖   ❖

The *mali* rode past the 42 bus stop where buses from the villages outside Mysore came to a shuddering, shrieking halt on their way into the city centre. He slowed down, half expecting to see Uma in the vicinity. He looked around. The morning's pageant in this part of Mahalakshmi Gardens was playing itself out but there was no sign of Uma. He pedalled on, sweat running into his eyes.

At Bamboo Corner a group of rubbish collectors were having a meeting in the shade of the giant bamboo. Their blue jackets had been pulled over their saris and their carts stood parked in a neat line down 6th Main Road. Also under the bamboo, a couple of elderly women were stooped over the parched sward, trying to pick long blades of grass for their *pooja*. The Nachappas' dachshunds were out on their morning constitutional, their little legs plugging along inefficiently. Up and down the locality's streets, newspapers were being lobbed over gates into verandas and balconies. The steady rasps of brooms sweeping out yards interrupted the demented chatter of bulbuls. The shutter of the provision store on 11th Cross Road was half raised; inside, the shop owner was deep in prayer before a sandalwood carving of Ganesh.

Opposite the main gates of the Gardens, the *mali* ran into the Bhaskars' night watchman, squinting at the sun as he adjusted the clutch of plastic bags in his hands. The *mali* brought his bicycle to a halt, trailing his feet against the hot surface of the road.

'Left your shift late again?' he asked.

'Yes, all because of that bastard,' said the watchman, putting down some of his bags.

'Which bastard?'

'He is meant to relieve me at six but not even one day does he turn up on time. He is the purest type of bastard. The genuine article. One of these days I will bury him alive.'

The *mali* had heard details of the proposed interment numerous times and was keen to avoid a further account.

'You are always wandering around with countless bags every time I see you. Like an old woman you are,' he said with a laugh.

The watchman thought hard before responding.

'Of course, make fun, big man. How many months have you been trying to get close to that tasty item inside the house? Seems like your Uma has no appreciation for a hero like you.'

'These things take time.'

'Don't be simply buzzing for too long. The flower will droop and wilt.'

'Go home, *ajja*.'

'Eunuch.'

'Bastard.'

They parted good-naturedly.

The last of the early walkers were completing their final circuits in the Gardens. A huddle of retirees could usually be found by the main gates, caught up in an intense exchange of news: all that had happened in the last twenty-four hours. The last few years had seen an influx of iPod-clutching, midriff-baring, visor-wearing joggers, who had returned for good from Houston, Manchester or Auckland. The t'ai chi habitués were adrift in their practice in the southern corner of the Gardens. A relatively new phenomenon in Mysore, this still attracted the gaze of alarmed older gentlemen, their loose cotton pyjamas flapping as they strolled down the paths. An aggressive display in electric blue spandex was taking place on the monkey bars. The regulars were all there: the speed-walking couple with identical lacquered hairstyles; the man whose principal exertion appeared to be clapping at the *neem* trees; the three rotund, middle-aged brothers who spent their forty-minute amble discussing breakfast options; and the woman in the Yale T-shirt who ran backwards, regularly flicking her head back to avoid an ugly mishap.

On Gulmohar Road the *mali* paused to wipe his face. He had

tried to set off earlier than usual, knowing that his conduct needed to be exemplary over the next few days. *Amma's* eyes would be following him continually until she forgot about that missing sack of manure or found something else to occupy her mind. But he had slept badly and was now struggling to make it on time. He began pedalling again, past the large bungalows with their forbidding wrought-iron gates, the Spanish-style villas set in green quads and the corner house shaped like a violin. He finally turned into 7th Main Road and stopped outside a neat house, smaller than its neighbours, surrounded by a low compound wall.

Knowing he was in full view of the front windows, his features creased into an expression of honest industry. He wheeled the bicycle in through the gates and propped it up against one of the pillars of the carport. It looked like Uma had not arrived yet and so he stayed away from the front and back doors. The gravel on the path leading to the shed looked white in the dazzling sunshine. Deciding not to take on the blaze, he squatted in a small patch of shade under the dining room windows, sluggishly tracing his fingers through the desiccated soil. His days usually began with a steaming coffee, set down in his steel *lota* by Uma next to one of the sinks by the back door. He leant over the spent blossoms of the hibiscus shrubs. As a bead of sweat from his face dropped on to a bud's wrinkled lobe, he settled down to wait.

In the master bedroom Susheela inhaled deeply and tried to hoist herself up on her arms, fixing her gaze on the corniced ceiling. Her wrists seemed to be made of moist clay. She renewed her attempt, managed to hold the position for a few seconds, before setting her head back down on the mat. A strange pain had launched itself between her shoulder blades, as if to counterbalance the throbbing circle around her right ankle.

21

There was a time when she would have taken herself off to see Dr Bhat for any such complaint, even if it meant having to endure his hyperactive receptionist and the jolt of her vigorously hennaed hair. Such frequent visits to the doctor, however, had become embarrassing. Although his manner was always solicitous, he probably assumed that she had little else with which to occupy herself. She recalled their last conversation, which had taken place as the doctor scribbled on a pad.

'You must think I'm a hypochondriac, doctor, but truly, this cough has not gone for weeks,' she had said, wishing he would look at her, rather than at his own jerky hand.

'There is no need for any concern at all, you are absolutely in the pink,' he had responded, still failing to meet her gaze.

'But, after all, something must be causing it?'

'Without a doubt. But you please don't worry. I am here, no? How are your daughters? Doing well, I hope?'

'They are doing very well, thank you. They were also a little worried about this cough, you know. They have been pestering me to get it investigated.'

'Oh yes, good thing that you came to see me. The body is such a complicated instrument, isn't it? The important thing is to be happy and enjoy a positive outlook. Joyful thoughts, in fact.'

'Doctor, to be most frank with you, I don't think my thoughts are more or less joyful than anyone else's, but not everybody goes around having a strange cough for weeks.'

'That is true. But in worrying about such matters one forgets that cheerfulness is the true medicine in life. An elixir, in fact.'

Susheela had given up. She had taken his prescription, a tonic that was apparently beneficial for general health and all-round well-being, and left the clinic in a state far removed from the recommended joyfulness.

Apart from the ankle and the shoulder blades, the last three months had also seen the appearance of a patch of dry skin on one thigh and an unaccountable watering of her eyes every time she lay down. Susheela had learned stoicism and a benign neglect. She no longer discussed matters with the Nachappa boy, who was a junior doctor at St Theresa's, and avoided the temptation of consulting an online compendium of illnesses. Given the array of symptoms, no doubt she would be able to diagnose herself with everything from aphasia to scurvy.

Some aspects of aging were easier to accommodate than others. The trouble, she thought to herself, in her most private moments, was that having had a face once widely acknowledged to be beautiful, one could hardly be expected to make an accurate assessment of its current merits. Just as an old but treasured cardigan would fail to reveal its frayed seams and baggy sleeves to its devoted owner, Susheela had begun to suspect that she had been rendered blind to a number of indignities in her facial appearance.

When she looked at her face she saw a woman who looked perhaps fifty-four rather than sixty-four. She saw good skin, lighter than the matrimonially prized 'wheatish', large brown eyes flecked with hazel, a fiercely proportionate nose and a well-defined Cupid's bow that gently dropped her mouth into a soft vulnerability. She saw a slightly fleshy chin and a deep fold of skin that had somehow nudged its way to the top of her neck. She saw a deep dimple in her left cheek when she smiled and a faint crease radiating out under each eye from the top of her nose.

All this she saw but was this what everyone else saw too? And when they had seen it, what did they make of it? She knew very well that what anyone saw or thought about her looks did not matter ten *paise* at her age but, in spite of herself, she still felt the need to place herself within an assembly of women of her generation. She pictured a line of dumpy elderly women in shawls and Kanjeevaram silks, *chappals* slapping against the floor as they walked across a stage, adjusting their sashes and tiaras.

As for her body, on the other hand, there she was perfectly confident that she had not been spared any realisations on the subject of its decline. Over the years it was clear that her hips had widened, apparently seeking to conquer with bulk what could not be conquered by grace. She was conscious of a solidity in her upper arms that she could not remember from her youth. Her stomach, she felt, was a disgrace. Obstinate and insistent, it seemed to pillow around her, taking no notice whatsoever of her hostility. Where had this flesh come from? It was at least fifteen years since Susheela had properly regarded herself as slim but her changed form still took her a little by surprise.

Susheela turned her head to look at the clock on the bedside table. She rolled on to her side and then slowly stood up, feeling between her shoulder blades for the exact source of this new visitation. A short bath later, it seemed to have subsided as she uncoiled the thin cotton towel from around her head. Her hair was still a little wet and had settled in stubborn waves down to her shoulders. Above her ears, Reshmi, her hairdresser, had artfully left a few strands of subtle grey.

'In all good lies, there must be a little bit of truth,' Reshmi had pronounced.

The rest of Susheela's hair proclaimed itself a glossy black. It was a fiction that she felt that she owed to the world and one in which the world ought to collude gratefully. This was not so much a matter of vanity as mutual courtesy. She picked up a comb and began to run it through her hair, wincing as she broke through tangle after tangle. Every day the same: first the right side and then the left, and then sweeping motions over her crown and the back of her head, all culminating in a sad fuzz of jilted hair, plucked from her comb and dropped deftly into the waste-paper basket.

In the bottom drawer of the teak dresser in the dining room was a picture album, the pink and grey floral swirls on its cover a reminder of her early married life. A third of the way into this album, carefully pasted on to the lower half of the page, lay a photograph of Susheela at the age of twenty-four. This image of herself had over the years become embedded in her mind and she clung to it without ever having meant to do so.

The photograph had been taken on a trip to Mount Abu with her husband, Sridhar. The year was 1968. '*Mere saamne wali khidki mein*' crackled out of transistor radios in tea shops, university hostels and railway station waiting rooms. Indira Gandhi was in Thimphu, discussing democracy with the Bhutanese monarch. In Tamil Nadu bursts of agitation continued against the declaration of Hindi as India's primary official language. The Beatles transcendentally meditated in Rishikesh, a group of friends in tow, and, quite coincidentally, condoms were being distributed and marketed across rural India by the large tea, petroleum and chemical corporations in a government family-planning initiative.

The photograph's white border, mottled by an unidentifiable substance, had curled up at the corners and a yellow tinge had washed across the scene. Sridhar had taken the photograph in the early evening of their first day at the hill station. Susheela's sari, a green Japanese georgette with a brown geometric motif, seemed to shimmer in the light, although she would have been horrified at the suggestion that she might have been dressed in anything that lent itself to a daytime gleam. Her hair was perfect. She had resisted the vulgar pull of a Sadhana cut or a beehive but some limited backcombing had given her face the composition that she had sought. A couple of kiss curls were a further concession to the era but the glossy braid that hung heavily over her left shoulder was timeless. Her posture was stagey, right arm tilting awkwardly by her slender waist and her chin lowered in a reproduction of cinematic coyness. In the background, the clutter of structures on the hillside looked about to pitch into the orange waters of Nakki Lake.

The last time she had looked at the picture had been a couple of years ago when her daughter had been recovering from chicken pox. It was a humid June day and Priyanka had been lying in the sitting room, listlessly turning the pages of the album, one eye on the Wimbledon match unfolding on television.

'God, *amma*, you look just like Sharmila Tagore in this one,' she had said, rather incredulously, it had seemed to Susheela.

'Yes, maybe when she played a mother's role in her fifties,' had been Susheela's retort.

'No, really. I think it's the hair and the shiny shiny sari.'

The photo album continued to be confined to the dresser drawer.

Her hair done, Susheela stood up and got dressed, picking out a purple silk sari with a black border. She adjusted the angle of the dressing table mirror, moved across to close the bathroom door and then straightened the edge of the bedspread. As she went downstairs, she wondered why Uma had not yet arrived. Maybe she was up to something with the *mali*.

Uma's eyes opened just as the train heading south to Mayila-duthurai wheezed into Mysore Junction. Only a row of dilapidated sheds, a slope covered with banks of refuse and a collapsing chain-link fence separated her home from the outlying platforms of the station. The sky was a sooty grey in the gap that ran around the room between the wall and the corrugated iron roof. In the near darkness, Uma's eyes focused on the wooden frame of the picture of Shiva on the wall. The liquid eyes and the open palm would only be visible after another hour or so when the light filtered through the gap and the room's tiny window. Uma shifted slowly on the thin foam mattress. Her skin felt flushed and sticky, the sheet twisted into a clammy wreath underneath her.

In one corner of the room, a pipe with no tap extended over a square of lumpy cement, surrounded by an uneven brim. Apart from the mattress, the room also contained a tin trunk and a plastic chair. Placed on the trunk were a small mirror, a comb and a bar of soap. Uma sat up and tried to perform the deep breathing exercises that Bhargavi had shown her. *Pranayama* would help bring peace to the mind and take away all fears and negative thoughts, she had said. Uma closed her left nostril with her thumb and inhaled deeply through the right one. After a few tepid attempts she stopped. She kept losing count and was not sure she was following the correct order in any case. She would probably just have to learn to live with the negative thoughts, at least for today.

She reached for a small scarf and wound her thick, fractious curls into a tight coil at the nape of her neck. Once she had bathed, she would begin the process of marshalling them into place, drawing them into a neat braid. When she was about six or seven, the neighbourhood children had scored a complicated ditty involving her 'hair like steel wool' and 'skin like charcoal' before moving on to another victim some months later. Even after their overtures had ceased, the hair continued to be an issue: agonising sessions of her mother's firm tugs and jerks as she tried to bring order to the jet black kinks. The skin remained even more of an issue, a plague that was impossible to hide.

Uma unbolted the door and stepped outside. There was movement even at this early hour. Her neighbour's daughter walked past, a mewling toddler hitched to her waist. The sound of water drumming against plastic filled the air. Somewhere a radio droned out the news while its owner hawked loudly by the gutter. Uma picked up her two plastic pots and, rubbing the sleep out of her eyes, walked down the row of rooms to take her place in the morning queue at the tap. Parvathi, her neighbour, was already there and smiled weakly at her. It was too early to exchange any pleasantries. The earth around the tap had been churned into a grey sludge, trailing skeins of banana leaves and strips of newspaper. Uma shut her eyes and pressed her pots against her chest as she waited to reach the front of the queue.

At the opposite end of the row another queue was growing, this one for the toilet. Uma walked quickly back to her room, her muscles taut with the weight of the water. Dumping the pots behind the door, she made her way out again towards the toilet, clutching a mug of water. A rooster seemed to have joined the queue in front of her, jerking its head and puffing out its feathers, as if in an attempt to be escorted to the front. Uma looked down and waited. A man now stood behind her: she could see his cracked feet in the blue rubber *chappals*. The wait to use the toilet in the morning seemed to be getting longer these days. Maybe more people were living in the rooms in this row. Then there was also the landlord's teenaged son who had taken to smoking in the toilet, barricading himself in there for ten minutes at a time, leaving behind a rank fug and a floor covered in cigarette butts. As she waited, Uma felt an almost imperceptible tug at her sari, a sough that instantly made her stiffen. She stood very still. It happened again; a soft but deliberate graze against the backs of her legs. She did not turn around, praying that the toilet door would open. The feet in the blue rubber *chappals* seemed to have moved closer.

Just then a man emerged from the toilet, wiping his hands on a towel slung over his shoulder. Uma rushed in and firmly locked the door behind her.

Mala could feel the hot sand pulsating through her *chappals* as she walked down the gradual decline to the river. She slipped them off and for a second the blistering charge against the soles of her feet made her spine ache. Drawing up her sari a few inches, she stepped quickly into the water and gained instant deliverance. Here the river bed was nearly forty feet wide where it gently swung away towards the lean scrubland further downstream. The stately progress of eucalyptus trees on both sides of the river came to a halt as the steep banks dipped into this gentle grainy bowl. The sustained dry spell had assailed the river basin and the water level was in full retreat.

Despite the mid-morning heat, various groups had made their way across the scalding dune to the water's edge. Four young boys had stripped off to their shorts and raced into the river. Mala squinted at their brown bodies glancing off each other as they whooped at the world around them. Following some prearranged signal, the bodies disappeared for a few seconds before four pairs of inverted legs emerged in a row, pointing shakily at the sky.

A boy in trousers rolled up to the knee was offering to take people across the river and back for ten rupees.

'Madam, you want a boat ride?' he asked Mala.

She shook her head.

'It will be like heaven,' he said, his eyes rolling in earnestness.

Mala could not help smiling. But she shook her head again.

The boy looked crushed and then, quickly recovering, disappeared into the cluster of kiosks that inevitably sprang up in the fecund earth around tourist sites.

At the top of the dune, behind the low wall, one hundred and one stone steps led to a temple that faced the high lustre of the river. The temple's roof was supported by thirty-six pillars bearing inscriptions in praise of the resident deity. A frieze of rearing horses ran over the plinths that formed the base of the structure. At its main entrance, the fangs and bulbous eyes of the carved sentinel served as a warning to tourists unable to muster sufficient interest in the history of the shrine. Taking his cue from this figure, a priest stood on the uneven porch and looked bleakly at the figures below, before returning to the solace of a large potato bun.

Mala looked at her feet, strangely flat and wide in the rippling water, like brown table-tennis bats. She wiggled her toes and a puff of sediment rose up to obscure the dull glint of her toe ring. Sweat was now running down her back, the fierce heat basting her arms and her neck. She looked around for Girish, who was deep in conversation with the father of the boat-boy. It was his usual sociological burlesque: what is your native place, who lives with you, how many children, how old are they, what do you grow, where are your parents, how far is your native place? Mala had seen the performance countless times. Girish would never listen to the responses, preferring instead to stack up more questions, revelling in the beneficence of his camaraderie with the drivers, the guides and the porters.

This time the conversation had veered into local politics. The constituency's MLA had recently succumbed to his injuries following a disastrous attempt at skiing in Kufri. A by-election had been called and the opposition was taking full advantage of the district authority's failure to construct a bridge at Suvarnadurga, four kilometres away. In fact, plans for the bridge had been stewing for nearly a decade. Opinions had been canvassed, engineers had been consulted, funds had been allocated, contracts had been awarded and invoices had been raised. The bridge, however, remained unconstructed: a footnote in the life of the late MLA for Suvarnadurga.

Girish waved at Mala, gesturing towards the tea stalls. She shook the water off her feet, slipped on her *chappals* and walked heavily up the dune again, the coarse sand cleaving to her toes. Girish was seated at one of the few shaded tables. She had felt his gaze all the way up the dune but had kept looking down at the little gullies her feet were making in the sand. She sat down opposite him, wiping her neck with her *pallu*.

'So do you know about the myth?'

'No, what myth?'

'About the temple.'

When Mala looked blank, Girish continued: 'It seems that there was a just and responsible king who ruled this area in times of yore. He always looked after his subjects and made sure that they did not start filing public interest litigation cases.'

Mala flashed a hurried smile in response.

'The king was looking for a bride and began praying to the river god to assist him. Using the river god as marriage broker, you could say. So, after the king had prayed for many months, the river god was satisfied and offered him his daughter's hand in marriage. The daughter, it seems, was a very beautiful creature. And also very entertaining.'

The coffee and *vadas* he'd ordered arrived and Girish broke off to examine them. Satisfied, he popped half a *vada* into his mouth with a smudge of chutney, shuffling the hot mouthful around with his tongue until it was cool enough to swallow.

'Yes, so this daughter could tell amazing stories, dance beautifully and play lots of instruments. The king was completely bewitched and married her with no delay. But then what happened is that the king became obsessed with his new wife. He began neglecting his state affairs and all his subjects began to suffer. You could say that he was the model for our politicians today.'

A girl appeared at the table, holding out calendars for sale. Girish looked around impatiently for the tea boy. Within a few seconds, the girl darted away, her skirt billowing behind her.

'Anyway, neighbouring kingdoms began to make plans to attack this state and the subjects began to starve so they begged the river god to make the king come to his senses. It seems the river god appeared before the king and scolded him for his dereliction of duties. The king was very arrogant, thinking that he did not need the river god any more, now that he had his beautiful daughter. So the river god punished the king by making his daughter invisible.'

A fight had broken out between two stray dogs in the parking area and it was a minute or so before their ferocious barking receded into a series of cartoon yelps.

'Some people, I think, will question whether making a wife invisible is real punishment.'

Girish smiled at Mala and then continued.

'But the king was highly distraught. He began to pray again to the river god, agreeing to any kind of penance as long as his wife was returned to him in visible format. The river god agreed to return his daughter, but only on condition that the king pray non-stop for forty days, restore the good fortunes of his subjects and also build a temple where the river god could always see it.'

Mala's eyes ventured a glance at the next table as Girish spoke. A couple were holding hands across the table's ringed surface. The tea boy set down two bottles of cola, flimsy straws capering at the top. Red and green bangles clinked on the woman's lower arms as she traced little circles on her husband's palms with the tips of her fingernails.

Mala stole another look. The woman was wearing a white *salwar kameez*, the fitted bodice showing off her contours. She stretched out her arm and turned the two pens poking out of her husband's shirt pocket so that they would be correctly ranged for any impromptu drafting. Her hand moved upwards and her fingers swept through her husband's hair, brushing it away from his side parting. Spotting a crumb at the edge of his mouth, she flicked it away and ran her thumb across his bottom lip.

Mala turned back to Girish and their eyes locked. She looked down at her lap and then across at the spread of the sluggish river below. Girish reached out for the sole paper napkin sitting in a plastic tumbler on the table and began to wipe his hands meticulously.

The doorbell rang at a quarter past eleven, spooling out a joyless version of 'Edelweiss'.

'Actually on time,' thought Susheela as she smoothed down the front of her *pallu* and walked towards the door.

Sunaina Kamath made her usual entrance: she walked into any room as if expecting to interrupt a vibrant conference. Her apparent disappointment at being confronted by only Susheela and a potted philodendron was quickly swept away as she took off her sandals.

'How are you, Sush? This heat, I can't tell you. It gets worse every year.'

Behind Sunaina, Malini Gupta smiled woodenly as she took in her surroundings.

'I don't know whether it's the global warming or getting older or maybe both. But I definitely seem to feel the heat a lot more these days,' sighed Susheela. 'Please come, Malini. First time you're coming here, no?'

Sunaina sank into a brocade sofa.

'Oof, I think I'll just stay here for the rest of the day and not move.'

Slightly rested, she let out an abrupt chuckle. Her dimples gave her face a softer, more pliant aspect as she dabbed at her neck with a man's handkerchief. Sunaina's hair always looked as if she had walked into it quite by chance, the unyielding bob anxiously perched over her face. She stuffed the handkerchief into one of the many pouches in her handbag and looked ready for business.

Malini Gupta sat straight-backed on a leather and bamboo stool despite Susheela's attempts to navigate her towards the more comfortable corner armchair. Susheela saved herself some trouble and focused her attentions on Sunaina, it being widely known that Mrs Gupta's only interests were the cave paintings of Ajanta and the arthritis in her big toe.

The social call slid into its characteristic rhythm. More on the hot weather, children, other family, traffic, general health, specific health, completed building works, anticipated further building works, weight gain, weight loss, cooks, maids, drivers and gardeners.

Sunaina dragooned her way through topics like a seasoned politician, mindful of all reasonable views but keen to move on to other more significant issues. She was convinced that her uncompromising sense of community responsibility and benevolent participation gave her a nose for what mattered. If questioned, she would have been hard-pressed to define the community for which she toiled so industriously. In fact, the question would probably only have served to irritate her: the kind of mindless prattle that got in the way of people setting agendas and achieving objectives. Nevertheless, she recognised the importance of weighty nomenclature. Sunaina had always believed that if one invited gravitas, patronage and influence would automatically follow.

She was therefore an indispensable member of the Association of Concerned and Informed Citizens of Mysore, the chair of the Mysore North Civic Reform and Renewal Committee and the secretary of the Vontikoppal Ladies' League. No less impressive was her record in the inner circles of the Mahalakshmi Gardens Betterment Association and St Theresa's Humanities College Alumni Society. She also gave freely of her time to any number of spontaneous causes and supplicants.

In some quarters her tireless public efforts were viewed as a deliberate counterpoise to her husband's cantankerousness. A canny property developer, he seemed to relish his renowned irascibility, picking fights with even the *paan* seller outside Mindy's. The most recent outrage had been an ugly scene involving an overturned basket of chrysanthemums outside the Chamundeshwari temple. During her early married life, Sunaina had appeared to have a firm grip on her husband's unpredictability. She had regarded her handiwork with the pride of a dog trainer who had made a success of a particularly idiotic mongrel. But over the years the cur had reverted to form and ever more florid notes of apology had been required to appease her relatives and neighbours.

Susheela wondered when exactly Sunaina had begun to call her Sush. She was certainly the only person in the world to do so. Uma appeared briefly to serve the chilled juice and some light mid-morning snacks. Sunaina greeted the *malai chum chum* and the cashew *pakoras* with protestations, grudging acceptance and then a cheerful zeal. The air-conditioning system rattled away in the background.

'Oh Sush, you're really trying to finish me off,' Sunaina groaned, biting into another *chum chum*. 'Just after scaring us with all these health stories, you serve us these heart attacks.'

Malini Gupta had barely touched her plate. A corner had been nibbled off just one *pakora*. Susheela made a mental note.

Talk turned to Sunaina's nephew, whose disinclination to find paid employment troubled her like an ingrown toenail.

'At least he doesn't gamble or, you know, conduct himself in loose ways,' said Susheela.

'Birdwatching,' said Sunaina with disgust. 'That's the only thing he's interested in. Always leaping up to tell you that he spotted some crested crow with three legs.'

'But I suppose it doesn't do any *harm*.'

'It doesn't do any *good* either. He may be comfortably off, but as a life, what does it amount to, all this lying around in puddles, gazing at hens?'

Malini Gupta seemed to cheer up a little at the thought of the dismal prospects of Sunaina's nephew.

The morning's paper lay folded and pressed flat on the coffee table. The front page revealed that the High Court had granted a fresh stay order on any construction at the site of HeritageLand. The saga of the proposed theme park, one of Asia's largest, seemed almost immemorial. Every call of support or protest was eagerly absorbed into the civic ether as if the pitch for construction was the real entertainment envisaged by the park's creators. Almost every aspect of the project was endlessly debated in the local press, the choice of site and acquisition of land being the most controversial. The editor of the *Mysore Evening Sentinel* was unequivocal in his warning: 'If we don't hurry up and build the damn thing, the Chinese will do it, like they do everything else.'

'As for this so-called HeritageLand, I don't think we will ever see it in our lifetimes,' said Susheela.

'I am just sick and tired of hearing about it,' said Sunaina, her hands fluttering to her temples.

'Every day there is another press release, another exclusive. The park will only have five-star hotels, it will have five thousand fountains, it will be seen from space.'

'Apparently we will be able to experience a day in the life of Tipu Sultan there.'

'Didn't he spend his days flinging Britishers off a cliff?'

'Maybe that's what they intend, although I hope not. Think of the mess. Just when street cleaning has improved in our localities.'

Sunaina gulped the last of her juice like a stricken heroine.

A bee had somehow made its way into the dining room and its dull drone was interrupted by the thud of its deranged lunges at the closed window. Malini Gupta glanced at the moulded ends of the curtain rail, shifted on her stool and once again examined her uneaten *chum chum*.

'So, what made you late this morning?' asked the *mali*, as Uma carried a basin of dirty utensils to the outside washing area at the back of the house.

She gathered up the folds of her sari, tucked them between her thighs and squatted to turn the tap on. The *mali* walked around to one side of the tap and looked down at the top of her head.

'Definitely in a bad mood,' he said.

'*Amma* said there were plates under the pots on the upstairs balcony that need to be cleaned,' Uma said. The water sprayed halfway up her thin arms and wet the edges of her sari.

'Can you get me another cup of coffee? Even in this heat, my stomach is feeling cold inside.'

Uma did not respond. She quickly rinsed the last of the steel tumblers, laid it out on a mat in the sunshine and hurried back inside the house, without giving him another look.

The sun was lower in the sky but the dry heat still bore away with the same intensity. Seated on the low wall, Mala looked for the hyperactive boys but they were nowhere in sight. Girish sat next to her, his arm slung across her shoulders like a sandbag. He occasionally clicked his fingers as if in time to some mysterious strain unfolding in his head. A few minutes later he stood up and stretched.

'Time to go, Mala. We've got that journey back,' he said, heading towards the parking area.

The square of shade in which the car had been parked had pivoted around to the right, leaving it fully exposed to the day's fury. Its interior felt like a hot, fetid mouth and the seat began to brand Mala's back and thighs. Girish reversed out of the parking area and slowly began the descent down to the rutted road.

The car was fairly new. Its purchase had been preceded by lengthy consultations with colleagues and relatives. Girish had pored over motoring magazines, scoured road user websites and posted detailed queries on car information forums. The Maruti dealer had come to their home three times and had fielded countless telephone calls. Finally, the loan was arranged, the EMIs fixed and the vehicle delivered on an auspicious day, before Rahu reared up to cause any chaos. Girish had driven the car carefully to the Venkateshwara temple in Sitanagar, a marigold and jasmine garland looped over the bonnet. As the priest reeled off the blessing, Girish stared at the new number plate. His intermittently professed rationalism had been given the day off. Girish was not a man who liked to take chances.

The thrill of ownership had faded rapidly. Three months after the purchase, the blue hatchback looked drab and niggardly, parked by a pile of macadam left in the lane beyond their front gate. With the surging price of fuel, the car had already become of incidental use: shopping excursions, day trips, weddings. Girish continued to wash and polish the car conscientiously, having read about the dangers of oxidation.

As Girish eased the car into second gear, he glanced at Mala next to him. She had lowered the sun visor and her head was turned towards the window on her side. The condition of the road seemed, at least to Girish, to have worsened inexplicably over the course of the day. The car shuddered and bounced as Girish weaved around pits and potholes. Here and there a darker smear of tar indicated a hurried patching up, maybe in anticipation of a VIP visit or a festival procession.

The car passed through a village, extinguished for the afternoon, and turned on to the wider trunk road at the next junction. Mala continued to stare at the deserted land. The monotony of the dry paddy fields on either side was oppressive. Diamonds of stubble and loam rolled past, at times broken up by a meagre windbreak. Girish slowed down as they approached a bridge. As the car moved across it, Mala looked through the white railings to see that the river below had shrunk drastically. The anarchy of rocks and exhausted channels on the river bed resembled a strange moonscape. She noticed that someone had abandoned a bundle of clothes on the wall of a culvert. It was the only sign of softness in that unforgiving scene.

'Shall I open the windows? At least the breeze might help,' said Mala.

'No, too much dust. Just turn that vent more towards you.'

They were bearing down on a van that was cruising along in the middle of the road. Girish hooted impatiently and flashed his lights. The van seemed to begin moving into the left lane and then shifted again so it was squarely in the centre of the road.

'Look at this idiot. Who gives licences to these bloody fools?' Girish let out a series of sharp honks and flashed his lights again.

An arm emerged from the van, undulating in the air.

'What is this idiot doing? What the hell is that supposed to mean?' More hooting followed.

The arm continued to motion and then, a few seconds later, withdrew.

Girish moved to the extreme right of the road, his hand pressed down on the horn. There was no oncoming traffic but he still could not overtake.

'Is this fool crazy or deaf? If he wanted me to pass, why doesn't he move?' Girish nosed as close to the van as he could without causing a collision. His hooting was now just an endless, insistent blast.

The van began to gain speed, still in the middle of the road, and pulled away from the blue hatchback.

'Finally,' muttered Girish, adjusting his seat belt.

In an instant the van swerved sideways into the middle of the road and stopped, blocking the road. Girish slammed his foot on the brake and the car jolted to a halt, tearing violently at the uneven surface of the road.

Girish had taken his hand off the horn and a foreign silence descended. Mala turned to look at him. He was staring straight ahead, expressionless. The van's door opened on the driver's side. There was no further movement.

Girish's hands remained on the steering wheel, the veins fanning out like the talons of a bird of prey.

A man jumped out of the van. He was slight and athletic looking, dressed in jeans and a tight vest, his hair cropped short. He approached the car at a leisurely pace, swinging a length of cloth.

Mala whispered: 'Oh God, Girish, please don't say anything.'

The man knocked at Girish's window and then pressed his palm against the glass, his flesh pale and turgid. He knocked again, this time harder.

Girish opened the window. The man leant down: '*Lo bhosdike*, what's the problem?'

Girish stared blankly at him. Mala pushed her handbag with her feet into the far corner.

'I said, what's the problem?'

'There's no problem.'

'Really? You make a lot of noise for someone with no problems.'

'There's no problem.'

The man took a long look at Mala and then shrugged: 'If you say so, boss. Too much tension. You need to relax.'

Girish was silent.

'Okay boss, if you say no problem, then there really is no problem.'

The man took another look at Mala and then sauntered back to the van, still swinging the length of cloth. In a moment the van's engine fired up and it sped off.

The man's hand had left a greasy imprint on the window. Girish waited until the van was out of sight. He opened the door and spat into the road. Closing the door, he adjusted the mirror, restarted the ignition and began to move slowly forward.

Neither of them spoke for a few minutes until Girish looked sharply at Mala.

'What do you think I would have said?'

'What?'

'You told me not to say anything. What do you think I was going to say?'

'I don't know. Nothing. I just didn't want him to get angrier.'

'Because I don't know that much? That I should not make a crazy rowdy like him angry.'

'I didn't mean anything. I was just scared.'

They were approaching the bend in the road at Bannur. Billboards scudded past: models entwined in cords of gold, rows of premium quality rubber *chappals* and earnest invitations to MBA courses in Australia. A truck carrying wobbling stacks of timber lurched in front of them. On top of the planks sat a sallow-faced man, his dead eyes focused on some distant point.

The rest of the journey passed in silence.

CHAPTER TWO

Venky Gowda had only ever sustained one vision in his life: HeritageLand. He dreamed of a world where cutting-edge technology could harness the drama of the ancient epics and transport his compatriots to an alternate reality. When he slept, he twitched and kicked, mouthing his plans for a recreated Dandaka forest where the curious could follow in Lord Rama's footsteps, battle the Lankan army in an elaborate flume, cut off Shurpanakha's ears and nose with laser arrows, soar to the treetops in a mechanical Garuda. His cupboards were crammed with notes for a Kurukshetra War simulation involving luxury chariots and a buffet service. Napkins within his reach were covered with doodles of the Kailash Wonder Mountain and the Yamaraja Monorail.

Venky's first attempts at obtaining finance for the project had been met with bloodcurdling laughter. Had he considered the problem of locating a site, the cost of construction and equipment, the logistical difficulties, the power shortages, the possibility that HeritageLand would only attract roadside Romeos feverish at the thought of witnessing the dishabille of a shapely Draupadi?

These were all legitimate points, but Venky Gowda only had one vision. And he was not the type of man to turn his back on it. After years of conspiring and toadying, endless feasibility studies and costs analyses, an MBA from Ohio State University, a rhinoplasty procedure and, finally, marriage into the family of a powerful political grandee, his phantom fantasy world faced the prospect of becoming real. Perhaps the gods had finally decided to bless Venky, themselves waking up to the fact that their universe would be incomplete without a representation of their fight against evil in the twists and turns of a water slide. And that representation would rise in Mysore, erstwhile land of maharajas, India's second cleanest city and home of many talented snooker players.

Venture capitalists from Hong Kong were ready with finance, architects and engineers worked day and night on the park layout and, crucially, opinions had been canvassed among prominent Mysore residents. The editor of the *Mysore Evening Sentinel* gave the project a cautious welcome: it would be a good opportunity to showcase the country's traditions and culture but historical and doctrinal accuracy would be essential. Ahmed Pasha, President of the Mysore Enterprise Forum, could see only benefits accruing from HeritageLand. He speculated at length on the growth in the city's economy based on projected revenues from the theme park and also took the opportunity to publicise the fine merchandise in his own furniture showrooms. Priyadarshini Ramesh, proprietor of the Mysstiiqque chain of beauty salons, declared that she was not opposed to the plans on principle but her main concerns related to the park's aesthetic impact on the city.

'Class, not mass,' she said, stamping her beautifully pedicured foot. 'We don't want the whole thing turning into a cheap circus full of low types.'

Professor M M Malikarjuna of the university's linguistics department ignored the question entirely and instead renewed his appeal for better policing on the Manasagangotri campus in light of the number of youngsters openly canoodling there in broad daylight.

An overall impact assessment of HeritageLand resulted in the following conclusions: the theme park would bring enormous economic and cultural advantages to the city of Mysore, transforming it into a premier global tourist destination; any adverse environmental impact would be mitigated by the planting of trees on the park site and by the use of low-energy light bulbs; no obstacles could be envisaged in the grant of licences required for the park as all necessary inducements would be incorporated into its unofficial budget; the residents of Mysore, or in any case those who held any serious influence, would provide full support for the project as long as it was realised in the best possible taste.

A celebration party was held at the Mysore Regency Hotel where all the guests agreed that the head chef had outdone himself with his Hyderabadi chicken lollipops. The Secretary of the Mysore Regeneration Council made the mistake of bringing up the issue of the land yet to be acquired for the project site and was beaten down by several colleagues. There seemed little value in wringing their hands over a virtual fait accompli.

Susheela stood by the window peering at the hunched figure by the gate in the white vest and khaki shorts, a small basket in his right hand. She seldom allowed doubt to factor into her deductions, but this time she pursed her lips as she tried to make up her mind. Certainly he looked crude enough to signify someone with an uncouth mentality. She was sure it was him that she had seen on previous occasions.

The milky sky had begun to radiate a toast-like warmth and the smell of the Bhaskars' breakfast drifted over the compound wall. Pulling her *pallu* over her shoulders, Susheela began to walk briskly towards the man, who was now standing gazing up at a frangipani tree in full blossom.

'Excuse me, do you think this is acceptable?'

The man spun round, his reverie cut short by Susheela's tone.

'Every day I see you, helping yourself to flowers from my garden, as if this is some sort of free place for the public.'

'Madam, these are for prayers. Not for selling in the market. What harm is there?'

'The harm is that you are taking what is not yours. Every day you come here and just help yourself. Have you ever thought about whether I also need these flowers for my prayers?'

'Madam, you should not deprive God of these small offerings, wherever they come from.'

'God will be a lot happier with you if you keep your hands off my garden in the future.'

Susheela turned around, picked up a couple of dead leaves off the path and walked back into the house. The door shut with a sharp click.

Their lunches were packed. The *pongal* for their breakfast was ready. The coffee was dripping through the filter. Mala had paid the electricity bill the day before. She had washed the front steps first thing in the morning and drawn her standard *rangoli*: four diamonds intersecting in the middle of a large spiral. It was just after eight in the morning. Mala looked for a safety pin in the coin purse on the kitchen shelf and then glanced at her watch. Gayathri the maid was now ten minutes late. Girish liked her to be gone before he had his breakfast at a quarter to nine.

A couple of minutes later the gate bolt screeched across the stone floor and a shadow passed along one of the tiny front windows. Girish had said that they could afford a maid for an hour a day. Mala would have to get her to run a broom across the floor, mop all the rooms, wash the clothes hurriedly and clean the previous evening's plates and utensils. The rest was for Mala to manage.

Gayathri gave Mala a practised smile as she walked to the bathroom. Nothing was said of the lateness. In fact, these days Mala said very little to Gayathri at all. When she had first started working there, Gayathri had tried to indulge in some banter. But Mala's self-censorship had already begun to be a habit for her, one she was not going to break for the maid. Even though Mala knew that it was her place to assert herself, she felt uncomfortable in Gayathri's all too corporeal presence. She could not stop herself looking at the audacious swell of the maid's haunches when she crouched low to flick the wet rag under the dining table; her creamy brown belly that pushed through the thin fabric of her sari; her extravagant breasts scarcely contained by her sweat-stained blouse. How could she be so fat when she did physical work all day?

Mala had little knowledge of Gayathri's home life, having only got so far as to ascertain that she had no children. Gayathri's response to a query from Girish about her husband was: '*Aiya*, he comes and he goes.'

With that she had let out her long, throaty laugh, a perplexing noise that sounded like a series of quick hiccups, each being ambushed by the next.

There was no evidence of scabrous entertainments in Gayathri's life but there existed an air of gratification and an earthy zeal about her that Mala had not encountered before. She had once asked Girish if he thought Gayathri drank. He had immediately responded with an interrogation as to whether Mala had smelt alcohol on her breath, had she been acting strangely, was there something wrong with her work, had someone said anything? Well, why was she asking then?

Mala regretted ever having brought it up.

The letter was addressed to the Head of Customer Services at the regional electricity distribution company and ran to three pages of block text. The author, the Chief Executive Officer and majority shareholder of a small company based in the industrial corridor to the south of Mysore, was by turns deeply concerned, immensely frustrated and utterly scandalised. The power situation in Karnataka had reached such a nadir that, by hook or by crook, urgent measures were required, come what may, without which, rest assured, there would be extremely adverse consequences for the future of Mysore as an attractive investment area. Furthermore, this was nothing less than a clarion call for the state's reputation as a centre for the enhancement of development opportunities.

The letter's author recognised that the damage to the country's reputation as a rising superpower did not require elaboration but, nevertheless, felt compelled to enumerate all the associated dangers. The author also pointed out that there was neither rhyme nor reason, prudence nor perception, aim nor ambition in the state's power-supply policies. He graciously acknowledged the lack of long-term investment in the sector and the grave challenges posed by transmission leakages and power theft; even so, his only option was to highlight to the authorities the fact that there was simply no justification for the current dismal state of affairs.

Attached to the letter was a schedule detailing the dates and times of load-shedding, power holidays and voltage drops in the last six months, along with calculations of output decline, loss of revenue, and expenditure on alternate power supplies. The author sought a full and frank explanation for the unscheduled power losses and a complete and comprehensive plan for the avoidance of such eventualities in the future. If an adequate response was not forthcoming, each and every legitimate avenue would be explored by the author of the letter, including, but not limited to, judicial intervention. The author's final point was that the idea of a project such as HeritageLand being contemplated in Mysore would be comical were it not so insulting. The letter was copied to the Karnataka Electricity Regulatory Commission, the Mysore Enterprise Forum, the Mayor's office and the Federation of Indian Chambers of Commerce and Industry.

Girish slowly replaced the letter in a manila folder marked

'Urgent' with a faded red marker pen. The word was followed by a hurried slash, an exclamation mark that added a comedic exigency to the whole business: bungling officials skidding on banana skins and walking into doors as they scurried around, attempting to resolve the power crisis. He wished he could see the funny side, but there was not much laughter to be had on the second floor of Jyothi House at a quarter to three in the afternoon. A pile of quality assurance statements and various drafts of the customer grievance handling procedure sat on the corner of his desk. He flicked the folder on top of this pile, its edges crinkled with heat and sweat, the constituent layers accordioning out in a last mad dash.

A few minutes later Girish called the Director of Customer Relations again but was met by the same collapsed voice telling him in three languages that the mobile phone he was trying to call was either switched off or out of range. He tried the Director's secretary once more. Sarita answered on the second ring and stated again that sir was in a meeting but yes sir, she had already passed on the message sir, when sir had emerged for a break, and sir had said that he would call sir as soon as possible, but you know how these meetings are sir, especially the meetings with sir, so she really could not specifically inform sir as to when exactly sir would be free to speak to sir but, of course sir, without a doubt sir, she would make sure that she reminded sir when he next emerged, not to worry sir, thank you sir, good afternoon sir. Girish knew she was lying; he could picture her face, like a boulder wearing a *bindi*. He also knew he would call her again in half an hour and hated himself for it.

Susheela's left ear was beginning to smart so she transferred the receiver to her other side.

'We're having the downstairs bathroom redone. It's been such a torture, I can't tell you, and now that the workmen are finally in, life is even worse. Yesterday when I came back they had left the front door wide open and were nowhere to be seen. Now the stupid company has sent the wrong shower door and I'm going to have to sort all of that out,' said Priyanka, Susheela's elder daughter.

'I know, everything goes wrong at the same time,' said Susheela.

'Exactly. And Vivek's in Brussels again, so that's really helping. Actually he called last night but the line was so bad. It's been happening the last few times. I think they've sold him the same *dabba* mobile that they sold me, remember? And of course, he'll make me go and sort all of that out because he'll claim to be too busy. *Amma?* One sec, one sec, okay . . . just got to get this.'

Susheela's mouth felt dry and chalky as she listened to Priyanka's travails. She swallowed hard, having completely lost the thread of the conversation some minutes ago. This in itself was not unusual. Their fortnightly conversations had come to mean progressively less to Susheela. Of course, it was lovely to hear from Priyanka and there was still that warm ripple when she remembered things Susheela had mentioned the previous fortnight. But their worlds had caromed apart a few years ago and the ties had grown flaccid and indistinct. Priyanka's chatter now seemed like the background buzz from television or titbits gleaned from mobile phone conversations in the doctor's waiting room. There were vague allusions to Katherine and Carlos, Jude and Alice, Matt and Chris. The call would be interrupted at times by mumbled asides to her PA or her husband. Susheela had noticed that of late Priyanka seemed to have a stock set of questions that she would clatter through, often hurriedly ending the conversation, promising further detail by email. These emails would arrive a few days later, stippled with exclamation marks and breezy references to Merzbau installations, *shochu* bars, experimental dance and city breaks to Stockholm and Berlin.

Susheela had not consciously withdrawn from Priyanka's elaborate life. She would not even have recognised the growing distance as a consequence of her own actions. Her retreat was subliminally pre-emptive: she had begun an instinctive process of shutting out before she was cast as the lonely interfering mother gazing at her daughter sashaying into the distance. As far as Susheela was concerned, the important thing was that the precepts of form and propriety were maintained. So calls were made, emails read, cards sent. To proceed otherwise would be to descend into sloth and chaos.

Priyanka's job entailed something incomprehensible in London to do with capital markets. Where once this had been a matter of accomplishment and esteem, Susheela had quickly understood that the current mood was very different. It now seemed that most of the recent global financial scourges could be tracked back to Priyanka and the incumbents of her world. Heads shook slowly at Mysore dinner parties, expressing disgust at the greed and recklessness of these brash, aggressive bankers and the mercenary politicians who had allowed them to gamble away the futures of decent savers from Caracas to Chennai. Susheela's feelings remained ambivalent. Where once she had quietly skimmed along on the tide of her daughter's achievements, she now stood tacitly at the shore, facing the other way.

She would be affected as much as anyone else by the tribulations of global finance, a widow with no actively earned income. There was a sum of cash in fixed deposits garnering a comfortable amount of interest: a combination of accumulated savings, the pay-out from the life assurance company and the entitlement received from Sridhar's provident fund, following twenty-five odd years of service at House of Govind. She owned the house outright and had no debts. Her circumstances had never impelled her to examine closely the small portfolio of shares that she had inherited from

Sridhar. From all the talk on the news, she surmised that it was probably worth very little.

There were gifts from Priyanka too: a new television one Diwali; extravagant bouquets and jewellery on her birthday; and two or three times arbitrary cheques for thousands of rupees which Susheela had been embarrassed to accept but too disconcerted to refuse. There was talk now of sinking banks, plunging interest rates and the end of the property boom. Her instinctive response was to look into some belt-tightening options; not easily done, as she did not regard herself as remotely extravagant.

Priyanka had rung off. There was someone at the door and she had to be at her Pilates class in fifteen minutes. Susheela sat by the window, still holding the telephone, looking out at the front lawn. Swirls of pale green, brown and white roiled across the ground, enraged at the lack of water. The *mali* had left the hosepipe in a great coil in the middle of the lawn, as if to provoke it further. There was a sudden rushing noise, followed by a few beeps. The power had gone again.

She sighed and began to sort through some old envelopes in the magazine rack. The situation was quite different with her younger daughter Prema, who had left Mysore for California on a celebrated scholarship. Her work had eventually led her to a research post involving the application of genomic knowledge to the development of fertility drugs. Prema offered up little about her life. Her telephone calls were more irregular, her emails hardly worth mentioning. Her life seemed to revolve around the lab and weekend rock-climbing trips. Even so, Susheela felt an implicit candour there that seemed to be missing in those lengthy conversations with Priyanka. The call from Prema could last five minutes or half an hour, but Susheela remained a participant. They talked about the most useful exercises for lower back pain, Obama's sparkling speeches or the easiest way to get an intense smoky flavour in a *baingan bhartha*. Beyond these moments, Susheela knew that it would be advisable not to probe further. Prema was like a piece of parchment that revealed certain limited truths but which, if inspected too closely, would crumble into a fine dust.

Mala slowed down as she approached the busy junction, easing the scooter to one side. She had been living in Mysore for over two years but some of the routes still confused her with their sudden one-way systems and riots of side roads. City officials had helpfully provided a profusion of signs and arrows at this circle, but they all seemed to look skywards in despair. Matters were not improved by the proprietors of Sheethal Talkies, who had covered up a number of signposts with posters for their morning feature, *Desires of the Night*, a work chronicling the renaissance of a girl who moved to a large city from an inconsequential town. It was unlikely that Mala would ever have the opportunity to compare experiences with the film's central character but there were one or two similarities.

Mala had grown up in Konnapur, a three-road town choking in its own dust. It was famed for its Eeshwara temple, a Hoysala masterpiece that today sat among ramshackle lean-tos housing doleful purveyors of *pooja* items. Little hummocks of vermillion and turmeric rose amid baskets of chrysanthemums, jasmine and marigolds. Coconuts were piled into bushels under unsteady wooden tables. Framed photos of Shiva and Ganesh stood propped up next to brass plates containing twists of sandalwood paste, incense sticks, lozenges of camphor and glistening fans of betel leaves. A little further, at a slightly more respectful distance, a selection of *beedi* and *paan* shops nudged the periphery of the temple complex.

The temple was the town's spiritual and economic hub, providing focus for most of its devotees, traders, handlers, speculators, brokers, priests, academics, itinerants, beggars and charlatans. Mala's father, Babu, had paid his dues as a secondary school teacher, poet, real estate broker and areca nut dealer before ending up as a tour-guide-cum-travel agent. His business cards confirmed that he was a 'History and Heritage Specialist', thereby adding a scholarly sheen to his entrepreneurial activities. Dressed in over-sized dazzling white shirts and pleated navy trousers, Babu would tell tourists that he chose not to tie himself down with premises and staff, preferring instead to meet his potential clients in the hallowed domain of the temple courtyard. In his professional ministrations he was finely attuned to the fascinations and appetites of his clientele.

'Welcome, welcome to Konnapur's magnificent treasure,' he would say expansively, as if personally responsible for the temple's architecture.

'I can see that you have come here looking for something very special, and I don't mind telling you, beyond any doubt, you will find it.'

For teenaged gap-year drifters he spun salacious accounts involving multiple gods, endowing the mace, the trident and the conch with an unparalleled lewdness. To salvation-seeking freethinkers Babu elaborated on the transcendence of the self required to discover the eternal identity and, naturally, highlighted Konnapur's key role in various Vedic milestones. For wealthy North Indian dowagers he played up the Konnapur deity's impressive record in reversing astrological ill omens, granting male grand-children and bestowing longevity.

The truth was that while Babu tried to turn his natural resource-fulness and broad knowledge to some personal gain, his love for Konnapur and the Eeshwara temple was profound and enduring. Much of his childhood had been spent loitering around the shrine vestibule, sheltering behind the carved balustrades and watching swallows take off from the moulded lintels. There was little competition among Konnapur's open sewers and garbage-strewn alleys. Babu's investment in the temple, and his certain knowledge that destiny had no greater plans for him elsewhere, kept him rooted to the centre of Konnapur. If his embellishments of the temple's historical and architectural significance resulted in some modest additional income for him, what was the harm?

At the age of twenty-three, Babu's prospects had been scrupulously appraised by older family members as a precursor to marriage negotiations. Of course, as the saying went, parents would adore their child even if it were a bandicoot, but such subjective regard had to be put firmly to one side in the important business of nuptial assessments. Fortunately Babu's parents had never had to avail themselves of such undiscerning devotion, nor later face any harsh realities. Babu was tall and broad-shouldered, with an open, confident face that invited further analysis. As a man, however, his looks were hardly of the greatest significance.

Hailing from a prominent Brahmin family that could number among its antecedents several Sanskrit scholars, a tax collector, a leading astrophysicist and the founder of a hospice for destitute widows, the initial outlook had been buoyant. Allowances then had to be made for a schizophrenic aunt and a great-uncle who spent his Sundays dressed as a former maharani of Mysore. There was also some speculation regarding the occasional presence of Babu's father at an illegal gambling house. It was duly noted that Babu did not stand to inherit land of any great value, the bulk of the ancestral property having found its way into the hands of an alternate branch of the family. Being a graduate, his value had appreciated, but not by much. Years of Nehruvian planning and entrenched official venality had meant that he would still be adrift in a sea of lettered young men, unless a benevolent patron emerged to ease his passage into professional life. This was not an impossible occurrence. The astrophysicist's son still passed through Konnapur on occasion. As a senior official at Western Railway who lived in a sprawling pistachio-green mansion in Baroda, there were plenty of favours he could grant.

Most importantly though, Babu's personality conveyed the sense of a man sanctified by fate. His apparent confidence and social ease generated an assurance that could not help but conquer potential in-laws. Babu himself was more circumspect about his future. An opening at a local secondary school did not hold great promise. But he had to get married and he needed to make sure that he presented himself in the best possible light. As a result, Babu talked himself into a favourable alliance.

Rukmini's family owned great swathes of land around Konnapur. Her father's orchards and plantations were breathlessly enumerated by those who liked to keep abreast of such matters. In all likelihood the extent of his wealth was exaggerated in those provincial circles, thereby rendering his children even more attractive. His four sons and eight daughters could launch themselves into their adulthood with more than a degree of confidence.

Rukmini had been eager to study further, perhaps Hindi literature at college. This would have entailed moving to another town, an outlandish prospect for an unmarried woman. Rukmini accepted this fact, being above all a woman of great pragmatism, and resolved to throw herself into the life chosen for her with all the enthusiasm that she could muster. Happily she had avoided the fate of her sister, who had recently been coupled with a boss-eyed creature in a safari suit, albeit one with a safe full of gold; at least *her* husband was handsome, articulate and entertaining. It was a good start.

As time went on, however, it became apparent that Babu's perpetual élan was not going to fuel an ascendancy in any chosen field. True, there were occasional successes in his varied careers, but these instances of good fortune could not disguise the fact that the months and years had generally been difficult and unpredictable. Rukmini had been forced to sell off most of the land that she inherited to meet various expenses. The small amount of capital that was eventually left was cautiously converted into Unit Trust of India units, generating a modest but vital sum of interest. She would run her finger around the blue edges of the certificates, before locking them in the secure compartment of her Godrej wardrobe. Rukmini was not in any doubt that bemoaning her husband's fortunes would be futile and unbecoming. She had, after all, two daughters to raise and a labyrinth of social obligations through which to navigate.

In spite of the hardship, Rukmini felt that she had done well. Babu's loving regard had made up for the shortcomings; she still thrilled at the awareness of his sudden presence and the rush of so many memories. The first Sunday of the month had always been special. At about half past six in the evening Rukmini and Babu would leave the house, Babu's mother having concocted some fantastical event as a decoy for the children. The couple would then make their way to Sujatha Talkies for the early evening show. Depending on the film, there would either be an impatient tumult outside the cinema, manic ticket touts shoving their way towards anyone who looked desperate or simple, or a few layabouts keeping a weary eye on the stray dogs that padded around under the ticket window. It was always the same: a length of fresh jasmine, the cracked leather of the balcony seats, oil-roasted peanuts at the interval and the charge of Babu's hand on her hip as they groped their way down the dark aisle at the end of the film. Later it was *dosas* and coffee at Kwality Hotel, Babu putting on a new accent each time to try to get the attention of the waiters in the ear-splitting din, *osh bosh* Britisher, *ithe kithe* Punjabi, *apro kapro* Gujarati. The waiters were never amused, and rewarded Babu with looks that could curdle milk. Rukmini and Babu would leave in high spirits, the syrupy burn of the coffee coating their tongues, their table instantly seized by a hungry waiting couple.

At the Vishram Coffee House in Mysore, two public sector bank officials were having lunch.

'So, what news, sir?'

'You have to tell me.'

'So Kumar got promoted.'

'Why wouldn't they promote him, the buttock-licking *chamcha*.'

'Sir, it is a real shame that they didn't transport the filthy fellow to the moon with that space mission. And leave the bastard there.'

'The moon does not deserve such treatment. Not happy with ruining this country, the government has to go and destroy the whole galaxy too.'

'Chandrayaan-1, that rocket is called, sir. How many more will be sent?'

'If these satellites are anything like the Nehru-Gandhi family, there will be one every five or six years.'

'Sir, one more coffee?'

'Make it one by two.'

'You are correct, sir, about all this ruination. Every day things are getting worse. They will need to sort out all our social nuisances before that HeritageLand is built.'

'Very true. The whole world will be looking at us.'

'I tell you, sir, the current climate of criminality is too much. You know what happened with my aunt and an auto driver?'

'Your aunt?'

'Yes, sir. On my father's side. She suffered very serious verbal abuse and mental torture.'

'What happened?'

'She was walking to the market, sir, and this idiot slows down next to her. She thought he was just wanting a fare so she told him that she was not interested. Very nicely, she told him, sir, my aunt is not just any kind of woman.'

'Then?'

'Then he asked her to go with him to a lodge. Can you believe it, sir? My aunt is in her sixties.'

'What nonsense is this? What kind of bastards are becoming auto drivers these days?'

'That's what, sir, you will not believe. Two, three more times, he was inviting her to some lodge.'

'She should have just given him two tight slaps on each cheek.'

'She is a heart patient, sir. Diabetes, too.'

'That is beyond the limit. Beyond the limit, I say.'

The two sipped their coffees in silence for a couple of minutes. Two blonde women walked past their table and left the restaurant.

'Sir, all these yoga students who come here, they don't have jobs in their own countries?'

'No, it's a very difficult situation for them. No jobs, thrown out by their families, rejected by society. Yoga is their last chance to make something of their lives.'

'That is very sad, sir; maybe that is why they are all so thin?'

'All that worry, unhappiness, shame, financial pressure, and on top of that, doing yoga in this heat, eating bad food and getting loose motion. What else will happen?'

'It is strange how things change, sir. Here we are, two Indians eating big plate meals and wondering whether or not to have an extra sweet, and these poor foreigners trying so hard just to keep body and soul together.'

'That is what you call the march of history.'

'You are a poet, sir.'

'No, I am a simple man.'

'No sir, a poet.'

'All right.'

As Girish emerged from Staircase B of Jyothi House, he quickly checked under his arms for any unsightly sweat patches. He had ridiculed junior colleagues often enough for looking like rotund housewives in tight blouses. It would not do to fall into the same trap. He checked the time and stood under the building's main arch, determined not to return upstairs for at least an hour.

The adjacent picture framers had spilled out on to the pavement, spreading strips of plywood and pieces of card over a large tarpaulin sheet. Pictures, mainly of deities, were propped up against the front wall of the shop, in the tiny strip of shadow cast by the cracked eaves. Among the beatific blue faces, giant lotuses and gleaming crowns, there stood a monochrome image of Frank Zappa, patiently awaiting its turn. An officious young man appeared to be in charge, taking orders from waiting customers while also arguing into his mobile phone and shuffling sheets of carbon in a receipt book. A teenage boy squatted on the pavement, hammering nails into the back of a frame while keeping a watchful eye on his boss.

Girish thought about walking down a couple of blocks before getting a coffee but the heat was merciless and no one in his office would notice or care. He stepped into the restaurant across the road and it was only a matter of seconds before the milky confection arrived in a chipped glass. Girish sent the coffee back, asking for another glass, incurring the savage but silent wrath of the waiter.

The restaurant was relatively empty at this hour. An old film song played very softly: a solemn ode to the beauty of a country belle.

'Of course, everyone is at their desks, shuffling important bits of paper, mentally composing crucial memos and notices,' thought Girish.

He decided to make himself comfortable and looked around to see if any newspapers had been abandoned. The waiter returned with the coffee, this time in an intact but grimy glass.

Raised voices from across the street carried into the restaurant.

'Look what they have done to my Krishna! Look at my Krishna. Look!'

From where he was seated Girish could see a wiry woman with a hoarse voice in a state of extreme agitation. The usual idlers, starved of entertainment, had quickly gathered around to provide counsel and succour. The woman pointed to an image lying flat on the tarpaulin. A series of sooty smudges had appeared on the picture like smoke rings blown from those perfectly shaped roseate lips.

'Look there! At the mouth! Look!'

The young man had quickly ended his phone conversation and was now cuffing the back of the boy's head every time the woman pointed out the mishap.

'What are you hitting him for? He has not been anywhere near the picture. You have done this. Or else it was that donkey inside. Look at my Krishna!' screamed the woman.

'Please calm down,' said the young man.

'Criminal *sule magga. Ninna mukhake benki hakka.*'

'We'll fix it.'

'*Nachikedu, paapi mundemakkala.* May burning hot coals rain down on your dick.'

'*Che che*, is that a mouth or a sewage pipe?'

'May a stray dog fuck your wife from behind.'

'She is not my wife yet. The marriage is in six months.'

Girish paid for his coffee and left the restaurant. That was all people could find to do these days: shout like a fishwife and cause a huge scene over a few dirty marks. He walked on the shady side of the pavement towards Kabir Road, stepping around the arrangements of cheap sunglasses and wallets laid out on dirty sheets. He thought of looking in on a friend who worked at a newspaper around the corner but then changed his mind. He was in no mood to hear about the daily miseries involved in being a third-rate journalist for a tenth-rate rag. He turned into Anegundi Road and headed towards the recently opened mall near the Farooqia College of Pharmacy. At least it would be cool and there would not be any howling harpies to give him a headache.

As he approached the mall he stopped and thought about paying Mala a visit at work. If he waited half an hour or so she would probably be ready to leave. Maybe they could go and have *chaat* somewhere and then go to an evening show. A vision of them sitting in a crowded snack bar, Mala playing with the chain around her neck, flashed through his mind. The thought depressed him instantly. There was nothing left in him to give to an evening of spontaneous recreation. In any case, going to pick up Mala would entail walking back to Jyothi House to pick up his motorbike and he had no intention of returning there at least until he had managed to speak to the Director of Customer Relations. He turned around again, crossed the road, walked quickly through the metal detectors and disappeared behind the mall's dark sliding doors.

The towels had been hanging on the line all day and were baked crisp. Uma piled them into a brittle mound in a bucket and stashed the clothes pegs in the cubbyhole under the water tank. On the neighbouring roof terrace, Mr Bhaskar stomped from one end to the other, deep in thought. Uma could not understand why he chose to boomerang from one end of that small space to the other when there were at least half a dozen shady roads along which he could promenade; not to mention the neatly paved paths in the

Gardens. She had overheard Susheela mention the same thing to one of her friends the other day. The friend's response was that Mahalakshmi Gardens was a more agreeable place without the risk of running into Mr Bhaskar. A pleasant enquiry would inevitably lead to a long fulmination from the gentleman on the country's decay.

'Better that he just wears out his roof tiles than makes your ears drop off in desperation,' the friend had observed.

Uma heard the neighbouring gate clank shut as Bhargavi left for the day. She looked down over the parapet and saw her half run towards the end of the road, obviously trying to catch the 42 bus before it rumbled off northwards. Bhargavi had only worked for the Bhaskar family for about three months but had established herself as quite a presence in this corner of Mahalakshmi Gardens. Within her first few weeks she had ensured she was on friendly terms with almost all the watchmen and *malis*. By the end of the second month she had managed to organise a boycott of a local coffee stall; the owner had gravely injured a boy who worked for him following some minor infraction. Recently she had arranged jobs in the locality for a distant cousin and her daughter, ensuring that they were aware that their conduct reflected closely on her reputation in the area as an efficient fixer.

One of Bhargavi's new acolytes had declared: '*Akka* has a big heart. She is a good woman, very decent, very clean.'

Not everyone was a fan: 'What decent? What clean? Does she wash her *kundi* with Nirma?'

Bhargavi had cornered Uma by the dustcart one morning and introduced herself. Then, assuming a fiercely protective air, she probed into the circumstances of Uma's employment. How much was she paid, did she get her day off every week without fail, how was she treated, were there any problems, what meals did she get, any bonus, any gifts, what did her duties entail, who lived in the house, was there anything else she ought to know? Uma stared at this creature, not quite five feet tall, with her tightly oiled braid and the glossy mole in the middle of her forehead, who seemed to want to gather her up in the pleats of her sari. Uma was attuned to demarcations and boundaries. Her steps were the gentle footfalls of the careful navigator. Now she was faced by this tornado of unsolicited concern. While Uma had always been aware of the malice in prying eyes, Bhargavi's kind interest was exotic territory.

Uma had responded to Bhargavi hesitantly, unable to resist her onslaught, but at the same time clinging to her own customary defences. In time, she had come to see Bhargavi's actions in a different light. The genuine warmth and consideration were there, but they were sifted through with a desire to be needed. Bhargavi's own compulsions had led her to act as a friend in places where regard was only given in return for profit or abasement. Much of this had become clear to Uma as she watched Bhargavi's interventions. As she pushed herself to the fore she always told her mother's story, an example of a woman who would not be forced down or held back.

Bhargavi's mother had been born in a remote village in the Velikonda Hills, marooned on a bank of shale between two slow-moving streams. Her birth had been greeted with conventional disappointment, and then distress, as a bewildering fact became known about the newborn. The baby's tiny palms were devoid of lines; they were as smooth as one of the hundreds of grey pebbles washed clean by the listless streams. The palms were washed, oiled, massaged and repeatedly inspected under the glow of first light, in the bleached dazzle of noon and by the beam of a smoky lantern. They remained unblemished and unbroken, a reminder that here lay an infant with barely a past and, seemingly, no future. The creases that should have sealed her journey through life did not make an appearance in the weeks that followed, perhaps in protest at the life they foresaw. There were only two ways of looking at this unnatural occurrence: as a curse brought down on the whole community or a sacred sign indicating the arrival of a superior being. Unfortunately the lines had failed to materialise on female palms, in the home of a low caste potter, in a village marooned on a bank of shale in a forgotten corner of the Velikonda Hills. There was only one way that this story could end.

So Bhargavi's mother was not fated to join the ranks of glorious local miracles: the weeping marble deities; the babies emerging unscathed from cauldrons of hot oil; the temple domes sprouting out of forest earth. Branded a witch, as soon as puberty struck she was palmed off to a drunkard from a neighbouring village, thirty years her senior. Bhargavi was born four years later and, shortly after, mother and daughter left the Velikonda Hills to find the future they had been denied.

Bhargavi's mother had a dynamic imagination and a flinty streak of resourcefulness, both more useful than all the palm lines in the world. She reinvented herself as a healer using some practical midwifery skills, a flair for astrological neologisms, an education in the properties of various herbs and a store of common sense. Where particularly thorny cases were concerned, she flashed her naked palms at her patrons, silencing their doubts and hastening the efficacy of their treatment. Mother and daughter travelled from town to town, sourcing new remedies and clients, rapidly establishing a daunting reputation, and then, with impeccable judgment, moving on.

Upon her mother's death, Bhargavi had not taken on her work but had, in her own way, continued the therapeutic tradition. Lacking an education, she was locked into a narrow channel of options, but had decided that this would not prevent her from making common cause with others when the situation required it.

She had ended up in Mysore, starting out as a tailor's apprentice in exchange for a couple of meals a day. Later she had joined a garment factory that specialised in men's shirts destined for a supermarket chain in Germany. Her attempts at organising trade union membership among the young women at the factory soon saw her ordered off the premises and blacklisted in various quarters of the industrial area. Bhargavi had not gone quietly. She had returned at the end of each day's shift to talk to the women as they emerged from the cramped depot into the evening haze. Eventually, one of the security guards had warned her not to return, while standing on her toes, his carefully polished shoe enormous on top of her tiny feet. She had left the area but she was sure that she would return.

A week later she had found work at the Bhaskar house. Now Uma found herself the latest beneficiary of Bhargavi's solid determination and, as she watched her hurry out of sight, she was not sure whether she ought to be grateful or not.

Susheela began the long journey around the house, shutting windows and drawing curtains. The early evenings were the most difficult time. The tasks of the day were complete but the entrenchment of night was yet to begin. The gate lights would flicker into life along the streets of Mahalakshmi Gardens and the mosquitoes would begin their crepuscular investigations. The fridge would register its boredom with a prolonged sigh and every planet would pause in its orbit for a fraction of a second. She tried to delay turning on the television for as long as she possibly could, since it was, in her mind, a clear admission of defeat. She would pick up her current novel, the last unread section of the newspaper, the telephone book or an old copy of the *Reader's Digest*: anything that might stave off a descent towards that final recourse.

65

The intensely irritating thing about being a widow, apart from all the other intensely irritating things, was that she had been rendered void by most of their social set. In the immediate aftermath of Sridhar's death the messages of condolence had flooded in, as they should. The sombre visits, the enquiries as to the final days, the ceremonial panoply, everything had been correctly in place. It was after those first few months of bereavement that Susheela had dropped to the bottom like a sunken stone. Perhaps they thought that her grief would make her incapable of pleasant intercourse; perhaps they lacked the idiom required to extend a social courtesy to a woman missing a crucial appendage; perhaps they thought she would run off with one of their decrepit husbands; perhaps they had never warmed to her in the first place. Whatever the real reason, a curtain had fallen with a heavy thud over the invitations to bridge evenings at the Erskine Club, concerts at Jaganmohan Palace, drinks at the JW Golf Club and dinners at the Galleria by Tejasandra Lake. There were still the weddings, housewarmings and naming ceremonies, of course; anything where a woman with a dead husband could be seated in a corner among other women with dead husbands, so that they could all quietly discuss their loss.

Across the road, the Nachappa boy had just returned from work. As he reversed his car into the garage, a tinny version of 'Que Sera, Sera' sputtered out into the early darkness. Susheela admitted defeat and turned on the television. A news channel was relaying footage of the chaotic scenes witnessed in the Karnataka Legislative Assembly earlier in the day. A number of MLAs had stormed the Speaker's podium in protest at what they saw as continued procedural unfairness in the conduct of debates. The Speaker had been escorted to another part of the building for his own safety while his microphone was dismantled by a particularly zealous member of the House. Balled-up paper flew across the room and, in the background, two MLAs had hoisted a chair up on to their shoulders, an action whose legislative purpose remained unclear.

Susheela's mouth turned down in disgust at the sight of these hooligans who were in charge of running matters. What had the people of Karnataka ever done to deserve such representatives?

The newsreader announced impassively that one MLA had threatened to take poison in the House, at which point the Speaker had adjourned proceedings for the day before slipping away. The Assembly members had carried on with their protest against the disregard for parliamentary rules, apparently too absorbed to notice the adjournment.

'What we need is someone to just come and take charge and put all these *goondas* in their place,' thought Susheela. 'If you give a little bit of freedom to these thugs, they just abuse it.'

She flicked through the channels, looking for something indicative of a more enlightened society.

Mala slid open the glass doors of the cabinet and gingerly fluttered a duster over the ceramic debris of her late mother-in-law's life. Girish's mother had died some ten years ago in a flash flood while on pilgrimage to Badrinath. Discussions of a possible match between Mala and Girish were at an early stage when Rukmini and Mala's elder sister, Ambika, came to know of the tragedy. They had clucked appropriately, Rukmini's eyes gazing sadly into the middle distance, but there existed an unspoken contentment that came with the knowledge that Mala would not have to endure any mother-in-law related guerrilla warfare. Girish's stock had just risen.

A week after the wedding, when Mala arrived at the house in Sitanagar, she wondered whether it would have been preferable for the departed lady to have been present in the flesh. As a memory, Girish's mother weighed heavily on the rooms in the small house.

67

The garlanded photograph in the sitting room showed a skeletal woman who looked like she had just sat on a pin. Her love for frogs was apparent in the cabinet, which also contained spindly trophies from some forgotten sports day, an enigmatic award from the Indian Red Cross, a few pairs of castanets and a soapstone elephant with one eye. In the spare room a wheelchair she had once used now housed a couple of badminton rackets and a vase filled with plastic flowers. Her sewing machine still glowered in the master bedroom, her name painted across the base in a five-year-old's wobbly hand.

Mother-in-law or no mother-in-law, this was Mala's home now, although late at night a wave of bewilderment would still occasionally wash over her. What peculiar devices of hazard had led to her ending up in this house, with its low, streaky ceilings, married to a man twelve years older than her, dusting the ceramic frogs of a woman who had drowned a decade ago in the Alaknanda River?

Mala shut the cabinet doors, folded the duster into a tiny square and buried it in her lap as she sat down on the sofa. She turned the television on and had to sit through the last few minutes of a quiz show before the melancholy strains of the theme tune to her favourite soap came drifting out. The show was set in a mansion in Delhi, inhabited by a prominent family of industrialists. The patriarch of the family was in a contemplative stage of his life. The money had been made; now the legacy had to be moulded. His wife, the third in an imperious progression, had recently come under the influence of a shady *swami*, a god-man with a penchant for travel by private jet. The state of her rapidly unravelling psyche formed one of the soap's more prominent subplots.

The patriarch's three sons all lived in the same mansion, along with their glamorous wives. The eldest son was a ruthless work-aholic who managed to carve out a little time to conduct a rather obvious affair with his secretary. His wife symbolised the soul of the programme and was often shown in heart-rending close-ups, trying to make sense of the turbulent world around her. Her devotion to her family was matched only by her apparent inability to recognise infidelity in her husband, a man addicted to surreptitious text messaging and returning home freshly showered in the middle of the night.

The second son had not been endowed with a personality and was therefore reduced to looking craven and forlorn in various quarters of the large garden. His wife, on the other hand, tended to fizz and pop with storylines. The daughter of a powerful politician, she ran a major fashion house – primarily, it seemed, by making her senior employees sob in public. Her adroit manoeuvring had seen a rival designer arrested on terrorism charges weeks before the launch of the summer ready-to-wear collections. Now she found herself faking a pregnancy in order to achieve some as yet unrevealed ambition.

The third son ran a modelling agency, which allowed him to troop through the mansion with a string of coltish nymphs in full view of his epileptic wife. The actor who played this character seemed to have been cast mainly on account of his lustrous hair and the programme makers endeavoured to show it always in the best possible light. This son's best friend was an art gallery owner who spent much of his time appraising paintings in Paris and New York. There were strong indications that he was developing an unhealthy interest in the wife of the eldest son. As the soul of the programme, it was beyond dispute that she would not be permitted to engage in any unprincipled frolicking. There were, however, signs that she was responding in her own way to some amorous stirrings, and her struggle to contain her restiveness would no doubt take the show through the summer months and into the rainy season.

CHAPTER THREE

Weight loss was big business in Mysore and not simply as a consequence of the city's many yoga schools. For Faiza Jaleel, it was oxygen. As sole occupant of the lifestyle desk at the *Mysore Evening Sentinel*, her articles drew on the wispiest of details and then puffed out information and advice, steeped in the earnest vernacular of slimming. New gyms seemed to be springing up in Mysore practically every day. Dieting clubs had begun to make inroads into suburban kitchens. The new Dhamaka health club in Mahalakshmi Gardens claimed to have a formidable waiting list. Boxercise and jazzercise groups were convening on roof terraces, first floors of office blocks and in community halls. The readers of the *Mysore Evening Sentinel* were assured that Faiza would catalogue every fad and fancy.

In one poignant interview, Mrs Jethmalani of Jayalakshmipuram explained the difficulties she faced.

'It is true that these days temptations are very strong, but I think the real problem is in my genes,' she confessed to Faiza.

'In my genes and in my jeans,' she giggled, a second later.

It was lucky that Mrs Jethmalani was of a jolly disposition. She had joined her local laughing club, having heard impressive accounts of its health benefits. The club founder had assured her that with a positive attitude and the strong abdominal muscles engendered by communal hilarity, the pounds would simply fall off. Faiza had nodded sympathetically, switched her recorder off and returned to work.

Carbohydrates continued to get a bad press and a pall of dejection settled over a city of rice-eaters. The coconut seller outside Sheethal Talkies had begun to sell body-building supplements along with hashish and pirated DVDs. In Kuvempunagar and Gokulam, the Keralite Ayurvedic centres were offering consultations and massages to counter disproportionate weight gain. The enterprising general manager of Sri Venkatesh Traders had managed to procure several consignments of grapefruit essential oil after hearing about its virtues as an appetite suppressant.

Guests at parties and wedding receptions collared Faiza, eager to discuss the merits of burdock root in increasing metabolism. Stealing a look at her plate as she circulated, they would outline the ingredients of the latest miracle remedy for corpulence and describe the craze for veil-dancing or Zumba-*Natyam* routines. Faiza serenely absorbed the new intelligence while noting the relative girth of prominent socialites; she had an idea for a column called 'Society Snacking Secrets'.

At a diabetes fundraiser, Faiza had spotted Leena Lambha, a well-known item girl. Leena was currently the face and body of a company that manufactured plug-in belts guaranteeing a toned midriff through a patented thermodynamic system. Leena had been charming and candid. Nothing she had ever tried had been as successful as the toning belt.

Some of the seriously well-heeled had of course taken their cues from their intimates in Mumbai and Delhi, returning from foreign jaunts with a new litheness on show. Tummy tucks and gastric bands were expensive, especially when rates were converted into rupees; deluxe maintenance, however, always came at a price. Faiza had arranged to meet a dentist who was known to administer Botox injections, the only high-profile medical professional in the city to do so. Encouraging him to say anything interesting on the record was proving difficult but Faiza was indefatigable.

Nutritionist husband and wife team, Valmiki and Vanitha Govind, had seized the day. Their second book on the perfectly balanced

Indian diet had hit the shelves. Radio interviews, a lecture tour, cooking demonstrations in shopping malls and a column in a women's weekly had all followed. There was a rumour that the couple were in talks with both ETV and Suvarna, their televisual potential not having gone unnoticed. Not surprisingly, Faiza's calls to their office no longer yielded a ready response.

Faiza did not take these matters to heart. There was more than enough vitality in Mysore's cultural scene to prevent her dwelling on the inescapable injuries of a journalistic life. She had come to know that the authorities at St Catherine's College had permitted the producers of a new reality show to use their Senate Hall for the Mysore round of the show's auditions. An advertisement soon ran in the *Mysore Evening Sentinel* encouraging 'bubbly, overweight ladies' to take this unique opportunity to embark on a life-changing journey.

The show's producers had taken inspiration from a variety of cultural leitmotifs to put together a concept involving the anguish of weight gain, the enchantment of celebrity, the allure of a distant island and the rapture of the human condition. Six celebrities and six non-celebrities, all female and all stout, would be transported to a Mexican island where they would be encouraged to find their inner and outer beauty, all under the strictest medical supervision. The participants would be assessed on their success at transforming themselves and discovering hidden truths about their personalities, with the invaluable assistance of telephone voting from viewers at home. The show's publicist had already sent out communiqués heralding the identities of the high-octane judges: a former Miss Asia Pacific, celebrity nutritionists Valmiki and Vanitha Govind, a stuntman turned fight choreographer and the personal physician to a retired Chief Minister. There had been some concern that the reality format no longer held the pulling power of previous years. As a result, battalions of media monitors were dispatched, market researchers appointed and focus groups set up. The final conclusion, some months later, was inescapable. *Moti Ya Mast* would send the ratings into the stratosphere. Faiza, notebook in hand, would undoubtedly be watching.

For years, Susheela had been a fan of the tangy rather than the sweet. Her natural constituency was the lip-sucking sourness of limes, the quivering tartness of tamarind on her tongue and the acid sting of green mangoes. She had once made Sridhar drive back to his cousin's home in Indore, when they were nearly halfway to Bhopal, in order to pick up a jar of gooseberry pickle that she had left behind on the dining table.

Once she was in her fifties, though, there appeared a new arrival that laid waste to her established palate. Sugar made a grand entrance in Susheela's life. Of course in the past she had on occasion popped a festive *laddoo* into her mouth, a squidge of birthday cake or some steaming *prasada* after a Satyanarayan *pooja*. This new interest in sweet things, however, was unprecedented in range and depth. She remembered the first time that she had realised that something had changed beyond all doubt. It was at the wedding reception hosted by Cyril and Sanjana Fernandes for their daughter Maya. On a whim, Susheela had drifted past the dessert table and returned with a single scoop of fig and poppy seed ice cream in a scalloped silver bowl. The first mouthful had been an epiphany, an unclouded insight into the realms of other people's pleasure. The jammy trails of fig had yielded at just the right moment, offering up their nutty grains. The swirls of poppy seed were engaged in a creamy conspiracy and Susheela had unlocked each of their dark secrets. The dessert had feathered her mouth and throat and left her with no option. She returned to the buffet and then had to summon all her willpower to resist a third visit.

Maya Fernandes's marriage ended a year later with some unpleasant allegations on both sides but Susheela's sensory stimulation had endured. Puddings, pastries and *payasas* had floated into her gaze like stunned fireflies in a searchlight's sudden beam. The envelope of rich butter cream coddling the carrot cake from the coffee shop at the Mysore Regency; the tender resistance of plump raisins in a dollop of *pongal* cooked in hot *ghee*; the honeyed tang of freshly made *jalebis*, the sticky coil coming apart in her hands: Susheela's surrender had been complete.

As the driver slowed down at the traffic lights on Narayan Shastry Road, she told him to make a quick stop at the Plaza Sweet Mart. It would not take long to pick up a small box of *kaju pista* rolls. The driver worked for her on Mondays, Tuesdays and Wednesdays, by arrangement with Shantha Prasad, fellow resident of Mahalakshmi Gardens. Neither of them required a full-time driver and they were both agreed that it would be an extravagance. So a mutually convenient arrangement had been struck, with Susheela offering to let Shantha have the driver during the latter half of the week, including Saturdays. It was a sacrifice that Susheela hoped would be acknowledged by a similar act of kindness. This never came.

She was surprised to see that there was hardly a soul at the Plaza Sweet Mart. She made her selection and then walked down the road to pop in to Great Expectations. Ashok the owner stood up as soon as he saw her.

'Welcome madam, not been here for many days.'

'How are you? I came one evening, I think your daughter was here. Nice girl.'

'Thank you, madam. Looking for anything particular?'

'Any books on Ayurveda? But properly written please, not by some fraud who makes up any old rubbish. There are plenty of those. *Vata*, *pitta*, *kapha*, alpha, beta, gamma . . . as if no one will notice.'

Ashok smiled sadly, apparently wounded by the depths of chicanery in the publishing business, and busied himself at a display, looking for books that would not affront Susheela.

A mulch of sweet wrappers and plastic bags lay at the entrance to the cyber café. The sliding door sat uneasily in its groove, threatening to crash to the ground at any moment. Girish could not tell whether or not the place was open for business. He knocked on the door and, a few muffled noises later, the door slid open by a few inches. He could just about make out the face of a girl with a red *dupatta* loosely covering her head. She raised her eyebrows once in quick enquiry.

'Open?' asked Girish, an edge of annoyance creeping into his voice.

The girl raised her eyebrows again and stepped slowly to one side, pushing the door open by a few more inches.

Girish stepped into the dim room, turning his shoulders away from the girl in disgust. What kind of a business were these people running? Probably a front for some terrorist cell, a *mujahidin* network having decided that Sitanagar in Mysore would be the perfect base for their activities. One just never knew these days.

Six partitioned surfaces holding computer monitors had been crammed into the tiny area. The room had no windows and the only light was the murky indigo flicker from the grimy screens. The woman pointed at a computer in the corner and returned to her own screen. Girish squeezed into the space indicated and began his circuit. He had an email from his credit card company, one from Indian Railways and one from a colleague sending on a tedious list of differences between 'the smart Indian man' and 'the smart Indian woman'. He moved on to various news websites, barely absorbing the first few lines of a story before clicking on another link. Then he checked into a couple of motoring websites.

There was a knock on the door and the girl pushed her chair back with a screech. This time she had a hurried conversation with someone wearing a baseball cap and returned to the gloom of her station. A mosquito dived past his ear with its urgent whine. He once again resolved to buy a computer before the end of the following month. It was simply untenable that he should continue to come to this rank hole and pay money for the privilege.

Girish had profiles on three social networking sites, all featuring the same brief account. A couple of allusions to his seniority were buried in the short description of his career; there were half a dozen photographs taken during his honeymoon in Ooty; and he had added a list of interests which probably had contained elements of veracity at some point. He had no idea why he even logged on to these sites any more. They had brought neither stimulation to his social life nor favour in his career. As a creature of habit, he supposed that it was just something else that he had built into his routine. He did occasionally like to catch up on the current status of ex-colleagues and college mates. The truth was that he probably scrutinised their profiles a little more than occasionally; quite a bit more. But then wasn't that what these websites were for? To present a palatable record of your own life and to gawk at the signposts planted by your peers?

According to Mohit Joshi's profile he was now based in Singapore, in charge of IT systems for a finance company. There he was posing in front of a fountain on Sentosa Island with his fat wife and lumpy kids. He had apparently decided that he was of American stock. His latest post began: 'Hey wassup dudes! Howsit hanging?!' This was from a man who had not left Firozabad until he was nineteen. Mohit's friends on the website seemed to be similarly deluded simpletons, fleshy calves emerging from khaki shorts at various recreational locales.

A few weeks ago, Girish had been surprised to discover that Abhijit Dutta was now some big-shot television producer in Delhi. In fact, Girish had only thought of looking him up online when his name had flashed up on the credits of a programme on Star One. In a bored moment Girish had wanted confirmation, and Abhijit had popped up in at least twenty-five pages of Google hits. He had certainly moved on from the affable but nondescript entity he had been at university.

Girish's recollections of his time at university always fixed him at the centre of a charismatic group with a keen sense of purpose. He had chosen to go to a well-regarded college, part of Delhi University, wanting to escape the reach of his provincial background. But once settled in his cheerless shared room in the men's hostel, surges of panic had begun to break over him. Faced by the adamant indifference of college cliques, sequestered in an alien city, for the first time he had cause to question his assumed route to success.

Some months later, a more senior student had come to Girish's rescue, spotting him at a debating society meeting. A final year mathematician, active in student politics, he had begun shepherding Girish to meetings and rallies, gabbling into his face every time a local party bigwig made an appearance on campus. At first Girish had gratefully tailed his new mentor, hugely relieved at this turn of events. The appearance of energetic activity that marked out the student politicians gave him an identity that he craved, in the face of the wealthier and more confident undergraduates who snaked around the campus. They were able to procure first day, first show balcony tickets at any cinema and tease out knowing laughter from girls in bright *churidars* at the local eateries. Girish had come to take his academic excellence for granted and needed some other insignia in that unfamiliar new world.

In time, he had become more actively involved in student politics, persuaded by his new circle that his contribution would be essential. He knew he could speak well (or, as he preferred, 'orate') and it was the admiration and exhortations of his associates, rather than any natural ambition or ideology, that was the impetus to his political activities. He began by absorbing the methods of the student union apparatchiks. The murky patterns of patronage and intimidation practised by the mainstream parties were reflected within the student union factions, abetting the rise of a number of muscular political personalities on campus. A student organisation affiliated to a major party would identify particular colleges where block votes could easily be delivered. It would then attempt to manipulate admissions procedures there to ensure that efficient student campaigners would gain entry to the college.

The political causes espoused at these colleges were becoming increasingly circumscribed: agitation for the reversal of college disciplinary sanctions against a student union official; a forced boycott of lectures following the announcement of inopportune union election dates; and protests demanding the release of an election candidate, arrested for unlawful possession of firearms. Girish quickly came to understand the nature of these operations but was untroubled by their complexion or by the alternate voices within the student community calling for a union clean up. The practice of politics was dirty and there was little to be gained from being blind to that fact. Girish was now speaking eloquently before appreciative audiences, was involved in strategy meetings and writing speeches for campus heavyweights. This was the real draw.

In Girish's final year, rumblings began to sound that the government was finally going to implement the recommendations of the Mandal Commission: the introduction of quotas for 'backward' classes for recruitment to public sector jobs and admission to government universities. The proposed extension of the state's affirmative action policies meant that almost half of all government jobs and university places were to be reserved for members of lower castes. It did not take long for the college student body's position to become clear, dominated as it was by upper castes. The organisations on campus were, however, getting mixed signals from the major political parties, who were unsure where to nail their colours, still debating whether the proposals amounted only to inconsequential government bluster. In a change from the usual internal politicking, rival student organisations began to come together to protest against the Mandal recommendations, convinced that upper caste youth were being dispossessed of the opportunities that were available to them.

Girish suddenly found himself in a widening fissure, a situation that demanded action. His participation thus far had seemed almost abstract, his interests lying in the execution rather than in the achievement. Now as demonstrations and walk-outs began to gather momentum across North Indian universities, Girish and his peers were called upon to articulate a very specific opposition to this new wave of social reconstruction.

Girish had always known that as a Brahmin of limited means, he would have to be the product of his own diligence and resourcefulness. This had never been a concern as he was secure in his assessment of his academic abilities and had begun to believe in the mantra of merit and efficiency that would finally open doors in a secular, democratic India. Caste was not a factor that needed to feature in these calculations. Its natural habitat was the remote feudal dust plains and tribal thickets of a different modernity. For Girish, caste had become a personal matter, a private cultural identity bound up only with the desultory practice of rituals in the kitchen and the *pooja* room.

But the shifting configurations of state patronage meant that his caste identity had reared up in a public arena to make him feel that his future was under assault. High levels of caste-based reservations had existed for years in South India but his awareness of them had been dim. It was only now that his consciousness snagged on the jagged tip of the protests erupting all around him. The student agitation in a number of North Indian cities was becoming increasingly violent. In Delhi a group of students from Girish's college had tried to barricade parts of Race Course Road and Kemal Ataturk Road, both points a short distance from the Prime Minister's official residence. Another group had attacked a police station in Moti Bagh, reports of arrests of students and custodial brutality having made their way back to the campus. This new realm of action was a jurisdiction too far for Girish, the supercilious wordsmith: he had never conceived of a reality beyond his finely crafted speeches.

Not long after he had spoken at a debating society meeting, the publication of an image in newspapers and magazines sent a devastating charge through the arteries of the urban elite. In one horrifying instant, a young man in a pale blue T-shirt, his upper body consumed by flames, faced the camera's lens with an ossified grimace. The student was a commerce undergraduate who had walked into a busy junction outside his South Delhi college, doused his body with kerosene and set himself on fire in protest at the government's decision to implement the Mandal recommendations. A number of self-immolations followed in other cities, each appalling incident polarising positions further. The serial debater, however, became curiously silent, fading into the dim hallways of his student hostel. His absence was noted but not acted upon in the frenzy of those eventful days.

Girish put an end to all his political activities and distanced himself from anyone who was likely to seek an explanation for his desertion. Instead he focused his energies on his studies, reaping an impressive number of gold medals by the time he graduated the following year. His activist days were never to return. They left only a hard certainty, like a cyst under his skin, that the world into which he was about to launch himself was one where, at the stroke of a pen, the meritorious could be ousted and their rewards expropriated. Girish returned to Mysore, the gait of a martyr already assimilated.

A distant rumble grew into a more discernible pattern of shouts and hand-clapping. At first it sounded like crowd noises from a radio but it was soon clear that this was something quite different. Susheela looked up from the book that she was holding.

'What's happening?' she asked.

At that moment Ashok's mobile phone rang and he apologetically put his hand up to Susheela as he answered it. She watched him as he murmured into the phone. The clamour seemed to be getting louder.

'Madam, that was my son. Seems there is some agitation in the city. Those theme park farmers.'

'What theme park farmers?'

'They are having a *dharna* in the city today and I think there has been some trouble.'

Ashok looked grave and walked towards the door, beyond which the street seemed unusually forsaken. His mobile phone rang again and he answered it standing in the doorway, looking in both directions.

Susheela put her book down and moved to the window. Through the gaps in the wooden shelving she could see only a few pedestrians, a trickle of two-wheelers grumbling past and no autorickshaws at all.

The theme park farmers. There had been something in the paper about them, but with the endless reporting on the progress of

HeritageLand, Susheela found it difficult to recall exactly who was aggrieved and for what reason.

'Madam, I think I am going to have to shut the shop. They have closed both sides of MG Road and I think there has been a *lathi* charge.'

Susheela reached into her handbag for her mobile phone. She looked in every compartment, a hot rush spreading over her neck and chest. Then she searched again through the bag, tearing at zips and plunging her hand into linty corners, and then looked up at Ashok. There was a ghostly lull in the street outside but layered with invisible waves of ferment, an upheaval that did not give many clues as to its complexion.

'I don't have my phone with me. I must have left it in the car. I don't know how to reach the driver,' said Susheela.

'Where is your driver?'

'I don't know. If there is no parking, he normally just goes round the block a few times but today, I don't know, he must be stuck somewhere on the other side. And I don't have his number here.'

Ashok's phone rang again and he began nodding as he walked back towards his desk.

A police siren began to sound a couple of streets away: a grudging, plaintive noise. Moments later another siren joined the first, the loops of discordant caution appearing to surround the shop. The sound of the protest rose and fell like the swash of a distant ocean. As Susheela listened, a roar went up, followed quickly by a blast of whistles.

Ashok looked up for a moment and then continued talking quietly into his phone. Susheela looked out into the street again but there was no further indication of events unfolding a few blocks away. She chewed on the inside of her mouth. She was furious with herself for having left her phone in the car, furious at the driver for not noticing and furious at this ridiculous predicament where law-abiding members of society could not go about their business because of a bunch of disaffected thugs looking to cause trouble.

The crash of a shutter coming down next door sounded much louder than it ought to have done.

Ashok finished his call.

'They have burnt a bus near KR Circle. I think the police have sealed off most of the area.'

'What are we going to do?'

'Madam, I'm very sorry but I have to close the shop. These *goondas* will start throwing stones through the windows any minute now. They don't need an excuse.'

Susheela stared blankly at him.

'Don't worry, madam, I have my scooter here. I only live about twenty minutes away. You can come home with me and call someone to pick you up. My wife is at home. Please don't worry, everything will be fine. I just don't think we should stay here any longer, you know; anything can happen.'

'You're going to so much trouble. But you're right, we can't stay here. I think . . . thank you so much.'

Ashok took all the notes out of the cash register, snapped a rubber band around them and tucked them into his pocket. He locked the door to the stock room and switched the lights and fan off.

'Okay madam, we can go now.'

They left the shop and Ashok locked the main door and quickly wound down and secured the shutter. More than half of the shops in the street were closed and no vehicles were moving. The trouble sounded more distinct now. A body of shouts, police whistles, a strange drumming and occasional loud bursts that sounded like fireworks. The empty pavement glistened in the noon glare.

'Madam, one minute, madam. Don't worry, I'm coming straight back.'

Susheela stared in horror as Ashok darted quickly down a side street and disappeared out of view.

The protest had begun with tractors parked all around KR Circle, blocking all the traffic going towards Devaraja Urs Road. The farmers had formed a human chain around the statue of Maharaja Krishnaraja Wodeyar mounted at the centre of the circle. Two groups had unfurled large banners where the assembled camera crews would be able to frame them with ease. Further down, a couple of trucks blocked the area around Gandhi Square. A number of speakers had stood up under the clock tower, each taking it in turns with the microphone rigged up to a small van on the other side of the square.

The 'theme park farmers', as they had come to be known, were not the prominent agriculturalists whose vast acreages had borne fruitful political connections and clout. They were the anxious custodians of small tracts, already divided up many times over successive generations, and destined for further apportionment. Their place in the new economic order was even more unclear than the intentions of the sympathetic-sounding surveyors, consultants and brokers who were now making weekly visits to their homes. In recent months, a network of community leaders and NGO representatives had also been making those same journeys, contradicting the reassuring statements of the previous visitors and firing up more speculation and hearsay.

It was these community leaders who had organised the KR Circle protest. Their message was simple. The government was pulling at the loose thread of their livelihoods, rapidly unwinding them, turning a perfectly serviceable garment into a length of useless yarn that would not clothe their wives and children. Farmers who had already been tricked into selling their land for the new theme park and link roads had been given insulting levels of compensation. The weight of the state's enforcement machinery was now being used to harass those farmers still refusing to sell their land.

All the concerned parties were becoming increasingly restive in anticipation of the High Court's decision on the legality of the land acquisition notices and the calculation of compensation. But as far as the protestors were concerned, they had to keep shouting loudly. There was no need to think that the battle was drawing to an end as it was far from clear that the judges would side with the farmers. To make matters worse, there were also strong rumours that some of the land, instead of being used for the theme park, would be resold to developers at an eye-watering premium, who in turn would parcel off the land and dispose of it at exponentially inflated rates.

For its part, the government saw the matter with unimpeachable clarity. It had already provided – voluntarily, it wished to stress – vast quantities of indisputable evidence to demonstrate that the completion of HeritageLand was vital for the development of the region. Not only would it generate large amounts of wealth for all persons residing within the catchment area, it would add to the prestige and standing of the whole state. The government expressed unmitigated outrage at the suggestion that any land would be misappropriated by officials and sold on to developers. If such mean-spirited allegations were being levelled at the government, it demanded proof of the existence of these base intentions. The state had already guaranteed that the land acquisition would not take place for any unconscionable transactions, so it was unable to understand the nature of the farmers' discontent. The government strongly suspected that the opposition was simply stirring up the emotions of these poor sons of the soil in order to make trouble in advance of the Assembly elections. If that were the case, the opposition had sunk to depths that the current legislators had never imagined possible. The government called upon all right-thinking members of the opposition to desist from this mischief as it was unethical, unconscionable and, most of all, un-Indian.

The assertions had gone back and forth during meetings, in newspapers, on television, at rallies and outside judges' chambers. It was, however, an unfortunate but incontrovertible truth that even the most eloquently phrased arguments could be displaced by a rock hurled from behind a parked tractor or a *lathi* rammed into the sinews of a field hand from Nanjangud. It would probably never be known which came first, the rock or the *lathi*. But what followed was documented with great precision and made it into most Mysore sitting rooms in a couple of hours as hyperactive spates of breaking news.

A row had broken out at one end of the road, where a truck had tipped out a heap of sand, encroaching on the strip of tar next to some half laid pipes.

'Oh, oh, is this your father's road? Take your rubbish and dump it somewhere else.'

A man in his mid-twenties had come running up to the side of the truck, gesturing at the sand.

The truck driver stopped drumming his fingers on the steering wheel and looked at the man.

'Take my father's name again and see what I do,' he said.

'How can you just block the road like this? We are having a function at home and a hundred people are coming down this way. What will they think?' asked the man, squinting up at the driver, his hand shading his eyes.

'I don't know anything about that. I am just doing what the building people told me. Go and speak to them inside,' said the truck driver.

Shankar was about to challenge the driver further but then

changed his mind. It was too hot, there were still so many things left to organise and he knew that the sand would never make its way back into the truck. He walked back home, his mobile phone pressed against his ear, calling a rickshaw driver to make sure that his wife's grandparents would be picked up in an hour, and then calling a distant cousin whom he had forgotten to invite. Better to confess now than to have to deal with the consequences of not inviting him at all.

The area in front of his house was covered by a bright red canopy, nailed down on to wooden poles on either side of the road. Rows of trestle tables and folding chairs occupied the centre of the road, providing shelter to a number of opportunistic stray dogs that would be banished later. A number of his mother's female relatives were standing in the doorway of his house and in its tiny front courtyard. A handful of Mysore silks crowded against some hand-loom cottons in the paltry shade cast by a tilting coconut tree; the talk was of the persecution effected by the school holidays. Shankar squeezed past the women and looked around for his wife, Janaki. He entered the house, walked down the dark corridor and knocked on the locked bedroom door. Janaki's sister let him in and shut the door again. He smiled sheepishly at Janaki's mother and Uma, who were sitting on a mat in the corner.

Janaki was lying on the bed, directly under the fan, its revolutions only sending down coils of feverish air. Her heavy green and gold sari seemed to weigh her down like a shroud and the sweat on her face had left her forehead spattered with pale patches where her powder had smeared.

'What other tortures have you got planned for me? Huh?' she asked, without opening her eyes.

'Are you not well?' asked Shankar.

Janaki did not respond. Shankar looked at Uma and Janaki's mother for assistance.

'Please Janaki, it's only a few hours, then you know you'll be going to your mother's house for six months. Or however long you want. Please, just for today,' he begged.

Janaki opened her eyes and the expression in them softened.

'Okay, don't be tense. I said I would do it, so I will. I just don't want to go and sit out there among those women until the last minute. You don't know what it's like being seven months pregnant and having to dress up like a festival cow, that too in the middle of summer. Now go, even your breath is making this room hotter.'

It was commonly acknowledged in their circle that Janaki had been extremely lucky in marrying Shankar, a handsome young man who was doing very well and, it was surmised, would do even better. He had started out as the apprentice to a small-time carpenter but had quickly learnt his trade and sought work in the expanding industrial area south of Mysore. A loan from a government scheme for small-scale entrepreneurs had meant that he had soon been able to start his own workshop. He had recently opened a second unit, taken on extra staff and was now able to meet large orders for cabinets and fittings from a chain of sports equipment shops in the city.

Janaki had met Shankar when he was still working on the industrial estate and she as a ladies' underwear salesgirl at Padmaja's Panty Palace in Vidyaranyapuram. Their first encounter had been at a Dasara exhibition a few years ago. Shankar had bumped into Janaki and her cousins, one of whom he had spoken to a few times at the local scooter repair shop. Janaki, a firm atheist, had been lured to the celebrations by the promise of unbeatable food stalls at the exhibition grounds. It was by the *pani puri* stand that Shankar had managed to get a proper look at her. Undoubtedly she had a special allure, with her eyes the colour of cloudy resin and her prominent cheekbones. Her looks collared the unworldly young man but it was her gritty self-possession that made her irresistible that afternoon. Over the course of the first couple of hours she had laid bare her unorthodox views on the festival, her evaluation of the snacks on offer and her plans to go to the evening computer classes run by the Tribhuvan Trust. Her preliminary interest in his life was something new too. Shankar was not in the habit of sharing details of his ambitions, but the confidences, imparted quietly amid the shouts of dancers and the crash of cymbals, seemed strangely apt.

Their relationship had proceeded tentatively at first. Shankar was unsure whether Janaki, even with her singularity, would appreciate his unsolicited attentions. He was, after all, a new and unendorsed acquaintance. A few weeks later, following Janaki's words of encouragement, he soon found himself waiting for her at dawn under the *gulmohar* trees by Tejasandra Lake or, in the evenings, keeping a gallant distance from the alarming window display at her place of work. For her part, Janaki had plunged into Shankar as she threw herself into the business of living: with complete absorption. In spite of the nature of Shankar's first gifts to Janaki – a tiger-print mobile phone case, a talking plastic heart and, once, a dozen eggs – within a few weeks they were spending most of their time off together. One Sunday afternoon Shankar took her to a secluded spot in Mysore Zoo, a stone in his throat, apprehension stinging his eyes. There he asked her to be his wife and she agreed, interrupted only by the irate shrieks from the gorilla enclosure.

The tag that now attached itself to Shankar was that of an adoring husband, still intoxicated by the heady balms given off by his beautiful wife. Neighbours and relatives observed with an affectionate wistfulness, or more often with self-righteous disdain, that Janaki was feted and indulged like a queen. Why was he spending so much money on a lavish send-off for his wife? Surely for a young couple like them a modest feast with only close family would have done. Didn't he know that he should only stretch his legs as far as his pallet allowed? All this *dhoom-dhaam* show, inviting half the town and making such a spectacle; she must have insisted on it. It was plain to see in the way she marched around. Over the next few months she would be at her mother's place but no doubt her writ would run large even from there.

Susheela stepped over a pile of magazines dumped at the entrance to the alley. She made her way slowly between the decaying walls on either side, streaked with ancient seepages and faded strips of film posters. Every few seconds she turned around to look back at the entrance to the alley, a rectangle of metallic light at the end of the desolate passage. The soles of her feet felt smooth and slippery, as if her sandals would slide off her feet at any moment. Small gaps between the buildings led to even narrower alleys. They were all empty. There was no sign of Ashok and even the stray dogs seemed to have disappeared from their haunts. She caught the acrid edges of the stench of burning rubber and looked up at the sky. A channel of brilliant blue wove its way above the upper stories of the shabby offices and warehouses on either side of the alley. Her eyes began to play tricks on her as the windows studding each floor began to vault and reel along the walls.

Susheela made her way back to the main road, once again stepping carefully over the stack of magazines. The heat was intense and she could now see smoke pluming over a nearby building. She leant back against a shaded section of the wall outside Great Expectations, her eyes shut, the windows now little blazing squares, swirling uncontrollably behind her eyelids. She was ready to believe the worst: that Ashok had abandoned her on this empty street, pulsing with unrealised violence and fully consummated fear. In Mahalakshmi Gardens a silent dread dragged its train over polished floors and stairs, through lush verandas, along driveways, past borders of coleus and lantana, under the pergola by the southern gate to the Gardens and into the latticed pavilion that gave on to the lotus pond. Now that dread had stalked Susheela into the centre of Mysore, trampling its veil on the hot asphalt.

'Excuse me.'

Susheela's heart lurched and she opened her eyes.

A man in his late sixties, or perhaps early seventies, stood before her, a look of concerned enquiry softening his brown eyes.

Susheela stared at the man, unable to comprehend this chain of events.

'I'm sorry, but are you okay? You know about the trouble in the city?'

Susheela nodded but her throat was too dry to speak.

'Please, it's not safe to stay here.'

A moment later he added: 'I'm sure we have met. If I'm not wrong, you're a friend of Sunaina Kamath's.'

Susheela nodded, although she was quite sure that she had never seen him before.

The man obviously decided that he needed to be a little more firm.

'Are you waiting for someone? Because, believe me, you should not be here by yourself like this.'

Susheela was explaining her predicament to the man when Ashok returned, jumping neatly up the few steps to where they were standing.

'So sorry, madam. I'm ready now. Shall we go?'

Susheela did not respond. Ashok continued to look at her sheepishly.

The man turned to him, his voice curt: 'Thank you for the offer but I will see the lady home.'

Turning to Susheela, he said: 'My car is in the basement of Prithvi House. If you don't mind walking with me just till there, I can drop you home. I am sure the roads on our side will be clear.'

Susheela nodded again, still tightly clasping the bag of *kaju pista* rolls from Plaza Sweet Mart.

The trestle tables had been covered with floral paper, the steel plates and tumblers wiped dry and the first batch of guests were patiently waiting for the servers to bring the food around. Uma had left Janaki reapplying her make-up and stood at some distance from the guests under the canopy. Particularly distinguished relatives, the elderly and the children would eat first, and once they had vacated their places, the young married couples, Shankar's business contacts and bachelor friends would take their seats. After their plates had been cleared, more distant family members and latecomers would be served before the final round of stragglers and community flotsam.

Janaki would have been appalled to see Uma alone, waiting out her turn in front of a pile of broken concrete slabs, a diffident and courteous half-smile fixed on her face. But Uma was not one to cultivate controversy by breaking established norms. She knew that she was already marked in the neighbourhood as someone requiring scrutiny, a woman living on her own with no apparent family ties. She had arrived at the row of tiny rooms with a history firmly laced up and stowed in some obscure compartment. Her guarded responses offered no clues and when the rumours began to uncoil around her, their frequency and intricacy were not surprising.

According to some local gossipmongers, Uma had arrived in Mysore from one of Bangalore's satellite towns where her lover had savaged her husband with a machete, most probably at her instigation. The lover was now said to be awaiting trial at Parappana Agrahara jail while Uma tried to create a new identity for herself elsewhere. Another account that had percolated through the narrow alleys was that Uma had been compelled to leave her husband's house in disgrace after seducing her father-in-law. Her apparent attempts at wringing cash and property out of the old man had failed and led to her exile in this bleak corner, below the network of sidings at Mysore Junction. There were other stories too: narrations that elicited spiky comment and drawn-out deductions.

Uma kept her counsel. She woke early and left for Mahalakshmi Gardens six days a week, returning only after seven in the evening. On the days when she had no packet of leftovers, she would stop at the provision store on the main road and buy a quarter-litre packet of yoghurt and, on occasion, some greens from one of the carts. She spoke to no one on the short walk past the Muslim cemetery and the coin-operated telephone clamped to a pole on the corner. As she walked down her row, she kept her eyes lowered and only lifted them once she had closed and bolted the door of her room.

It was almost a miracle that she and Janaki had ever spoken. At the time, Janaki had just moved in to Shankar's small house on the periphery of the squalid sprawl. Their paths had crossed a few times while Uma was looking for work and Janaki had taken a liking to Uma's sedate poise. Janaki had never probed into Uma's past but she felt duty-bound to support a lone woman who was refusing to choke in the neighbourhood's hostile smog. Janaki herself had been the target of malevolent gossip from a young age and had seen the dirty edges of everything that it touched. She knew that it was up to her to make the effort; if not, Uma would probably allow herself to fade away, bleaching back into the dirt-streaked walls around her.

'Uma, not eaten yet? Please go ahead, the next batch is just starting,' said Shankar as he brushed past her, weighed down with a pail each of *ghee* rice and *sambar*.

'I think I'll wait for Janaki.'

'No no, you better eat. She says she wants to eat inside later, away from the crowd. Actually what she said was a lot ruder than that,' Shankar lowered his voice, before heading towards the tables.

Janaki emerged from the house, led by Shankar's mother and aunt. A chair was quickly found for her and placed in the middle of the front courtyard. As she lowered herself into the chair, Janaki caught Uma's eye and beckoned her over.

Uma made her way past the canopy, through the thronged courtyard and leant down towards Janaki.

'What are you doing standing over there by yourself like a police constable? How was the food?' asked Janaki.

'It was very good.'

'You should tell Shankar; he has hardly been able to sleep. He was sure the caterers would ruin everything today.'

'So what time are you leaving for your mother's house?'

Janaki's voice became a throaty whisper: 'No idea. They have to make sure the sun, moon and every single planet are in the right position before I am allowed to fart, let alone leave here for six months.'

'They only want to make sure nothing goes wrong.'

'So you have my mother's address; make sure you come and see me next week or the week after. I will have nothing to do there but eat and sleep so plenty of time to talk. You'll come, no?'

'I'll definitely come.'

'Also, I've told Shankar to come and see you now and then. If you need any help for anything, you just ask him.'

'What help will I need? Really, there's no need to trouble him.'

Janaki's face took on a picture of theatrical outrage: 'After all the trouble he has given me? Look at me sitting here in this heat like a buffalo.'

Under the shade of the canopy, a teenager was pointing his camera at the servers, having assigned himself the role of official photographer of the event. Patches of sweat had made his white shirt translucent and an agonising concentration invaded his face. Among the seated guests, hair was hurriedly tamed, *pallus* were straightened and noses wiped: preparations the photographer chose to ignore as he made his way along the tables.

A mother said to her child: '*Ai gube, channag* smile *maado*. Face like a *kumbalakai*.'

In the washing area set up for the caterers, Shankar had just finished giving instructions to some young boys. He turned round and, seeing Janaki sitting in the courtyard, made an exaggerated bow in her direction, a saucy grin animating his features.

The car made its way out of the Prithvi House basement and sped along Sayyaji Rao Road where a couple of police barriers had been dragged to the side of the road and then abandoned. Angry discs of smoke wheeled up into the sky from a point behind the bazaar that lined one side of the street. A few cars were still on the road, all moving out of the city centre in the direction of Tejasandra Lake. A man lay on the ground in the shade of a mimosa tree at the Nelson Mandela Road junction. The position of his limbs gave no clue as to whether this was just respite from the heat or something more sinister.

Susheela had managed to ascertain that Sunaina's friend was called Jaydev and that he lived only fifteen minutes away from her in Yadavagiri. After that she had retreated into the air-conditioned chill of the car's interior, her temples throbbing and her throat sore. Jaydev's gaze moved from the mirror to the deserted road ahead and back. It was only when they were finally moving along the southern edge of the lake that he spoke.

'There is some water on the back seat if you want.'

'No, thank you.'

It occurred to Susheela that her response might have come across as brusque, so she added: 'I am just so relieved to be nearly home.'

She thought her voice sounded strangely loud and high-pitched.

Jaydev shook his head: 'Even Mysore can be a scary place these days.'

Susheela noticed that Jaydev's leather watchstrap was loose and that the watch had slid a third of the way down his arm. His hands, settled firmly on the steering wheel, had a prominent network of veins that crowded their way into his knuckles. The cold air circulating in the car had made the silver hairs on his arms rise. All of a sudden Susheela became aware of the fact that this was the first time since Sridhar's death that she had sat in the passenger seat of a car, being driven somewhere by a man. The car's low croon weighed heavily on her as the forced intimacy of the moment began to make her feel restless. The car's interior smelt of clean seats and a hint of jasmine. A CD of Carnatic violin music lay on the dashboard.

'I must thank you once again. God knows how long I would have been stuck there or what would have happened,' she said, needing to fill the space with words.

'No, no, please. It's just lucky I was passing. I actually got delayed waiting at my accountant's office while he was stuck somewhere and couldn't get into the city. Must be the same story everywhere. Anyway, at least we managed to escape from the mob. Just like in a movie.'

Jaydev turned to smile at Susheela.

She kept talking: 'The trouble is these days there is no community spirit. If you are a farmer or whatever and you want to agitate for something, there is no concern for how your actions will affect everyone else. Your aim needs to be achieved at any cost and the rest can all go to hell.'

Jaydev looked like he was listening to her intently but did not respond.

'I mean, especially for senior citizens, it is like we don't exist. We can't cross these crazy roads, we can't barge into queues like youngsters, we can't endlessly ask people to do things without going mad,' said Susheela.

The car was approaching Mahalakshmi Gardens, silent at this time of the afternoon.

Susheela laughed. 'I'm sorry. You have been kind enough to give me a lift and here I am, turning into one of those crazy raving people. It's right at the end of this road.'

'Not at all. I think speaking one's mind is one of the privileges of getting old. Let's face it, there aren't too many others,' said Jaydev.

Susheela smiled. The *mali* had come running to open the gate and the car pulled in to the driveway. Susheela got out of the car and noticed that the driver was still not back. She began to wonder whether something serious had happened.

She leant into the car and said, 'I really don't know how to thank you. Please come inside for some coffee?'

'No, thank you. Maybe some other time. I also need to get home.'

Susheela stood in the doorway, waving as Jaydev reversed out of the gates. As she turned to go inside the house, her throat felt inflamed and her head still ached. All she wanted to do was wash the grime off her body and lie down until the night air brought some relief.

Girish could hear the rasp of drawers being pulled open in the bedroom. There was a clang as the door of the metal cupboard swung open and hit the corner of a chair. The room fell silent for a few moments before he heard the muffled sigh of something being lifted on to the bed. The cupboard door clicked back into place and the drawers were eased back with a jiggle. Mala emerged from the bedroom, a few loose strands of hair hanging limply by the sides of her face. Her forehead and nose glistened and a flush was forming on the skin between her collarbones, like a wet stain under a piece of muslin.

'Some electricity man had come here to cut the supply. He said we hadn't paid the bill,' she said, leaning against the door.

'I thought you said you had paid it.'

'I did pay it. I told him that but I couldn't find the receipt. That's what I was looking for just now. He said he's coming back later.'

'That would be a great thing, no? The regional deputy chief of customer relations for electricity has not paid his own bill and so his current is cut.'

'I told you, I *have* paid it. I just need to find the receipt. If they didn't have such useless records, they would know that I have paid it.'

'You better find it before he comes back.'

'I know that.'

'I am not going to bother calling someone up to sort all this out at the office, if that's what you're expecting.'

'I was looking for it just now. I'll find it.'

Mala sat down next to Girish and added as an afterthought: 'If you are so worried about it all, maybe next time you should pay it yourself and not leave everything to me.'

Her hand lay on the waxy surface of the sofa, fingers curled upwards. Girish began to press down on them with his hand. He continued to look straight ahead; only a slight spasm in his jaw hinting at any effort. The heel of his hand crushed her fingers, a commanding force bearing down through the heft of his neck and shoulder.

Mala flinched.

'No, stop it, please. That's really hurting.'

Girish grabbed her hand and began to force it upwards. Mala's fingers were trapped in a ridge of pain and her wrist began to tremble under the strain.

'What are you doing? Stop it.' Mala wrenched her hand away, pushing herself off the sofa.

Girish stood up.

The blow, when it came, was definitive. The impact of the slap loosened a tooth, rattled the glass cabinet doors, cracked the paving stones by the gate, split the trunk of an ancient tamarind tree in the lane outside, sent an alley dog skittering away in terror, collapsed the humpback bridge that led to the main road and caused a lone cold wave to begin rising over the surface of distant Tejasandra Lake.

PART TWO

Monsoon

CHAPTER FOUR

THE senior executives of the Mysore Tourism Authority (MTA) were worried. Their critics in the local and trade press were becoming increasingly vocal.

'We need dynamic individuals who will take resolute action to rescue our ailing tourism industry,' thundered a front page article in the *Mysore Evening Sentinel*.

A leading hotel owner, interviewed at a travel fair, had been more blunt: 'This band of baboons simply moves around from one luxury hotel to another, enjoying free hospitality and talking nonsense at their good-for-nothing events. I can tell you one thing, they are most certainly not welcome at my hotel.'

The information from associations of tour operators, travel agents and hotel owners was not encouraging. A survey across Tier I and Tier II cities by a market analysis firm showed a disquieting ignorance of Mysore's main attractions, coupled with a worrying lack of interest. There was no doubt that serious efforts would have to be made to enhance the city's lustre. The momentum had to build since the beginning of construction at HeritageLand kept slipping every few months.

The MTA quickly rejected any kind of international onslaught. The focus quite clearly needed to be the Indian market, as large numbers of domestic tourists were travelling further and more frequently, with apparently ever-increasing holiday budgets. In any case, as far as overseas tourists were concerned, overtures could be made at a later stage for Mysore's prominent inclusion in the Ministry of Tourism's Incredible India campaign.

The MTA, not known for its radical promotional strategies, had at first decided to play it safe. It seemed that the most logical step would be to recruit a popular Hindi film personality to become Mysore's brand ambassador. An immediate issue had been the inability to identify a high- or medium-profile star with any connection to Mysore or its environs. A number of board members also began to question whether a close association with a major star would really capture the appeal of Brand Mysore. After all, if remunerated adequately, these luminaries were willing to lend their faces to everything from prickly heat powder to motorcycle engine oil.

The next suggestion was to approach reformed rowdy-sheeter and rising Kannada cine star, Nuclear Thimma, to represent Mysore. His hit songs were causing a sensation among the key youth demographic in South India and he had lived for many years opposite a mutton stall just yards from Mysore Junction. But he simply did not have the required national allure and his unfortunate past was an insurmountable obstacle. The idea was scrapped.

The board of executives decided that specialist assistance was required and set up a number of meetings with advertising agencies and brand consultants. A full briefing was sent out to the relevant representatives, pitches were prepared and the business of illuminating Mysore began in earnest. The ideas put forward by the various creative departments ranged from the inane to the fantastical, a fact that did little to achieve consensus among the members of the MTA's board of executives. The elephant in the room was of course the many delays in the development of HeritageLand, a subject that was taboo in this sensitive congregation, many of whom felt faint at the mere thought of offending Venky Gowda.

After another round of meetings at various heritage properties, it was agreed that the proposal that offended the least number of people was the 'Geneva of the East' campaign. A team of consultants had drawn on Tejasandra Lake for inspiration and found that it had the potential to transform Mysore into a simulacrum of the Swiss city. The campaign would centre on the great range of attractions around the lake, from the Anuraag Kalakshetra and the museums at one end of the lake's shore to the Galleria's upmarket shops and restaurants at the other. Given the enduring affection for Switzerland among the Indian middle classes, brought up on a surfeit of films featuring chiffon-clad heroines on Alpine slopes, the campaign was certain to evoke the perfect melange of old-world sophistication and a suitably aspirational aesthetic. City officials on the board assured their colleagues that there would be a rapid improvement in basic services around the lake, including drainage and waste collection, in order to give credence to the key aims of the campaign.

Support for the 'Geneva of the East' campaign at the MTA was far from universal. A number of board members expressed their reservations in bald terms. One of the more pessimistic views was that it would simply invite ridicule and contempt, succeeding only in singling Mysore out as a city of deluded imbeciles. Another detractor felt that the campaign reeked of colonial sycophancy. He was later compelled to add that he was perfectly aware that Switzerland had not been in possession of any colonies and that he was gravely disappointed that some of his colleagues could not grasp simple critical concepts.

A further series of meetings were called in an attempt to make a final decision. As discussions continued, one fact became clear: the pulsing need for HeritageLand was being felt more keenly than ever.

The jets of water from the sprinklers at the Mysore Regency Hotel shot up like silver streamers on the expansive front lawn. The sprinklers were fed by an enormous reserve tank, which in turn drew upon one of two bore wells on the property. A third had run dry a few years ago. Mysore's public water supply was somewhat unreliable even at the height of the rainy season, so this year, after five dry months, expectations were not great. In any case, Mysore's custodians of luxe were accustomed to navigating their way around the shortcomings of the municipal authorities. The hotel often purchased water from private suppliers and the results were more than satisfactory. A healthy thicket of palms by the main gate provided the security guards with some shade. On the borders below the wide verandas the camellias were flourishing, and despite the prolonged summer their leaves had retained their imperial gloss.

The driveway curved around the front lawn and stopped at the grand Indo-Saracenic foyer. A turbaned doorman opened car doors to allow visitors to walk up the mosaic steps towards the front desk, burnished with furniture wax and the best hospitality training. The mahogany writing desk in a corner of the room was said to be a replica of the one owned by Sethu Lakshmi Bayi, Maharani of Travancore. The windows next to the reception hardly let in any light as they were almost covered by a lunatic cascade of allamanda vines that dropped to the ground outside. The reception area was lit by the amber cups of a Hyderabadi chandelier, their glow reflected in the shards of mirror that studded the occasional tables. On the other side of the front desk, a set of brass doors led to the veranda bar, the Burra Peg.

The hotel had always been popular with British and French tourists, and these days select Russian and Chinese guests too. Security had recently been tightened and cars were inspected with particular care when the occupants were young men displaying an unnatural intensity. On most Saturday evenings during auspicious months a white marquee would be hoisted up over the lawn, strings of milky lights looped between its poles. A happy couple would accept the assembled company's best wishes, drifting around the tables covered in stiff alabaster damask and strewn with miniature candles and champagne roses. At a given moment, the band would start up in a riot of congratulatory blasts, and a few moments later the hotel switchboard would be jammed with calls from furious hotel guests.

A few discreetly placed paving stones skirted around the edges of the front lawn to the staff entrance, located at the back of the hotel and screened off by an imposing bamboo. Here the ravages of the summer were more apparent. Ashen tufts on the ground in front of the laundry had been abandoned to their fate. The hydrangeas lining the unloading bay were globes of mauve dust waiting for a rare gust to blow them apart.

Mala looked at her watch as she approached the staff entrance. She was slightly early so she stood in the shade of the bamboo for a few seconds, wiping the back of her neck with a handkerchief.

Inside the hotel, in a small office behind the front desk, the other two employees of the accounts department were already at work. Mr Tanveer was the 'in-charge', a responsibility he bore with all due solemnity. Given to bouts of pronounced anxiety, his predisposition was given away by the habitual expression on his face, that of a man who had just fallen down a well. He tried, at least at the outset, to take a generous view of his friends and colleagues but found that his confidence was seldom rewarded, a fact that often instigated a theological enquiry: why had God created man, if not to disappoint Mr Tanveer? Apart from his unyielding commitment to his duties, he was also known for the startling array of items he carried in the pockets of his trousers. A hole punch, a self-help book, an unripe mango and a spanner had all been produced, at one time or another, from those seemingly bottomless repositories.

Opposite Mr Tanveer sat Shipra, originally from Mumbai, noted at work for her large hands, which she liked to adorn with numerous turquoise rings.

'Shipraji, did you check those figures from yesterday? What had that girl done?' asked Mr Tanveer, his head suddenly shooting up.

'No idea, sir. Here, I have redone part of the report but should I finish the whole thing?'

'No, can you speak to her when she comes in and kindly do the needful? Try and make her understand again what has to be done and ask her to finish it by business close.'

'Okay sir, surely I'll do that.'

Mr Tanveer sighed, his expression tightening into even greater distress.

'You know, this is what happens when people get jobs through influence. After that they can just make merry but it all falls on someone else's head,' he said.

'Is she from some big-shot family?'

'No no, she is from some small, godforsaken place, but her brother-in-law is that Anand.'

'Which Anand?'

'G S Anand.'

'Which Anand?'

'What which-Anand which-Anand, I'm telling you, no? That fellow who owns Exospace.'

'Oh I see.' Shipra still looked blank.

'Yes. So he asked our big man to give this girl a position and now they have put her here. Our misfortune.'

'There are so many capable people, sir, with no hope of getting a job and look here.'

'I know. What can you do?'

Shipra adjusted one of her rings.

'But sir, maybe she'll learn. You never know.'

Mr Tanveer's head shot up again: 'Shipraji, she will not learn. That much I know.'

108

Mala's parents had always agreed that the important thing was for her to graduate. The field of study was not of great importance as, it had to be admitted, she had never shown a strong aptitude in any particular area. The point was that a degree was essential for any kind of economic independence, and of course, even married women needed to be economically independent these days. A modest donation had enabled her to secure a place at the private RMV College. Rather surprisingly, a marriage proposal had arrived while she was still in the second year of her commerce degree. The young man in question was, however, a translator at a small publishing house and probably did not earn enough to support himself, let alone a family.

Rukmini had refused to even consider the offer. As far as possible, she was determined not to condemn her daughters to a life of the constant mental arithmetic that came with paring and pruning the budget. Babu had reached the same conclusion too, although perhaps swayed by a different consideration: the output of the publishing house in question seemed limited mainly to a tawdry range of detective novels set in the red-light districts of Chennai. In any case, Mala needed to complete her degree; then the quest for a husband could begin in earnest.

Mala's days at RMV College seemed to sound a knell towards an indeterminate future. She would wake each morning at half past five, bathe, light the two small *ghee* lamps in front of the picture of Ganesh and pray solidly for half an hour. Before leaving for college she would engage in a couple of hours of consolidation, going over the previous day's lectures and diligently asterisking key points with an encircled 'NB'. Later she would arrive at the wrought-iron gates of the college, her rucksack crammed with texts on corporate accounting and marketing principles, her notebooks colour-coded and covered with the incontinent loops of her handwriting. In the last month before examinations she would sit on the back steps of the house in the tawny haze of early morning, her lips mouthing the knowledge that had to be jammed into her brain, a bowl of almonds soaked in milk cradled in her lap.

At the end of her final year the results were as expected: undistinguished but not mortifying.

'Anyway, she is not going to head off to be a collector. It will do,' her elder sister Ambika had said.

A few years earlier Ambika had graduated with a first class degree in engineering and was now married to a surgeon who called her 'white white face'. There had never been any doubt that Ambika would attract a creditable alliance. Even as a fifteen-year-old, her face had frequently been compared to the carved idol of the deity at the Mahagauri temple in Konnapur. Added to her milky skin and expressive eyes, these features meant that Ambika was married by the time she was twenty-three. True that by then she had begun to put on the extra weight, but what did it matter? Once she was married, she was married. Now that her husband had set up his own nursing home she was actively involved in its administration and was hardly ever seen in Konnapur. Her brisk efficiency kept the forty-bed facility running smoothly and the couple had plans to open a new wing for gynaecological services.

As Ambika's husband liked to point out: 'There is no boom and bust in life and death.'

A couple of months after the graduation ceremony, Mala began to dedicate herself to the process of finding a husband, putting in the same kind of studious preparation that had structured her college days. She kept a watchful eye on her weight, stayed out of the sun and continued praying. Every morning she applied a gram flour and rose-water face pack and twice a week massaged her scalp with a paste made from six tablespoons of yoghurt, half a banana, two teaspoons of honey and a tablespoon of lemon juice. On the day that her photos were to be taken, she had a special hibiscus facial at Soundharya Beauty Parlour and her hair was carefully blow-dried for the first time, notwithstanding Rukmini's firmly held belief that hairdryers only led to baldness. The photographer was encouraging: he was confident that she would find a wonderful life partner within weeks. He assured Rukmini that he had developed a sixth sense in such matters, having been in the business for over thirty years.

The marriage broker that Rukmini visited was less conciliatory.

'Look madam, I don't cheat my clients, I don't make false promises, I don't say that the sun rises in the west. I have to give you an honest assessment. She doesn't have height, only a B.Com, colour okay, features passable and – I am sorry, but I am only repeating what you have said – there is no question of much property or money. In our community, the question of dowry does not arise, thank God, but still, people look at these things. And you want what everyone wants: a good-looking boy from the right caste, with a good education, good family background, good job, good prospects and a good horoscope match. At the moment, I don't know; you will just have to leave it with me. Let's see what happens,' she had said, scrutinising Mala's photos with a practised severity.

Rukmini had left the marriage broker's house in a state of deep agitation. In her world people tended to speak in practised allusions, cloaking barbed truths in a mantle of assurances. Her throat contracted sharply as she realised that her second daughter faced an unforgiving few months.

The reality was that it took nearly two years. By the time a distant relative had suggested Girish's name, Mala's photos had been circulated as far as Pune and Coimbatore.

'A little puny.'

'Not bad looking but her nose is pretty bulbous, no?'

'The boy is too tall, see her height. It won't look good.'

'She's fine, she's nice; it's just that he has seen someone that he really liked.'

'Nothing doing.'

After a while, Rukmini simply stopped making the follow-up calls. She maintained a garrulous optimism for the benefit of her husband and daughters and was careful not to relay any adverse comments to them. The message she passed on was always that 'something did not suit, you know what people are like, they are never straightforward.'

Babu had suggested that it would be good for Mala to find a different focus while they waited for marital matters to arrange themselves. A few weeks later she found a part-time job as an accounts assistant at a PUC college. On her second day there Mala discovered that any fiscal propriety enforced by the school board was a matter purely of historical interest. The college accountant to whom she had to report was rarely to be seen and a similar level of absenteeism flourished among the other members of staff and the students. Her mornings were spent in a dusty room at a desk supporting numerous ancient ledgers and what appeared to be a computer of similar vintage.

Mala dutifully turned up on time every day and left the office just before lunch. In the intervening hours there was not much to disturb her nervous ruminations. At that point the future seemed like a place of fantasy to Mala, peopled by spectres adrift in a nebulous realm of responsibilities. Occasionally a student would pop into the room with a query and then drift away. Some mornings Mala would copy type a few pages of a newspaper article or an old report and then, upon completion, erase all the words. Much of the time she looked out at groups of girls and boys in the compound who would congregate in the shade of a *neem* tree, framed by the jagged edges of the glass in the office's broken window.

Months later, by the time talks had begun with Girish's aunt,

Mala had given up the job. She was more than willing to be guided in life by those better informed than her, but even she could see that there was absolutely no benefit to be gained from spending any more time in that sepulchral space. At that point Ambika had offered to step in and provide her with an administrative position at the nursing home. It would keep her from sitting at home and she might learn some new skills. But Rukmini had felt that Mala was better off at home in Konnapur where prospective husbands could meet her and her parents. It had become a habit not to ask Mala for her views. She had been denied the vernacular of agency for so long that her reticence merely glanced off the bulwark of parental concern.

The interest from Girish's aunt came at an opportune time but it was not without its complications. The twelve-year age gap was hardly ideal and, crucially, Rukmini and Babu had wanted to know why Girish was not yet married. In theory, someone like him should not have had many problems finding a girl, and yet there he was, a man single at the age of thirty-five. Was there some health condition in the family, a long-term girlfriend who had finally spurned him or, God forbid, a foreign wife in America? The family intermediary had not been able to ascertain the precise reason for Girish's single status. She could only surmise that there might have been some sort of romantic disappointment but the crucial factors were all in place: he was tall and slim, had excellent antecedents, an exemplary academic record and a good job at a state electricity distribution company. Tragically, his mother had drowned while on a pilgrimage and his father had since moved to an *ashram* in Kerala. There was one brother, a wealthy business-man, also in Mysore, and a scattering of decent relatives elsewhere. Apart from his age there was nothing to indicate that he was not a good match. Besides, Mala had been sitting at home for nearly two years now. The family intermediary was certainly not the kind of person who would presume to tell them what to do. She had simply presented the facts.

Four months later Girish and Mala were married and on their honeymoon in Ooty.

The papaya seller meandered down 7ᵗʰ Main in Mahalakshmi Gardens most mornings between ten and half past ten. His cry usually began as a bellicose challenge; by the time he had negotiated his way to the final syllable, it emerged as a squall of triumph.

'Uma, look in the basket. Is there a papaya for tomorrow?' asked Susheela, from the armchair in the sitting room.

'Yes, *amma*, there is.'

Uma's voice was always only just audible, as if greater volume would instigate a sudden vocal collapse.

A few moments later she moved into the sitting room, sweeping the floor with a brisk circular motion. Susheela took off her reading glasses, folded up the newspaper and stood up to move to a different part of the room.

'No sign of any rain,' she announced, looking sternly through the patio doors.

The brittle whisper of the broom continued against the floor.

Susheela sighed and walked towards the bookshelves. She had no idea what it would take to get any conversation out of this girl. She did not expect Uma to discuss politics or philosophy but even coaxing out a bland observation seemed impossible.

Uma had come to her on the recommendation of a friend in Yadavagiri. She had only been working with them for an hour each day but the friend could confirm that her work was neat and she arrived mostly on time. Susheela had sent word that she wanted to see Uma. Her previous maid had moved away and she needed to employ someone else in a hurry. She had already asked two girls to come to the house for a preliminary assessment. The first had arrived on the back of a pink scooter, tittering into a mobile phone. Susheela had stared at her long silver fingernails and the jangly accessories that hung off her handbag. Would this girl scrub pans or just use the house as a convenient base to conduct sundry love affairs? The second said her name was Jolly. As if that weren't bad enough, she had turned up three hours late, taken a good look at every room in the house and decided that the job was not for her.

'Perhaps she did not care for my choice of curtains,' Susheela had remarked to Priyanka, with a voice that could slash through sisal.

Uma seemed the type who would be grateful to work in a decent house. She had arrived slightly early, dressed in a plain yellow sari, the *pallu* pulled over her slender shoulders. Susheela noticed that her neck was bare. A single gold bangle glinted against her dark wrist. She was engaged on trial for a month, her breakfast and lunch would be taken care of and she would get Sundays off.

Susheela could not find any fault with Uma's work but this wraithlike behaviour was beginning to irritate her. She was not accustomed to people in her pay rejecting an invitation to conversation.

Susheela tried again: 'The corporation men were outside earlier. Did they say when they would finish all the digging?'

'No, *amma*, I didn't see them.'

Uma left the room without making eye contact, her anklets tinkling faintly with each step.

Susheela climbed the stairs, her tread heavy. She went into the study, opened a drawer and began to look through a freezer bag full of old cheque book stubs.

❖   ❖   ❖

As soon as Mala arrived home she reached into the plastic bag and picked out a mango. She held it under the harsh spray from the tap and then dried it, swaddling it in the kitchen towel. She placed the fruit on a board and pushed a knife through the skin into its immodestly ripe flesh. The heady smell intensified at once and redoubled its attack on her senses. Expertly she judged the presence of the stone's edges and extracted it without letting any of the honeyed pulp go to waste. She sliced the fruit into five rectangles. Picking up the largest piece, she pushed her hair back, leant over the kitchen sink and sucked hard on the skin. Her tongue burrowed into the belly of the mango and her lips closed around its juices. Mala's eyes were shut; suspended in the darkness of her absorption, she negotiated every fibre in the fruit's marrow.

She gulped noisily and, putting aside the mangled skin, reached for another slice and sank her teeth into it. Unaware that her pleasure was now audible, she drew more of the flesh into her mouth, her grunts escaping into the air. She lifted her hand and plugged her lips around her knuckles to catch the juice that was beginning to trickle towards her wrist. Her tongue skimmed across the trails in the fruit left by her teeth. She wrung out the last of the slice.

A troublesome shred was caught between her front teeth, trying to provoke her into interrupting her gratification. Mala ignored it and slid a strip of peel out through her pursed lips. She reached for the mango's stone, cocooned in its rich sheath, and slipped it into her mouth. Her lower teeth grated against the knobby ridge at its heart as she stripped it clean. Easing the stone into her fist, she bit down on the tip and then swallowed hard.

She picked up another piece and then paused. Sensing a presence she spun around, flinging the fruit into the sink.

Gayathri stood at the kitchen door. Neither woman spoke until Gayathri let out a rasping guffaw.

'Enjoy, enjoy! They are the last ones of the season, after all,' she grinned.

A tuft of fruit clung to Mala's chin. Juice was dripping off her fingers onto the floor. She stared at Gayathri, a vicious flush spreading up from her neck to her ears.

Gayathri's face settled into a detached repose.

'I came to return the three hundred rupees that you lent me. Shall I just leave it here?' she asked.

Mala looked at the notes, rolled tightly in Gayathri's hand. She nodded, turned back to the sink and began to wash the juice off her hands.

Uma gathered her sari around her haunches as she squatted down to grate a coconut. Her hands made rapid, practised motions around the blade, its serrated edges devouring the white flesh.

'Uma, what news?'

Uma looked up at Bhargavi's head, which had suddenly appeared over the compound wall.

'Nothing at all. What about you?' asked Uma.

'Oh just working, going home, sleeping and back to work. And did I tell you? My landlord died.'

'No, was he sick?'

'He was all right. It was suicide. He drank pesticide and died at the hospital. Couldn't take any more harassment from his wife. For once, it was the husband that drank poison, eh?'

'So the wife is your new landlady?'

'Yes, I don't know whether she will keep the place or sell it. So I may need to move soon.'

Uma wiped the blade clean with a corner of her *pallu* and stood up with the plate of grated coconut.

'I'll see you,' she said.

'No wait, did you see the police jeep on 6th Main yesterday morning?' asked Bhargavi.

'No.'

'They had come for the man from the blue house, you know, the one with all those dogs.'

Bhargavi paused for any indications of excitement and, receiving none, went on: 'I found out from the watchman. The woman who lives there with him is not his wife, her husband is in Bombay, some MP or MLA. She left him there to come to live with this man, so the husband used his influence to put a police case on him, saying he kidnapped his wife.'

Uma did not look entirely convinced that such intrigues could be playing out on 6th Main.

'It's true; anyway, that's what the watchman said. The police took that poor man away to the lock-up last night and when they came back this morning, his face looked like a pumpkin. The woman has not come home since yesterday so God knows what has happened to her.'

'I have never seen her. Or him.'

'Too late to see either of them now I think.'

'I'll see you. I'm going inside.'

'Okay, but keep your ears open for once. If you find out anything, let me know.'

'I didn't know they had a watchman during the day,' said Mala, as the uniformed guard gave them a jaunty salute and opened the gates.

'Well, you know Anand is a big man now, he probably has all kinds of mafia dons wanting to kidnap him,' replied Girish, parking the blue hatchback behind his sister-in-law Lavanya's silver Lexus.

Mala looked at Girish, not sure if he was being serious.

'Take the fruit basket,' said Girish, giving himself a quick glance in the rear-view mirror before getting out of the car.

The fruit basket had featured prominently in the day's itinerary. The initial plan had been to pick something up at the usual fruit stall in Sitanagar. But an inspection of the selection there had revealed a mound of shrivelled oranges and an ailing watermelon. Girish had then driven to Devaraja Market where he had chosen a suitably carnivalesque combination, only to find that the vendor intended to place his selection in an ugly plastic basket, covered with some grease-spattered cellophane.

The search had then begun for a more acceptable receptacle. The bamboo bazaar only stocked large bushels and trays and the man at one of the general stores had tried to sell Girish a basin that he swore was a fruit bowl. Finally, they had retreated to a shopping mall, where a number of themed fruit hampers were on display in the food section. Mala gazed at the Lovers' Delight, the Aroma-therapy Special and the Cheese N' Wine Deluxe, not even daring to look at the prices. Girish proclaimed that the entire range was in some way deficient and stalked off towards the household department. Half an hour later they emerged from the mall with a small woven basket and made their way back to Devaraja Market, where the vendor had callously returned Girish's selection to their original positions in his arrangement.

Mala now picked up the basket and followed Girish to the front door. Girish's brother Anand lived in a large Yadavagiri property that he had bought about three years ago. The house was completely incoherent in layout and style as each successive owner had indulged an architectural vision, or corrected an apparent lack of embellishment, with scant regard for the overall composition of the building. The result was bewildering. The ground floor extended across the site like a cubist fantasy: three giant blocks of equal size, arranged like a three-leaf clover. The first floor, resembling a Swiss ski chalet, seemed to have dropped from the sky quite by chance, attaching itself en route to a trio of pretty Juliet balconies. Above the first floor, a Gaudiesque turret rose up to menacing effect, competing for attention with a stately dome, dotted with a number of portholes. The full impact of the house was like being brought face to face with a deranged aunt who had decided to wear all her party dresses on the same day.

Lavanya opened the door as they approached it.

'I thought I heard the gate.' She winked, waving them in.

In the sitting room *Richie Rich*, dubbed into Hindi, boomed out of the 52-inch plasma screen on the far wall. Anand was seated cross-legged on the thick cream carpet, sporting a tiger mask, a pink *dupatta* wrapped around his head. As Girish and Mala walked into the room, he began to lift himself up.

'Ah, come in, come in. You have my permission. I am the maharani of the jungle, you see,' he explained.

Standing next to the armchair was his daughter Shruthi, a green *dupatta* tied around her neck, waving a steel whisk.

'*Appa*, I told you that you have to roar loudly before you say anything. That's how all the other animals in the jungle know that you are going to speak,' said Shruthi.

Anand looked suitably chastised as he unwound the *dupatta* and stood up.

Lavanya switched off the television and, surveying the jungle inhabitants' paraphernalia strewn across the sitting-room floor, called out to the maid.

Turning to Girish and Mala, she said: 'Look at me, still in my exercise clothes. Since coming back from the gym, these monkeys have not given me even one second's peace. I'll just change and come, okay. You'll have some pineapple juice, no? Or tender coconut? Anand, see if Girish wants a beer.'

She went upstairs, her gait deliberate and ceremonial, as if aware that there could be an audience.

Girish shook his head from the enormous cream leather sofa. As Anand wandered off to speak to the maid, Girish looked at Mala sitting opposite him. Even though she had recently started to wear make-up when they went out, she still looked absurdly young: like a PUC student who had been dolled up for a skit at the school's annual variety show. She was still clutching the fruit basket. The whole effect made it seem like she was going to burst into a harvest folk song.

'What are you still holding it for? Give it to Lavanya when she comes down,' he muttered to Mala.

He turned to smile at Shruthi who had retreated to the far end of the room. Her preoccupation with the whisk seemed to have increased but she still managed to show a modicum of interest in her aunt and uncle.

'Shruthi, why are you hiding there? Come and tell me how your holidays were. Where did you go? What did you do?' asked Girish.

'We went to Bangkok,' mumbled Shruthi.

'Wonderful! So tell me, what did you see there?'

'Lots of temples.'

'Lots of temples, okay. What else?'

At this point Shruthi shrugged and slipped upstairs too.

The maid came into the room with four glasses of juice and set them down on the coffee table. Anand followed, smiling expansively, as befitted someone who wished his brother and sister-in-law to make themselves completely at home.

Anand was three years younger than Girish. Expectations for the younger brother had never been great. In fact, in some quarters there had been a grim apprehension that he would fall in with the wrong type of people and be responsible for his poor mother's early demise. As it happened, one of those fears was proved accurate, although for reasons connected to the overloading of boats on the Alaknanda River, rather than any unmeritorious conduct on the part of Anand. Academically undistinguished, he had drifted into a job as a sales representative for automobile components and then moved on to a shadowy enterprise involving a number of cable operators in Sitanagar. It was only after extricating himself from those arrangements that Anand had wandered into the world that would make his name.

About ten years ago, on a hunch, he had gone into partnership with a friend and purchased the right to put up two advertising hoardings at a nondescript junction near the Bangalore–Mysore road. At the time, the section of the road separated a disused chemical plant from a belt of sugar cane fields at the northern periphery of Mysore. The junction's main role had been to channel trucks and other goods vehicles to and from the state highway. But Mysore's growth meant that the city's boundaries began to carve away at the surrounding agricultural land, laying new extensions and sectors on top of fields of paddy and sugar cane. Within six months of Anand's purchase, plans for the allocation of residential sites in the northern layouts were complete; a year later, the chemical plant had been demolished; and soon after that there was a brisk trade in real estate spoils from the area.

As the metropolitan contours of Mysore shifted, Anand's entre-preneurial vision tapered to a fine point. The friend was discarded and the partnership transformed itself into Anand and Co, later Exospace Media, a company that sought to requisition all of Mysore's outdoor territory for its huge commercial canvas. Nothing was safe from Anand's keen gaze: bus shelters, station platforms, roadside banners and street dividers. As the months went by, park railings, tree guards, gantries on construction sites and mobile phone masts were all commandeered for his business strategy. Some years ago, in a pioneering coup for the city, he had negotiated the use of one side of a private apartment block to sell life assurance; the apartment owners' association had resisted the move strongly until the financial rewards had been fully elucidated.

While Anand supplied limitless perspicacity and drive, he was assisted by a team of skilful affiliates. Carefully cultivated contacts at the civic administration headquarters meant that all relevant licences and certificates of compliance were issued whenever required. A couple of associates at the Mysore Regeneration Council kept him fully informed with regard to developments to the city's landscape. A number of his well-wishers in the city's network of organised criminals ensured that the small-time operators putting up illegal hoardings were encouraged to consider other vocations.

A disgruntled hoarding owner had observed: 'G S Anand is shameless. If his wife is looking the other way, he will even try and put an advertisement on her bare buttocks.'

As the traditional out-of-home advertising market in Karnataka became saturated, Anand, taking his cue from the big players in Mumbai and Delhi, hitched his wagon to the new technologies that offered greater rewards. By then he had moved into the first of his bungalows in Yadavagiri and felt it unbecoming that he should be considered the type of person who would have his mobile phone number daubed on a roadside sheet of metal. His company moved into the production of customised digital advertising screens at train stations and interactive displays for shopping malls, cinemas and exhibitions. His latest flagship project was a complex system of interlocking panels that would flash the benefits of a mobile phone network to commuters from the side of a planned flyover. He had also recently managed to net a lucrative contract to install digital advertising monitors in all the lifts in Mysore's newest private hospital. The next stage in his career had only just begun. There were still entire ranges of products that the middle classes were completely unaware that they required; Anand was putting in place all the architecture he needed to communicate the necessary messages effectively and profitably.

The first that Susheela had heard of this business was in an article in *Scope*, headed 'Silver sweethearts: Second time round for seniors'. Apparently the trend was increasingly noticeable; or rather, had been noticed by one Vaishali Mehta, deputy features editor of the magazine. Older men and women were striking out again, refusing to disappear into their newspapers and knitting. If Ms Mehta were to be believed, most of the coffee shops in Delhi and Bangalore were occupied by septuagenarians on their third dates. The Internet, it seemed, had liberated an entire generation of metropolitan seniors who could now invite romance and marriage back into their lives. The article made it sound like no park bench was safe, no restaurant out of bounds and no theatre free from the triumphant cries of carousing pensioners.

Susheela had always assumed that dating and matrimonial web-sites were only for youngsters and perverts. Now her curiosity was piqued. A handful of online searches showed her that a fair number of seniors were locked in a lamentable bid to reclaim their youth. Apparently there was no humiliation that they would not endure in an attempt to turn back the clock. Susheela jammed her reading glasses further up the bridge of her nose: some of these characters were even older than her.

On one website a sixty-six-year-old individual who called himself Avinash stated that his wife Brinda had passed away three years ago. Surely these people would not use their real names? Avinash claimed to have a deep interest in philosophy and stressed that his family members were all highly educated professional people, living all over the globe. He also bore more than a passing resemblance to the old Hindi film villain Pran. Avinash was seeking a well-educated wife or companion, slim or slender, between the ages of thirty-five and fifty. Susheela could only presume that none of Avinash's erudite, internationally settled relatives had access to the Internet.

She clicked on another photo. Narendra, aged sixty-eight, from Bangalore, had felt the need to include a lengthy description of his career trajectory in the medical equipment manufacturing industry. He was divorced. His wife, he stated, had 'indulged in some unruly behaviour at the express instigation of her family members and others,' the consequences of which were fairly apparent. Narendra was looking for a Hindu wife who would be pleasant by nature, devoted and adaptable.

At what point had so many people taken leave of their senses? One man proclaimed with no shame that he was working in Afghanistan and wanted his future wife to accompany him there. As if it was not enough that the unfortunate woman would have all her husband's details advertised across cyberspace, this man wanted to take her to a place where she would be mercilessly abused by the Taliban. Of course, there were a number of seemingly normal older men who looked perfectly well meaning. Yet some temporary mania had sent them all scurrying off to find wives when they could barely stand up unassisted.

Susheela turned her attention to the women. There seemed to be a number of Anglo-Indian women in their sixties seeking husbands, a fact which did not surprise her. One Bengali woman's profile had been created by her daughter who claimed to be speaking on her behalf. Was the poor woman even aware of the existence of this website or would her daughter simply present her with a long line of geriatric suitors one day, a *swayamvar* for the superannuated? At least many of the women had seen fit to refrain from publishing their photos. Susheela did, however, spot one very decent-looking lady in a Kanjeevaram sari with a gentle smile. Meena lived in

Mumbai and stated that she was looking for a 'second innings' with a caring man who would respect her independence. How had her family allowed her to get involved in such things? Susheela heard the phone ring and quickly logged off, her thoughts still fixated on Meena. She really hoped she would not end up with that man in Afghanistan.

'So what news in the world of power supply? More load-shedding? There will have to be since the rains are late this year,' observed Anand, pouring himself a beer. 'You're sure you don't want one?'

Girish shook his head.

'Well, if the population goes on increasing and demand keeps going through the roof, what can anyone do? No increase in supply will be able to keep up,' said Girish sourly.

'What you people need to do is stop giving those farmers all that free electricity. At least you will improve your revenue streams and be able to invest in capacity.'

'Not all farmers get free electricity.'

'The ones who don't just stick their line anywhere and steal it. And you people take no action, the police take no action, no one does anything. If it were up to me, I would have a few of their leaders thrown in jail and see how much power they can steal after that.'

'It's easy for people like you to talk. It's not that easy to police the lines. Plus the rich farmers' groups are very powerful in delivering votes. So they will always get what they want.'

Mala had followed Lavanya into the kitchen.

'Where was the need to bring all these fruits? So formal you've become,' said Lavanya. Then, turning to the maid: 'Manju, put these fruits in the fridge. And that basket you can take. You might need it for something.'

In spite of the fact that Mala was married to the elder of

the brothers, her age, background and experience meant that a recalibration of familial norms had been necessary. Certainly, that much had become evident the first time she had met Lavanya, a week before her wedding.

'You will not have any problems in Mysore,' Lavanya had said, while adjusting Mala's *pallu*. 'Anand knows everyone.'

Mala had quickly learnt that her role in her relationship with Lavanya was to be that of an eager pupil, curious and admiring in equal measure. For her part, Lavanya would by turn explain or advise, treating Mala with a complacent grace. Mala was sure that as long as she stuck to these parameters, she would be able to avoid any potential unpleasantness or conflict. She had the measure of the intricate difficulties in Girish's relationship with his brother and sister-in-law and she now felt responsible for preventing any manifestations of his prickly discontentment in their presence. Her powers were circumscribed but she could certainly play the part she had been assigned with an earnest vigour.

Lavanya reached for a brochure that was resting on the microwave.

'Look Mala, I want to show you something. But please, we haven't told people so not a word to anyone, okay?'

Mala looked at the brochure's thick sleeve: an aerial shot of an arc of glittering villas set in a landscape of palms and jewelled lawns. The name of this Shangri-La was Terra Blanca, 'Mysore's most exclusive lifestyle enclave' according to the serpentine calligraphy on the first page. Mala began to turn the pages reverentially.

'I didn't even know they had such places in India,' she said.

'Yes,' breathed Lavanya, as if Mala's comment had buried within it a primal truth.

'Are you thinking of moving here?' asked Mala.

'Not thinking! We have already booked one of the villas on the western side of the development,' said Lavanya.

'Really? I can't believe it!'

'Really, really, really!'

'These houses, I mean villas, are amazing but this is also such a nice house in such a good area. Will you really sell it and leave?'

'Mala, this place was good for us but our needs are also changing. The main thing is security. They have 24-hour armed guards and cameras at Terra Blanca and they are very careful about whom they let in. Shruthi can play outside with no problems. And you know, they are also very strict about who can buy a house there. We will be with other people like us.'

Mala's face was a picture of elation.

'And just look at the facilities. There's an excellent school there, a shopping complex, a cinema and a mini-amphitheatre for weddings and other functions,' continued Lavanya, seizing the brochure and jabbing at the relevant pages.

'The swimming pools look so nice,' said Mala.

'Everything is nice! Look at the fitness centre and the spa. And it even has its own medical facility and fire department.'

Mala reached out for the brochure, like she would for an infant. As she thought up a few more questions to ask Lavanya, she allowed herself to be relieved that the conversation was taking place in the kitchen.

As Uma walked home, the wind grew stronger, filling the air with a fine sediment that lodged itself in the corners of her eyes and coated the roof of her mouth. It was Saturday evening and there was already a huddle of early drinkers trying to attract the attention of the man behind the counter at Raksha Wines. A woman sitting on the pavement had clearly given up the struggle for the time being. As Uma walked past her, she looked up, her eyes raw with need. Uma glanced at her and kept walking.

Emerging from the chaos outside Raksha Wines, a man in his thirties, with a face like a pair of pincers, called out to Uma.

'Eh, don't pretend you can't hear me,' he yelled at her receding form.

The man was a local fixer. In the greasy world of municipal graft, his was one of a number of names that could prove useful in ensuring a desired outcome. Providing all due funds were made available on time, his areas of expertise were legion: a speedy landline connection, multiple SIM cards without proof of address, an expedited income certificate from the *tahsildar's* office, domestic gas cylinders without delay and the prompt registration of land title documents. His weekend swagger was not one produced by large quantities of local whiskey, but instead by the sense of distinction that came from providing a public service in a mutilated system.

Uma needed nothing from that world and had no reason to stop to see what the man wanted. She paused outside an unassuming temple, tucked into a small courtyard next to a printing press. The temple was frequented exclusively by the low caste inhabitants of the surrounding sprawl. Others preferred to worship at the two temples on the main road, where presumably the deities were better equipped to deal with the ordinary concerns of members of the upper castes. It was time for the evening *aarthi* and a long but orderly queue stretched out of the temple entrance. Uma decided not to join the queue. Instead she slipped off her *chappals* in the road, folded her palms and bowed her head in prayer.

A few minutes later she was making her way down the row to her room. A number of children nearly crashed into her on the narrow path as they raced towards the hill leading up to Mysore Junction; there were rumours of fireworks. The white belt of one of the girls' dresses had come undone and fallen into a pool of dirty water outside the door of Uma's room. She picked it up and laid it flat across the top of a tyre that had been left leaning against the wall.

Uma's room was in darkness. The power cut had already lasted over two hours and it was entirely possible that it would continue through the night. The monsoons had still not arrived and the water levels remained low in all the hydroelectric dams that served the state. Uma lit a candle below the picture of Shiva. She picked up a cloth hanging on a hook, dipped it into a bucket of water and dabbed at her upper arms. She lifted her hair up and swabbed the back of her neck, her upper chest and her face. She then moved to the washing area and poured a judicious amount of water on to her feet, massaging her arches and running a finger deep into the crevices between her toes. Picking up a towel, she wiped her feet dry and then lay on the mattress.

The wind outside sounded like silk being ripped. Under the picture of Shiva, the candle's flame shrank into a blue bead before leaping back to illuminate the unplastered brickwork behind it. The top of Shiva's face was in shadow but Uma could see his palm raised in approbation. She forced herself to concentrate on the hand and its munificence. The flame's rhythms grew less erratic and the dim light began to pull on Uma's temples and cheeks, gradually drawing her into a murky delirium far beyond sleep.

It was a reverberation at the door that restored her to the darkness of the room. The flame had died and all she could make out were the sky's distant pleats in the gap between the wall and the roof. The wind had dropped but a different sound had taken its place: what seemed like the leaden resonance of a man's voice imitating the wind. Uma turned on to her side and faced the door. The sound faded. Moments later she started as something clattered against the door, perhaps a handful of gravel. She slowly sat up, her eyes shut, listening. All she could make out was the barking of a faraway dog, steady and mechanical. She continued to sit upright, her arms clasped around her knees, computing the textures of the night.

When the scratching at the door began, she recognised it

instantly. By now she was familiar with the long, uneven rasps against the grain of the wood that sounded like they were being drawn along her scalp. From her first few weeks in Mysore she had been the target of opportunistic advances and arrogant demands which followed the same sinister pattern, whatever their provenance. The sound continued for a minute or so before ending abruptly; a low cough followed and then some receding footsteps.

Uma opened her eyes and looked through the gap between the wall and the roof. A navy wash was leaching across the sky in an almost imperceptible advance. She closed her eyes again.

CHAPTER FIVE

The quarterly general meeting of the Mahalakshmi Gardens Betterment Association (MGBA) was scheduled for seven in the evening at the function hall of the Erskine Club. The MGBA had been set up nearly fifteen years ago as a reaction to the municipal authorities' steady indifference to the provision of essential amenities in the area. The objects of the Association were ambitious: once the local community's activist potential had been harnessed to resolve the neighbourhood's problems, the same faculties would be directed towards uplifting more disadvantaged localities and creating a sense of unity in Mysore. Unfortunately the last decade and a half had seen the pioneers of local welfare becoming mired in a swamp of issues very close to home. As a result, the more philanthropic aspirations had been postponed indefinitely.

Sunaina Kamath had recently taken over as the chairperson of the MGBA's Executive Committee, in what the previous incumbent, Mr Nandakishore, regarded as a savage coup. She had sent out a memo reminding members that under Article 54 of the articles of association no officer of the Executive Committee could stand for re-election for a third term, a rule that served to terminate Mr Nandakishore's excellent stewardship. He had grudgingly stepped aside but was determined to ensure that the MGBA would not be deprived of his years of experience in matters of civic importance.

The general meeting had originally been due to take place a week earlier but a violent downpour had meant that many of the MGBA members had stayed at home. In spite of the sparse attendance, Sunaina had been minded to continue with proceedings.

Mr Nandakishore, however, reached into the same constitutional arsenal that she had previously raided and introduced a point of order with regard to the conduct of general meetings. He was surprised to note that Mrs Kamath intended to proceed with the general meeting despite the inevitable violation of Article 14 of the MGBA's articles of association. The provision required a quorum of thirty members for the transaction of any Association business. Mr Nandakishore's careful calculation had arrived at a figure of only twenty-nine. After a hurried discussion with some of the Executive Committee members, Sunaina had adjourned the meeting in an asphyxiated voice. In the car park of the Erskine Club that evening, Mr Nandakishore strode through the stinging rain with his head held very erect.

The second attempt at the meeting was far more successful. It was a clear evening with a punchy freshness in the air and the car park at the Erskine Club was almost full. When Susheela arrived, most of the seats inside the Club's function room were occupied, even though she was a good twenty minutes early. She walked to the front of the room, smiling warmly at fellow residents who were either currently in her circle or who had left it without causing offence. She sat down in the front row where a few seats remained and continued to look around the room, trying to make her scrutiny look as casual as possible. A tap on her shoulder made her turn expectantly in her seat.

It was Jaydev: 'Hello again. It seems we only meet in situations of high drama.'

Susheela immediately looked embarrassed, not expecting to be reminded again, and certainly not at an MGBA meeting, of her strange vulnerability on that day.

'Hello, what a surprise to see you here. What brings you to our neck of the woods to witness our little dramas, as you say?' asked Susheela.

'Sunaina and Ramesh have promised to take me to a new Italian restaurant by Tejasandra Lake after the meeting. Being an old man with far too much time on my hands, I have followed them here to make sure that they don't give me the slip.'

'I certainly hope the food is worth it, if it means you have to sit through discussions about our garbage and traffic lights and so forth.'

'Let me just move forward instead of leaning like this. Is that seat free?'

The seat next to Susheela was usually free these days.

At that point Vaidehi Ramachandra gently squeezed Susheela's elbow on her other side.

'How are you Susheela? I haven't seen you for such a long time,' said Vaidehi morosely.

'That's true, how busy we become without even knowing why,' said Susheela, with as much regret as she could marshal.

'I'm glad that I've seen you here,' said Vaidehi, cheering up and rummaging in a Shanta Silk House plastic bag. 'I have been meaning to give you this for a long time but kept missing you.'

Susheela watched the ominous movements being made by Vaidehi's hands, all the time conscious of Jaydev looking on.

Vaidehi pulled out a pamphlet and presented it to Susheela with a flourish. Under an image of a coastal sunset, the front page read: 'The Twilight Terrain, A Guide to the Final Paths to the Almighty by the Mokshvihar Spiritual Trust'. If the unequivocal wording were excised, on the face of it, the pamphlet could just as easily have been a guide to honeymooning in Goa.

Susheela scanned the inside pages, which offered vignettes of rudderless pensioners who had eventually discovered the Mokshvihar lecture programmes and trademarked MokshDhyana group meditation techniques. The rest of the pamphlet was devoted to an extensive biography of the Trust founder, a charismatic humanitarian who frequently toured the world with his message of sanctity and salvation.

Susheela glanced at Jaydev, who appeared to be spellbound by some object in the vicinity of his knees. Around them, even more people had arrived and the pre-meeting chatter echoed loudly through the hall. To one side of the dais, two young men in waist-coats and bow ties were setting out more cups and saucers on a long table.

Susheela looked up at Vaidehi, whose face had settled into an expression of beatific encouragement.

'Don't say anything about it now. You need time to go home and reflect on what is said there. If you have any questions later, please come and ask me,' said Vaidehi, turning to face the front again, satisfied but with an air of modesty. She was, after all, only the messenger.

Susheela thanked her and put the pamphlet into her handbag.

She had never really questioned the complexion of her spiritual fibre: she believed in God, knew she lived a principled life and performed the correct rituals on festival days with an undeniable precision. She would no more have considered becoming an atheist than she would the cultivation of marijuana on her front lawn. But the truth was that she found it difficult to entrust other beings, mortal or celestial, with the business of running an organised existence. Even when Sridhar had been diagnosed with prostate cancer, she had not sought relief in appeals to the divine. Her natural instinct had been to throw herself into finding the best oncologist, keeping an unfaltering watch on the hospital staff, ensuring the maximum possible comfort in his daily routine and communicating regularly with those who needed to be kept informed of his progress. When her sister-in-law had suggested a special *pooja* for Sridhar's well-being, Susheela had quickly slotted it in on an auspicious day free of other commitments and made brisk enquiries on acceptable rates for caterers.

Vaidehi Ramachandra's overtures did not offend her from the point of view of scripture or orthodoxy. What Susheela did not care for was the presumption that there was a space in her life that needed to be filled or that she was adrift in a sea of moral doubt. The fact that Vaidehi felt entitled to give Susheela advice on her spiritual nourishment was no less irritating: she was hardly a friend, habitually wore her sari two inches above her ankles and her husband had made his fortune selling steel utensils in an alley behind Shivrampet.

Jaydev leant in towards Susheela and said under his breath: 'So when are you off to the *ashram*?'

'Please, not now. She might hear you.'

'I don't think so. She looks like she is in some sort of trance.'

'Please Mr Jaydev, here is not the place.'

'All I am asking is that you allow me to wish you all the best on your journey to salvation.'

Susheela could no longer stifle her smile, but persisted in looking straight ahead at the bowl of chrysanthemums on the Executive Committee's table.

At that point Sunaina and her colleagues on the Committee took their seats on the dais, the Treasurer stamped on the floor a number of times and the assembly was called to order.

As Girish had told Mala that he would pick her up in the evening, she had left her scooter at home and had got a rickshaw in to work. When she left the main gates of the Mysore Regency Hotel at half past five, she saw him across the road, standing by his motorbike, reading the evening paper. The rain had been heavy the night before and she had to skirt around the pools of water in the road, avoiding the onslaught of cars and rickshaws that splashed their way through.

Their first stop was a sari shop near Hardinge Circle, crisp pleats of turquoise and mauve silk fanning across the bolsters in one of the window displays. In the other, the mannequins appeared to be about to launch into a martial routine, their arms slicing at the neon air around them. Despite Mala's protests, Girish had insisted that she should at least have a look. She was bound to see something irresistible.

It was wedding season and the shop was busy. Impassive matrons consulted lists scribbled on pages torn from their grandchildren's exercise books and huddled conferences were breaking out on the little stools provided for customers. Shop girls circulated with steel *lotas* of intensely sugared coffee and cold *badaam* milk, made from a cheap packet mix, as noted by the more discerning clientele. Here the service was still steeped in the traditions of canny servility; the haughty appraisals and polished merchandising of the new boutiques at the Tejasandra Galleria were a world away. Sari after sari was rapidly unfolded, *pallus* shaken out, borders smoothed flat: a ballet of drapes and furls. Despite the small size of the store, the offerings seemed endless. A teenaged boy leapt about barefoot on bales at the back of the shop, locating additional stock, although to the untutored it simply looked like the crazed caper of a Nilgiri mountain goat. Nothing was deemed unavailable; runners were despatched to nearby warehouses or convincing alternatives were seamlessly conjured up.

Girish was always an enthusiastic participant in such an environment. He thrived on the theatre of transaction and grasped eagerly at his roles. These were the occasions where Mala relaxed and fed off his enthusiasm as he became the disappointed fiancé or the outraged bystander. She ran her finger over a *zardozi* leaf on a sari, the embroidery scratching against her skin. Girish's face was flushed in the crowded room, a film of moisture spreading above his lips and across the back of his neck. His eyes flashed at Mala, an intimate connection made in the shop's thick air, over the heads of two sisters who were examining a length of printed crepe. He was leaning on the counter, his fingers resting on the rounded steel edge, a tiny pulse thrilling in the soft dip under his thumb. Mala noticed that his belt clasp was hanging loose between the sharp creases at the top of his trousers. She smiled at him as he narrowed his eyes at the salesman whose hands were acting out a livelihood being wrung dry.

'We can always try Srinivas and Sons,' she said, on cue.

A refreshed scene of offer and counter-offer, declaration and protestation, finally culminated in them leaving the shop with a plastic bag containing two saris wrapped in brown paper.

They wandered past one of the many electronics shops on the same street. A stack of DVD players in their boxes stood on the pavement outside the shop. A buck-toothed boy in a baseball cap urged them to go inside to take just one look at the rest of the stock. Girish ignored him and walked on towards Sheethal Talkies.

'Where to now? Do you want to look at some jewellery?' he asked Mala, twisting around in the throng on the street.

'No, I think that's enough for today. What do you want to do?'

'Are you hungry? Let's go to the food court.'

Mala was not hungry. The smell of fried garlic from nearby food carts and the brawny wafts of kerosene from their stoves were making her feel nauseous. A muted ache was taking form somewhere behind her temples.

They made their way across the busy intersection to Sri Harsha Road, walked past Woodlands Theatre and Maurya Residency, turning towards the new shopping centre that had leapt into the centre of old Mysore. The giant hoardings outside the mall advertised a new range of teak furniture, heavily discounted as a result of a condition termed 'Monsoon Mania'. In front of the metal detectors, girls with fresh jasmine in their hair were aggressively thrusting flyers for cut-price home cinema systems into the hands of shoppers.

Inside the mall, Girish and Mala trawled up a series of escalators, negotiating pyramids of non-stick cookware, bins of cheap towels and bed sheets, racks of crumpled shirts and a display of framed landscape prints. A remix of a Hindi film song bore into Mala's head as they reached the fourth floor. The food court was partially screened off from the shop floor by a set of cardboard palm trees. Under paper cut-outs of pizzas and burgers, which hung in dense clumps from the ceiling, a couple of dour security guards circulated around the tables, trying to spot anyone who had smuggled in eatables from outside.

The food court had a complicated payment system involving the purchase of colour-coded coupons from different counters, depending on the type of cuisine. On their first visit, it had taken them half an hour to understand the intricacies of the system and another fifteen minutes to realise that they had paid for the wrong number of dishes.

Mala slid quickly towards the one free table, her lip curling in disgust when she spotted a greasy noodle on the tabletop. She looked around for the boy as Girish went to inspect the demented array of menu displays and special offers. On the next table three men were hunched over a mobile phone, shoulders shaking with mirth. They must have been brothers; as they leant back, Mala could see that they all had the same upturned noses. On her other side an elderly woman was staring at her with vapid eyes. Mala looked away, arching her back in an attempt to get comfortable on the tiny chair.

Girish returned, reciting: 'Fried-rice-hakka-noodles-*aloo-paratha*-onion-*paratha*-veg-pizza-veg-club-sandwich-chilly-*paneer-dahi-puri-sev-puri-masala-dosa*-paper-*dosa*.'

'Plain *dosa*,' said Mala.

Girish spun smartly around and initiated the complex procedures necessary to order some food. At the next table, the woman continued to stare vacantly in Mala's direction. The boy arrived and gave the table a half-hearted swab. After he had gone, Mala took a paper towel out of her handbag and wiped the surface dry. The skin on her wrists looked raw and had begun to peel. She put her hands in her lap and tried to exhale her headache.

The agenda for this quarter's MGBA meeting was not particularly heavy. There were the perennial updates on waste collection and street lighting. A number of members were keen to discuss the two incidents of chain snatching that had been reported recently. Mrs Urs of West Garden Road leant forward and told the group that the crime wave was taking a psychological toll: she had begun to have a recurring nightmare in which a tattooed man locked her in the servants' toilet and made off with her collection of antique snuff boxes. Sunaina nodded as these concerns were aired and then read out a statement from the sub-inspector at the Mahalakshmi Gardens police station, its reassuring message lost in her melodramatic delivery.

Jacob D'Souza, the Secretary of the MGBA, wished to draw attention to the proposed tree-felling on Fergusson Road. He was keen to stress that he did not subscribe to the view that the road-widening project was essential to the city's development; on the contrary, he advocated the preservation of the jacaranda trees that gave Fergusson Road its unique character. Mr D'Souza's moving description of his childhood spent in the trees' lilac shadows introduced a nostalgia to the meeting that was not universally appreciated. A caustic voice at the back of the room suggested that discussion of the issue was premature. The tree-felling proposal was in its infancy and it was unlikely that any firm decision would be taken for some time. Luckily for Mr D'Souza, municipal inertia was as great a boon as it was a curse.

The meeting then moved on to the issue of the enormous hoarding at Shastri Circle. Many of those present were agreed that the visual pollution being visited upon them had now reached unacceptable levels. After all, what was the point of paying these exorbitant amounts for a corner site facing the Gardens if the view was going to be sabotaged by a fifteen-foot advertisement for a water purifier?

The issue had, however, only now made it formally on to the agenda of an MGBA meeting. The hoarding which had caused the present anxiety advertised a luxury jewellery brand: the giant face of a supermodel, an emerald ring in the form of a peacock clasped between her lips, snaring drivers and pedestrians at the traffic lights below. The hoarding had existed at Shastri Circle for a number of years without objection, its staid parade of mobile phone handsets, high-interest savings packages and family cars apparently tolerated by local residents. But there was something about the current image that had awakened a sense of disquiet. The members present at the meeting could hardly condemn the image for its subject, luxury branded jewellery having made its way into many of the home-security lockers in Mahalakshmi Gardens; nor was there any transgression as a result of inappropriate skin-show. Instead the composition of the image and a highly charged quality in the model's eyes gave an impression of unreserved improperness. Unsightly intrusions on the urban landscape when coupled with unfettered female carnality had proved a step too far in Mahalakshmi Gardens.

The Executive Committee was urged to make representations to city officials without delay and, if possible, a direct appeal to the Mayor's office. It was implicit in the assembly's objections that the correspondence would stress the negative impact of indiscriminate signage on the locality, without setting out the particular impressions generated by the supermodel with a ring in her mouth.

There were a few items of little consequence raised as 'Any Other Business', some concluding remarks from Sunaina and then the customary vote of thanks. As the members of the Executive Committee stood up, Sunaina glared victoriously at Mr Nandakishore who was seated in the second row. Her bob seemed even more anxious today, a frizzy tangle on the crown of her head seeking to secede from the rest of her hair. She stepped down from the dais and looked around for her husband Ramesh.

'The rascal, I knew he would miss the meeting,' she said, as she waved distractedly to various people.

Little groups had begun to form by the table of refreshments and the function room door. The manager of the Erskine Club had made an appearance, the club crest resplendent on his dark blazer, as if to remind the MGBA members that, regardless of the importance afforded to their association, they remained on club premises. Mr Nandakishore had decided to avoid the office-holders of the Executive Committee and began to engage some new members in conversation. After all, Article 2B of the association's constitution included among its purposes the aim of 'promoting unfettered camaraderie and congenial fellowship among the Members and all residents of Mahalakshmi Gardens.'

'That was very interesting,' said Jaydev. 'True people power in action.'

'It's easy for people like you to laugh at us. But if we just sat at home, this place would turn into a slum like so many other parts of Mysore,' said Susheela tartly.

'I was being serious,' protested Jaydev. 'I have never been to a meeting like this. Where I live most people are always abroad at their children's homes anyway.'

'We have to take care of ourselves,' said Susheela, her tone softening.

She looked around the room and then stood up.

'I will take my leave, Mr Jaydev. Enjoy your dinner,' she said.

'Why don't you join us?'

'Oh no, I didn't mean to ask for an invitation.'

'Of course not, but it would be very nice if you could join us. It's only Sunaina and Ramesh, whom you know.'

'That's very kind of you, but I should really get home.'

'To read the Mokshvihar pamphlet?'

'Yes, maybe. You have no idea what my spiritual needs are.'

'I think your soul will be better nourished with a plate of delicious pasta than a lecture given by some mad guru.'

'No please, I really don't want to barge in on your evening like this.'

'Fine, if you won't listen to me, maybe you'll listen to Sunaina. Here she is.'

Sunaina had found Ramesh playing billiards in another room and was now approaching Jaydev and Susheela, still fuelled by her post-meeting adrenalin.

'Sush, I didn't even see you and here you are in the front row,' she said.

'I have just been telling Susheelaji that she absolutely must come with us to La Whatever-it's-called tonight,' said Jaydev.

'And I have been telling Mr Jaydev that I simply cannot charge in uninvited.'

'You're invited now, *na*? What do you need, Sush, an embossed card with tassels?' asked Sunaina. 'You'll love this place. Last time I had the tiramisu, I swear, they had to carry me out of there.'

And with that, Susheela found herself being shepherded towards the Kamaths' car.

'Ramesh, if you try and have another peg here, I swear I'll bury you in that flower bed,' said Sunaina.

Susheela caught Jaydev's eye and smiled. As they left the club, the manager bid them a curt good night. There was a chance he had heard the allusion to destruction of club property and, if so, had no doubt taken a dim view.

On the way out of the mall, Girish wanted to stop off in the electronics department for a few minutes. They walked through a crowd watching a demonstration for a new model of hotplate and reached the computer section. Girish immediately engaged one of the sales assistants in a conversation about laptops. Mala looked around for a seat but there was nothing in sight.

Across the aisle, a scene from a film played on a giant television screen. A disgruntled young man strode through the foyer of a hospital holding a machine gun as nurses and porters leapt away in terror. The man walked into the lift, shoving aside a squat, bejewelled man holding a briefcase, and stared bleakly at the floor indicator as he was taken to the fifth floor. The film's background music pounded out of the television's powerful speakers, each strike of the bass making Mala's chest contract. She leant against a rack of DVDs and prayed that Girish would finish soon.

The hero of the film was now making his way down a corridor, swatting away security guards with just one arm, his pace not slowing. A brave doctor tried to lasso the hero with his stethoscope but was sent crashing into a gurney for his troubles. The hero then walked into a ward and violently pulled at a curtain behind which a hook-nosed man lay shivering in bed.

'*Bewarsi, halka nanna magane, ill bidhgondidhya ninnu?*'

There followed a summary of the torment suffered by the hero's family members at the hands of the man with the hook nose, delivered by the hero in an emotional address to those members of the hospital staff still present. The scene ended, in predictably gory fashion, with the patient being gunned down while trying to escape down the staff staircase.

Three college girls stood near the television screen, acutely conscious of a couple of young men pretending to look at a catalogue a few steps away. One of the girls shifted her weight from one leg to the other while flicking ambiguous glances at the men. Her tall friend was bolder and smiled in their direction. After some discussion the catalogue was discarded and the men approached the girls. There was a bold offer of a mint and a silvery laugh of acceptance. The group headed off, one of the men pausing to primp his hair as he caught sight of his reflection in a toaster.

Girish was still talking to the sales assistant and their heads bobbed in unison as they leant over a computer. At one point, with his hands outstretched, he mimed one car taking over another and they both laughed. The bright overhead lights gave the air a faint blue tinge and an almost metallic sheen to Girish's hair. His posture was that of a serious buyer, knowledgeable but open to suggestion, a man in control.

Mala's headache was now a seething, churning beast mauling her nerves and tissue. She decided to perch on the end of a wooden block that supported a mobile phone display. Instantly a member of staff appeared, eager to use this opportunity to put some training into practice.

'Madam, sitting here is not allowed,' she said primly.

'I'm sorry. I got very giddy. I'm not feeling well.'

The woman's expression changed: 'Are you on your own, madam? Should I call someone?'

Mala stood up.

'No, thank you. My husband is here. We are just leaving.'

Mala looked around for Girish but he was nowhere to be seen. At the food court she had hardly touched her *dosa* but Girish had insisted that she try some of his fried rice. The smell of the starchy steam and the dollop of ketchup's artificial sweetness now began to repeat on her. She had a word with the sales assistant who had been talking to Girish but he shrugged and continued with some paperwork. A burst of applause from a group behind her made her turn around. The hotplate demonstration had come to an end and the audience was dispersing, the company representative thrilled with the success of his last joke.

The tiles on the floor seemed to shift suddenly as Mala held on to a pillar to regain her balance. Wave after wave of nausea consumed her as she swallowed hard, willing every fibre to check her body's runaway impulses. She sank to her knees, feeling the sweat breaking out on her face. A woman behind her called out for help. Within seconds Mala was vomiting on the shop floor, kneeling in front of the row of laptops. There was a searing sensation in her nostrils and the heaves seemed to go on and on.

As a sales assistant rushed off to alert the section manager, Girish appeared in the aisle, his eyes drawn to the hunched figure on the floor. In his hand he held a surprise gift for Mala: a small diary bound in creamy yellow felt.

When Susheela and Sridhar left Mysore for Bhopal in the late seventies, the area around Tejasandra Lake had been a swampy wasteland, famed mainly for the tenacity of its mosquitoes and the stench of the dense algae washed up on the lake's shores. The only conceivable reasons for venturing there were to stave off hunger by catching some of the lake's toxic carp or to dispose secretly of a dead body. When they returned to Mysore from Delhi, following Sridhar's retirement, the state government had finally released a substantial tranche of funds to clean up the lake's fetid waters. A stew of sewage, pesticides, cattle remains, automobile lubricants, medical waste and plastics, the lake had been named one of the top ten environmental scandals in a nationwide study carried out by a prominent NGO. The clean-up operation had taken another four years to complete, but nonetheless it was a major success for the state's environmental record.

Some time later a Deputy Commissioner blessed with unusual foresight and dedication had ensured that a flood defence was erected on the western shore, above which wound a stately promenade, modelled on Pondicherry's Avenue Goubert. The rest of the development then simply fell into place like a series of golf balls slowly tumbling into their holes. The Museum of Folklore had been a longstanding promise from the Department of Culture. Endowments from a number of international arts organisations led to its rapid completion, its modernist design ensuring manifestations of rapture and revolt in equal measure among the city's consumers of culture. Supporters of the building lauded the mettle of the architects who had set Mysore free from an orientalist vision of domes and arches. Its detractors lamented the lack of harmony between the exterior of the museum and its collections of tribal and folk art from all over India. Most of the rest simply boggled at the price of the entry tickets.

Expensive tickets were not a problem at the Mysore Archaeology Museum, which also arrived at Tejasandra Lake. The government-run museum had previously been located in the centre of the city, in a building so cramped and decrepit that its demolition was a peerless act of kindness. The fossils and antiquities happily made their new home in a three-storey structure with uninterrupted views of the lake's majestic sweep.

The Tejasandra Galleria was next in line at the lakeside: a grand labyrinth of shops and restaurants, flawlessly preserved by arctic air-conditioning and hushed adulation. In its early days, valet parking had been introduced in an attempt to shore up its exclusive credentials. It transpired, however, that even the best-heeled Mysore shoppers displayed a degree of nervousness when strangers tried to take over the wheels of their cars.

The last major addition to the waterside community was the Anuraag Kalakshetra, a small but luxurious concert hall, courtesy of an infamous tobacco baron and his passion for Carnatic music. It had quickly become a crucial part of the city's cultural landscape, hosting an array of music and dance programmes while also housing a small café that served excellent apricot tarts.

The group from the Mahalakshmi Gardens Betterment Association arrived at the Tejasandra Galleria in high spirits. In the car, Sunaina had enjoyed telling a story involving the Acting Mayor of Mysore, a second-year medical student and a false-bottomed suitcase. They took the glass lift to the fifth floor, where a reproduction matinee idol seated them at a table by one of La Vetta's huge lake-facing windows.

Sunaina, ever-conscious of her currency, made her way around the tables looking eminent yet accessible, not unlike a dignitary seeking re-election. Ramesh followed, reflecting that Jaydev was in many senses fortunate to be a widower. As a napkin fluttered into her lap, Susheela experienced the velvety rush of sudden and splendid gratification. Her sense of expectation and participation had narrowed to such an extent that this accidental social reconnection almost drew her breath like a plunge into icy depths. The elegant stems of the wine glasses, the soft chocolate of the suede-panelled walls and the low buzz of sophisticated chatter began to loosen the pins and bolts that had clamped tightly down on her appetites.

'Have a glass, Sush. Don't worry, if you get merry and fall in the lake I'll jump in after you,' said Sunaina, as the waiter began to pour the wine with ritual attention.

'We'll have our own wet sari sequence,' smirked Ramesh to Jaydev.

'Don't be so lewd,' said Sunaina, thoroughly enjoying the idea that she could be part of some risqué song-and-dance routine.

Susheela picked up the glass of wine and took a small sip, being extremely suspicious of anything that could cloud her judgment. She had only been tipsy twice in her life. The first occasion was at a party in Delhi's Vasant Vihar in the late eighties. She had collapsed onto a swing on the balcony and spent the rest of the evening trying to remember the hostess's maiden name. The second time was at a restaurant in London the evening of Priyanka's graduation: after her third glass of champagne, on her way back from the ladies' room, Susheela had mistakenly sat down at a table with three Russian businessmen. Inevitably, the family ribbing had been endless.

'It's so lovely that we have places like this now in Mysore,' said Sunaina. 'I remember when cream cakes at the Southern Star were the height of luxury.'

'Nothing wrong with those cream cakes,' protested Jaydev.

'No, of course not,' Sunaina swatted at his comment. 'But you know, the fact that we can be proud of places in our home town, in front of anyone from anywhere in the world, that's something, no?'

An attractive woman wove past their table and Susheela scrutinised her taut midriff.

'It's been so long since I went out this late,' said Jaydev. 'In the last few months, I've been avoiding driving into town at night. The glare of oncoming headlights, can't take it any more.'

'You should have told me before, *na*? If you want to go anywhere, I can take you,' said Sunaina.

'I am sure you would, if I asked you,' said Jaydev, smiling. He paused and added: 'But after all this time, it's having to ask that's the problem.'

'You men, with your silly pride. I swear, you all create most of your own problems. You know Pradeep Nair? I went to see him in hospital this morning. He looked so awful. He has to have a kidney transplant and even then, who knows how long he will live. All because he kept refusing to have check-ups. His poor wife; who will remember her name after he's gone? He was always the life and soul.'

Jaydev glanced at Susheela but she kept her face expressionless.

'It was just too horrible to see,' continued Sunaina. 'Poor man is in a shared ward as well. Can you believe it, there are no private rooms available at Northfield Wellness or at J S Desai. I was speaking to one of the directors of Northfield. Dr K Narendra? He sits on a board with me. Anyway, he was saying the private rooms are full of foreigners these days. They are all flocking here because it's so much cheaper for them to have surgery than back home. Lovely little holiday, get a new knee, buy some souvenirs, take a few photos and then return in two weeks. In the meantime, we are all pushed into the common wards with God only knows what kind of diseases.'

Susheela turned to look at the quiet shimmer stretching out below the windows. The wine had softened all her synapses and the liquid amber of the lights reflected in the lake seemed to mirror her easy composure. Around her, the tinkling hum of the restaurant sounded like it was rising from the waters below, a carefully composed liturgy being offered up in praise. As she gazed at the lake, the gentle play on its surface led to a series of shifts in its aspect, all of them captivating.

Sunaina excused herself, having spotted the new chairperson of the Vontikoppal Ladies' League.

'Have you met Twinkle? She's a bit stiff, but still quite adorable. Maybe you don't know, but she once had tea with Princess Diana,' she said.

'Why would Princess Diana have tea with *her*?' asked Susheela.

'I don't know, something to do with illiterate housewives, or was it vagrants? Anyway, Twinkie said that she almost melted into Diana's eyes. The compassion simply *rolled* off her.'

'For the vagrants or for Twinkie?' asked Jaydev.

'Oh hush, Twinkie is fully *crème de la*. I must go over and say hello.'

'She is always so busy,' said Ramesh, his voice beginning to quaver at the thought of the neglect he suffered.

There was no response so he too left, claiming he had to make a call.

A strange new silence enveloped the table. Susheela's face was still turned towards the window, her hands locked under her chin.

'Lost in your thoughts?' asked Jaydev.

'It's so beautiful out there, it's almost making me sad.'

Susheela expected him to ask her why, but he looked at the water and simply nodded.

The motorbike swerved into a great arc and roared back towards Uma. It was only when the driver was within touching distance that she realised that it was Shankar. He was wearing a pair of sunglasses that made him look like a seedy gangster and Uma was relieved when he took them off.

'Uma, I'm glad I saw you. Janaki's not happy with you. Why haven't you called her?'

'I wanted to but . . . how is she? Almost the due date now.'

'She's okay; she's like a bomb ready to explode. She told me to drag you to her mother's place if I see you. I'm going there now. Come with me if you want.'

'I can't come now. Tell her I promise I'll come on another day.'

'She wants you to phone her. Here, take her number again,' said Shankar, reaching for his phone.

Uma did not look at his outstretched hand.

'You write it for me,' she said.

'Oh, so then you can say that you couldn't make out my hand-writing? Here, take the pen. I'm not going to let you blame it on me,' laughed Shankar.

'I can't write,' she said flatly.

'Okay look, I'll write it on this,' he said, tearing off the end of a receipt. 'Ask someone to dial it for you from the coin phone, but make sure you call her. I think she's worried about you.'

Uma took the fold of paper and tucked it into her blouse.

Shankar eased his sunglasses back on and turned the motorbike back around. A moment later he turned his head and asked: 'Everything is all right?'

'Everything is fine,' said Uma and walked on towards the pennants flying high above Mysore Junction.

In the distance, the ochre light in a turret at Amba Vilas Palace guttered into the darkness.

The next day was a Saturday and Girish had left the house early. The morning hours seemed to stretch indefinitely like acres of molten tar. Mala stood in the doorway, arms folded tightly against her chest. The hot air around her throbbed like a heartbeat and the leaves overhead were engaged in a sly susurration. It was sure to rain. She had brought the clothes in earlier and they now sat in neat ironed piles on their bed: Girish's handkerchiefs, socks, short-sleeved casual shirts, short-sleeved formal shirts, long-sleeved casual shirts, long-sleeved formal shirts, work trousers, casual trousers, vests, underwear, long *kurtas*, short *kurtas* and pyjamas. Her own petticoats and saris she would do later. The sky gradually began to darken. An autorickshaw piled high with gas cylinders blocked one end of the narrow lane. Goats daintily stepped past the vehicle, guided by the deep guttural 'uhhhnnnhuh' of their herder, a wiry young girl in a faded *salwar kameez*. As the goats approached, Mala became aware of the time and her pulse quickened. Girish would be home soon.

She went back into the house and the sudden darkness made her stop. The room only had two tiny windows covered in steel mesh, which both looked out on to their neighbour's sagging brick wall. At times Mala thought that she was beginning to shrink into this carapace of a room, that one day her mother or her sister would arrive to find her lying in the dust outside, enclosed in this shell along with the Rexine sofa set and her mother-in-law's Air India Maharajas. She turned the television on, thought better of it, switched it off, before turning it on and then off one more time. She sat down at the dining table and listened for sounds of Girish's return.

She did not have long to wait before she heard the fading thrum of his motorbike in the lane. She stood up at once and went to the kitchen, where she listened for further sounds. Her relationship with her husband was increasingly managed by aural concentration, an association mediated by thumps, creaks and knocks. She was fiercely attentive to clues left by his footsteps, the pitch at which he cleared his throat, the rustling of newspapers and, in particular, the way in which he called out her name.

'Maa-laa.'

Or 'Ma-la*aa*,' with a slight lilt at the end.

Or '*Mah*-la.'

Or 'Ma-luh,' quickly exhaled.

These divinations had become a vital mechanism of governance for her. Sometimes she would stand in the kitchen while Girish was asleep trying to foresee his mood when he woke up. Rasping snores, repeated creaks of the bed frame, a gentle wheeze followed by a whistle of breath: they were all drawn into her computations.

She had become an expert at eliminating the sounds of her own breathing lest she miss some vital sign from the man lying on the bed in his checked pyjama and white vest. Her strategy was simple. She had to adapt her conduct so that no part of it could be perceived as a brazen challenge. Yet she needed to gather information and this was provided by the wholly unremarkable soundtrack to Girish's quotidian movements. Of course her prognoses were hardly foolproof. The sound of his shoes hitting the back of the cupboard was not always the sign of a gnarled frustration; his conversations with the Prabhakar boys, who were playing badminton in the lane, did not always mean that he would be charming for the rest of the evening. But generally a connoisseur could tell.

There were other subtle signs to look out for too. How long he spent in the bathroom shaving, whether he shut and bolted the door or not after he returned from work, the number of times he stepped into the backyard to answer calls on his mobile phone. Every day Mala added to her cache of intelligence. Sound administration required it of her and habit only served to reinforce the practice.

As Mala stood in the kitchen, she now listened for sounds from the bathroom. She heard the light being switched on and the slopping of water on the concrete floor as Girish washed his hands and feet. She began to get lunch ready, making sure there was no water on the steel plate and that the cabbage was piping hot. She laid the food on the table and waited by the window, her left heel automatically rubbing against her right ankle.

Girish walked into the kitchen and sat at the table. A crow had made its way on to the kitchen windowsill and was flapping against the frame: *tok tok.*

'Chase that thing away. It'll shit all over the window as usual.'

Mala shooed away the bird, knocking on the window and

breathing a sigh, relieved that he had spoken. Her mood lifted and she shut the window with a smart click of the latch. Spots of rain had begun to appear on the glass.

She moved to the table and began to spoon rice on to Girish's plate.

'Stop.'

Girish surveyed the rice and looked up at Mala. Her hand hovered over the bowl as she stared at the rice, its steam unfurling upwards. Her eyes turned towards Girish.

'Look at the rice. Is this how you like it? Dry, like sand?'

Mala put the spoon down.

'Tell me. Is this what you eat?'

The rain was falling much harder now, little eddies forming against the window.

'Sit.'

Girish had stood up and pushed his chair back. Mala looked at him, her calculations thrown into confusion, her ciphers in disarray.

'Sit. Why don't you sit?' Girish offered her his seat.

Mala sank into the chair and looked at the rice on the plate again. Three little mounds in a huddle, all more or less the same size.

Girish carefully rolled up his right sleeve and sank his fingers into the rice in the bowl. He scooped up some rice and smeared it across the top of Mala's head, working it into her parting with his thumb. The hand returned with more rice, slapping it on to her crown, kneading it into her hair, daubing the sides of her head with yet more rice. Mala's scalp tightened with fear. The heat from the rice made her face itch. Her eyes were firmly shut as she gripped the sides of the chair. Girish's hand kept returning. She could feel its weight, its heat, its motion. Bile flooded her mouth as she felt the steely edge of his ring graze her forehead. She gasped when a hot surge spread in her lap and warm liquid began to trickle down her legs and over her ankles. She heard Girish put the *sambar* pot down on the table and carefully wash his hands at the kitchen sink. There was a thud on the kitchen window before he walked out of the room.

Mala stared down at the puddle of *sambar* on the floor. There were little pieces of onion glistening in her lap like jewels. Somewhere a scooter wouldn't start, the engine hawking repeatedly. A clod of rice fell to the floor over her shoulder and landed behind her chair. Her sari began to weigh down on her lap as the *sambar* cooled, the cotton clinging to the tops of her thighs. Outside, the rain had turned into a fine mizzle. Finally, after a couple of renewed efforts, the scooter started and roared away.

CHAPTER SIX

The editor of the *Mysore Evening Sentinel* was a quiet man. His face displayed a transcendental serenity, with eyes that seemed permanently half closed and a moustache that declared its maturity like a handsome banyan tree. His staff in the newspaper's offices on MG Road read an array of subtle signals into his silences, and over time endowed him with the powers of a mind reader, a clairvoyant and a skilled agony aunt. While in private he would probably have admitted that he was deficient in all of these areas, there was no doubt that in one field he was a true master: leaning back, keeping his ears open and letting warring parties fling prodigious amounts of mud at each other in his presence.

In the course of his many years in the business of local news, he had observed an MLA threaten an Assembly colleague with a bicycle chain; seen the former chairman of the Mysore Regeneration Council slapped by his mistress in a branch of the Canara Bank; and been witness to a number of undignified scenes at the *tahsildar's* office. A colourful version of these developments inevitably made it to the front page of the *Sentinel*. The editor's finest hour had come a short while after the capture of notorious serial killer Ratpoison Revathi in a marriage hall in Hunsur. The *Sentinel* website broke the news as a world exclusive and that evening's paper edition came with a pull-out supplement of India's most feared lady mass murderers.

The latest public spat attracting the attention of the *Sentinel's* journalists concerned the organisers of the first Mysore International Film Festival. The editor had first been alerted to some possible discord when he had noticed the tension between the artistic and programming directors of the festival at a publicity

157

event. As soon as the press conference was over, they each moved to a different section of the room and appeared to be trying to attract an audience of sympathetic supporters. The following morning, Faiza Jaleel was sent to wait outside the Sri Sri Srikantaiah Memorial Hall where the festival's committee was meeting for further deliberations. While the reporters of the *Sentinel* had on occasion been accused of shoddy journalism, wanton sensationalism and poor grammar, they had never been known to shy away from the rigours of endless vigils in the corridors of public buildings.

The stated aim of the film festival's committee was to broaden audience participation in non-commercial forms of cinema and to provide a holistic view of all aspects of the cinematic process. The programme would include the finest art-house offerings in English, Hindi, Kannada, Tamil, Telugu, Malayalam, Bengali and Odia. A special section on digital films and new media had been mooted but these ambitions were hurriedly thrust aside. It was decided that this particular festival did not aspire to screenings of trendy lesbian romps in Colaba apartments, shot on handheld cameras by returned NRIs trying to make a splash.

Previous discussions had focused on whether the international aspect of the festival should be dropped, given that participation from non-Indian film-makers appeared to be limited to a Maoist comedy from Nepal and a five-hour biopic made by an Iranian resident of Gokulam. Luckily there was one more foreign entry in due course: a Hungarian director's retelling of the story of the Sirens.

In the offices of the *Sentinel*, a clearer picture of the Supervisory Committee's difficulties was emerging. On strict condition of anonymity, a reliable source on the Committee had stated that the trouble began at a cocktail party when the artistic director had criticised the programming director's approach as overly commercial. Unfortunately the phrase used was 'shameless Bollywood whore' and it had been relayed, unmitigated, to the programming director. The injured gentleman had retaliated via a smear campaign accusing the artistic director of nepotism and corruption: the latter's wife had written the script for one of the films in contention for the closing night gala. Naturally the artistic director, a film historian of some repute, was incensed and had immediately called on his allies on the various sub-committees for their unqualified support. Further accusations and insinuations emerged over the next few months, piquant accounts in the *Sentinel* marking their passage.

The timing of the current difficulties was calamitous as considerable progress had already been made. The Principal Secretary's office at the Department of Culture had approved its participation some time ago and communications with the Directorate of Film Festivals were at an advanced stage. The chief sponsors had been confirmed as a mobile phone company and the state's largest producers of metal casings for electronic equipment.

Matters would probably have deteriorated further without the lucky intervention of a Singapore-based private bank, which agreed to step in as an additional main sponsor. The unexpected availability of further funds seemed to achieve a sudden convergence in the artistic vision of the two camps. In a matter of days, email subject headings became more optimistic, the event's organisers were given concrete instructions and a number of press events were hastily arranged.

It was decided that the festival opening gala would be held at the Anuraag Kalakshetra in December, at the height of the tourist season. The film chosen as the first screening was billed as a 'futuristic *jehadi* chamber drama' made by a prominent Malayali director who was apparently returning to form. As the festival took shape and publicity grew, a renaissance began to take place among the city's cultural stewards. Moribund projects were steered back to drawing boards, new funding applications were completed and a whole series of suggestions made themselves known on the letters page of the *Sentinel*. A novel exhilaration spread even to the Mysore Tourism Authority. Further soul-searching at Authority meetings had not yielded a fitting alternative to the 'Geneva of the East' theme; now the film festival's celebration of cinema at the edge of Tejasandra Lake seemed a brilliant opportunity to showcase the whole of Mysore in a jubilant lakeside setting.

A few weeks later the Authority called a press conference of its own where, in rhapsodic association with its commercial partners, it announced that Mysore's first Lake Utsava would take place on the Tejasandra Promenade, the day after the film festival's opening gala. A fitting prelude to the construction of HeritageLand, the Utsava would present a diverse selection of the city's talents along the lake shore, planting exhibitions of the work of local artists next to a Carnatic music tent, displays of street theatre alongside a parade of vintage cars. A dance stage featuring exponents of *bharatanatyam* and *kuchipudi*, a yoga fair, the obligatory food *mela* and a handicrafts bazaar would all be incorporated into the revelries.

The timetable was tight and the countdown had begun. Nominations to various new committees were finalised; site inspections were made; stakeholders, willing or not, were identified. The sap of a certain section of Mysore society began to spit and swirl through channels formerly clogged by indecision and civic torpor. HeritageLand or not, Mysore was preparing to face the world.

The first sprigs of intimacy revealed themselves in code, arrangements that both Jaydev and Susheela knew were crucial but which were never discussed. Susheela was taken aback to hear his voice the first time that he called, her surprise feathered by an enigmatic thrill. In the course of that first phone call, Jaydev did not say how he had got her number or on what pretext. But she had no doubt that the enquiry would have been made with a stolid discretion. That phone call had led to a few others, all made and received with the ease of a casual friendship but, for Susheela at any rate, ringed with the shards of a jagged anticipation. They did not speak of why they did not meet, despite living only fifteen minutes away. Their conversations took form around roomy imagined recesses that could accommodate any number of quirks of conduct or confession.

As the conversations unspooled, Susheela was surprised to find herself the target of friendly accusations and the butt of the most obvious jokes. It was an attention that was new, distracting and delicious. When Jaydev called, Susheela went into her bedroom, shut the door and settled onto the divan facing the windows. She was sure that Uma was completely uninterested in her phone calls but why take a chance? It was, she knew, ridiculous to even be thinking of risks or chances; her conversations with a seventy-year-old retired lawyer should concern absolutely no one else.

What was most surprising to Susheela was the number of conversations that they unlocked. She had not realised that she had that much to say. But the anecdotes and observations plunged out, a spontaneous flow that at first embarrassed her and then invigorated her. She found herself talking about Sridhar with an aching avidity, realising that some need to give voice to their life together had come fizzing up to the surface. Jaydev seemed genuinely interested in a man he would never meet and long-forgotten events began to lodge themselves in Susheela's ken from a distant space.

'After so many years of being together, I never thought about what it would be like to live without him. Even when he was very ill and we knew he would not survive, I didn't think about what it would be like. I was just too busy, there was always something to organise or I felt that I had to try and keep his spirits up.'

'And then it hits you weeks or months after they have gone.'

'Exactly. But I should have tried to be more mentally prepared; it's my own fault in a way. My daughter Priyanka always says that I have no imagination and she's probably right.'

'But how can you imagine loss, I mean *real* loss, until you experience it?'

'I don't know. But I just can't get away from the feeling that there must have been something I could have done to be better prepared.'

On another occasion she described to Jaydev those first tentative moments in her married life when she and Sridhar were still trying to map each other's emotional contours. Two months after their marriage, Sridhar had been transferred to Bhopal, the first in a series of moves that would eventually lead him to the position of Director of Finance for the whole of House of Govind. They had arrived at the staff quarters, only to be informed by the caretaker that part of the ceiling had collapsed in the bungalow assigned to them. They had been quite prepared to spend a few weeks in the company guesthouse until the house was rendered habitable again. But Mr Mishra, Sridhar's new boss, had been adamant that he would not commission such an injustice. A bulky man with glistening hair that looked like it had been squeezed out of a tube in little curlicues on to his head, he had insisted that the couple stay with him and his wife; otherwise he would never be able to forgive himself. Mrs Mishra had been less welcoming. A tall, joyless woman, like a length of driftwood wrapped in a silk sari, she had coldly fixed her gaze on the fragments of ceiling plaster while her husband put his arm around Sridhar's shoulder and ushered him towards a waiting Ambassador.

Sridhar and Susheela reluctantly spent six weeks staying with the Mishras. Any attempt at negotiating a passage to the company guesthouse was met by a jovial but solid admonishment from Mr Mishra and a disbelieving snort from his wife. It was a strange and unexpected beginning to their married life. Susheela's mornings were spent trying unsuccessfully to engage Mrs Mishra in conversation or following the cook around the enormous kitchen while he tried to shake her off.

In the afternoons Mrs Mishra went to her kitty parties, to which Susheela was pointedly not invited. She would lie on the bed in the spare room, under the hypnotic rotations of the ceiling fan, looking at the Constable print on the wall and listening to the sounds of Mrs Mishra's departure: sharp instructions to the maid, the turn of the lock in the fridge, the padlock being clipped into the telephone dial, the drawing of the curtains in the sitting room against the afternoon glare and the clicking of her heels on the mosaic floor towards the front door.

The evenings were only slightly better. The two couples would engage in a disjointed quadrille on the veranda, Mr Mishra encouraging Sridhar to join him in 'a bit of one's favourite poison' while Mrs Mishra stared grimly at the receding level of whiskey in the bottle. In between frenetic periods of warding off mosquitoes, Susheela would disappear into long reveries that drew her into reassuring tableaux of life as a normal newly married couple. Sridhar would end the evening lavishly drunk, having attempted to keep up with Mr Mishra in his enthusiastic consumption and unintelligible career advice. As the darkness around them grew into a star-strewn shroud, the boy would bring plate after plate of snacks that went untouched.

After the couples had retired for the night, Sridhar would apologise for their predicament, promising that if the ceiling was not fixed in a week, he would quit his job and they would leave

Bhopal for good. Susheela would nod distractedly, listening to the telltale pitch of the voices that could be heard on the other side of the bedroom wall: Mr Mishra's wheezing explanations that sounded like a broken harmonium and the snapping of sun-baked twigs that could only be Mrs Mishra's clipped retorts.

'So, can you imagine, if you bumped into Mrs Mishra today?' Jaydev asked.

'Oh God, please don't even say that as a joke. You know, I think I'd have to tell her that, regardless of her best efforts, I managed to pick my way into her fridge every afternoon and eat one of her horrible imported chocolate hearts.'

Jaydev's wife, Debashree, had suffered a stroke eight years ago and died a few months later. At the first mention of his late wife, Susheela found herself in foreign territory, her normal social equilibrium deserting her. Would it seem inappropriate for her to display greater curiosity or would a delicate circumvention of the topic appear uncaring? It suddenly dawned on her that men in their seventies with dead wives were not her forte. But Jaydev required neither prompting nor guiding. His allusions were brief but numerous.

Jaydev had known his wife, Debashree, at college. She was the first girl in his year to have her hair cut short and arrive at college on a bicycle. They had married in spite of the objections of Jaydev's mother, who for years afterwards spent hours detailing disastrous predictions for their future in her letters to him. He had once shown Debashree a letter in which his mother had claimed that not only would his wife abandon their children one day, she would do so by running off with one of her dissolute colleagues at the Institute of Education. Debashree's reaction had been typically brassy. She had written to her mother-in-law, setting out in laborious detail the combination of defects in each of her male colleagues that rendered them unsuitable for adulterous couplings.

The telephone wrapped Susheela and Jaydev in the folds of its invisibility, giving them a safe haven for their pauses and reflections. An hour would pass, sometimes two or three, before Susheela emerged from the bedroom, her capillaries swollen with the sound of Jaydev's measured voice, his quizzical teasing and that almost inaudible chuckle.

'Are you an only child?' he had once asked her.

'Yes, how did you know?'

'I can tell. You have that constant watchfulness that an only child has.'

'I am a sixty-four-year-old widow with knee pain and you think I have the constant watchfulness of an only child?'

She felt almost gratified when he had laughed so hard that it brought on a choking fit.

The gloom inside the room was so dense that it had a texture, like cotton wool ripped from a bale. Through the open window Mala could hear rainwater dripping off the roof into the choked gutter, the last sobs of the dying downpour. She looked at the clock on the bedside table. It was still only eleven o'clock. At half past nine she had called the office to let them know that she would not be coming in. Shipra had answered the phone, sounding bored and distant.

'Okay fine, are you coming in tomorrow? Actually, just hang on. Mr Tanveer wants to talk to you,' she had said.

'Ms Mala? What is the matter, not feeling well? What *exactly* seems to be the problem?'

Mala had explained that she had a migraine and, she thought, a temperature.

'That is *most* unfortunate, Ms Mala. Have you taken the opinion of a good doctor? Oh, I see. Well, you must not neglect these matters, of course. But I am sure that you will recover *very* soon; after all, you have youth on your side, not like us old fuddy-duddies. Shipra will call you later today to make sure you are not in need of anything. But in any case, I am sure we will see you tomorrow, isn't it?'

Mala lay in bed, looking at the damp patch where the wall met the ceiling. The surface of the wall had bubbled up like a pancake and now little flakes dangled over the dusty suitcases shoved on top of the cupboard. The last time they had been used was on the honeymoon to Ooty. On returning, as Mala had stood on the bed, reaching up to push them against the wall, she had suspected they might not be required again for a long time. She had been right. But now Girish had become obsessed with the idea of a trip to Sri Lanka, an indulgence they could not afford and which, as far as Mala could tell, held no significant attraction for either of them. The thought of following Girish around ruins or beaches far away from home made her want to cocoon herself away. It was taking every strand of equanimity to pilot her way through her everyday existence; the anxiety that would be engendered by new experiences on distant shores was terrifying.

There was a knock at the door. Gayathri had said she would be late today. Mala got out of bed and let her in. As usual, there was minimal conversation. Mala returned to the bedroom, sinking down on the sheets that seemed to have sucked in the moisture from the walls. She could hear Gayathri opening the windows in the sitting room.

She turned on to her side, away from the window, desperately tired but knowing sleep would not come. Living a secret life made innumerable claims. Every day she had to guard against the erosion of her will with a heightened watchfulness, induced at great cost and leaving her winded.

Mala had considered leaving Girish, but her conception of leaving was shapeless. It was only a vaguely sensed mood, not something that could yet be termed a real choice. She stumbled at the first steps, trying to recall a time before the essence of her life became violence and humiliation, alternating with boredom. The intervals between Girish's random acts of cruelty should have been periods of relief. But an enormous tedium took over and battered her with its slow, steady beat: the routine tasks that Mr Tanveer assigned her, looking equal parts stricken and suspicious; the organisation of life in that dark house, with its corners full of contempt and derision; Girish's lengthy speeches, girdling a subject on which he had decided she needed instruction.

Yet thoughts of any alternatives left her incapacitated, a sharp chill penetrating into her bones. When she married, Mala had made a mental break with her maternal home and Konnapur. She had departed for the legitimacy of adulthood. Picturing herself at home with her parents again was impossible, if it meant returning to Konnapur with nothing to show for her married life but the corrosive shame of her inability to make her husband love her.

Gayathri stuck her head around the door.

'Not well? What's the matter?' she asked.

'Headache.'

'Shall I quickly do the floor here?'

'No, just leave it. You can do it tomorrow.'

Gayathri nodded and walked to the bathroom, tunelessly humming a song; an odd sound that lay somewhere between a gasp and a croak.

The old man next door turned on his radio. His sitting-room window was so close to Mala's bedroom window that she could have stretched her arm out over the low wall and touched it. A radio play was in progress. A woman had been accused of infidelity and she was proclaiming her innocence. The tremors in her voice were wrapped in a static echo as she tried to defend herself against her accusers. A smooth baritone cut in, a voice with the lacquered timbre that made it ideal for radio. His mother and his brother had discovered the truth, said the male voice, and he preferred to believe the people who shared his blood, rather than a stray he had rescued and married out of misguided compassion. The wife's denials began afresh, swearing that she could never betray a man who had been so kind to her.

Gayathri walked into the room again.

'Finished for today. I'll see you tomorrow then.'

'Wait, can you do something for me before you go? Can you get me some tablets from the medical shop? Here take this chit, I've written down what I need.'

Gayathri nodded and reached for the note and the money. She turned to leave but then stopped.

'Not everything can be cured by a tablet, you know.'

Mala propped herself up on her arms: 'Meaning?'

'Nothing. I'll be back in five minutes. You better take some rest.'

With that, Gayathri left the room.

The lunchtime rush had thinned out at the Vishram Coffee House. The two public-sector bank officials had decided to take a late lunch and were at their usual table.

'That Prakash called me yesterday,' said the senior official, his eyes narrowing.

'What for, sir?'

'By mistake. I got the call but I didn't recognise the number. I answered it anyway and you know what?'

'No sir, what?'

'He asked me who *I* am. *He* calls *me* and he asks me who *I* am. Can you believe?'

'That man has no shame, sir.'

'Who is he to phone me and demand to know who I am?'

'His character is not at all good, sir. His background also.'

'I recognised his voice at once.'

'Did you tell him who you were, sir?'

'No, why should I? *He* is the one who called *me*. *He* should tell me who *he* is first.'

'Hundred per cent correct, sir.'

'If he calls me again and asks me who I am, I will really let him have it. *Kappalakke yeradu.*'

'No shame, sir. You can never teach such third-class people.'

'Can you believe how much they have started charging here for extra rice?'

'It's fully looting, sir.'

'*Che.*'

'Sir, this HeritageLand? You think it will ever be built?'

'Why not? Once those farmers shut their mouths, I have full faith in that project.'

'It says in the paper today that the Mughal Waterworld will be one of the greatest examples of engineering ever seen.'

'Very possible. We are the mother of invention, you know. Algebra, buttons, snakes and ladders, all invented here. Also, one rupee shampoo sachets and *idli manchurian.*'

'Very true, sir.'

'And let me tell you another thing, it will be a great opportunity for this city. I mean, who had heard of Florida before Disney World?'

'Nobody, sir.'

'What was there before?'

'Nothing, sir.'

'Just swamps and a few crocodiles. Now look at it.'

The junior bank official left the table to wash his hands and returned, wiping them with a neatly pressed handkerchief.

'Sir, they say that inflation has gone into negative figures – deflation.'

'My foot. They use some godforsaken measure that includes nothing useful that people buy. No food, no medical, no rent. I think it only counts made-in-China mobile phones, which are the only things coming down in price.'

'*Alwa*, sir, seriously. You tell the *aam aadmi* that the government thinks prices are only falling, what will he say?'

'Nothing. He will nod like a sheep and say, "No problem, sir; whatever you say, sir." People in this country will just accept anything. The things that go on here, you think they could happen in any other country?'

'No, sir. It is our cursed fate.'

'For example, you have some gangster with twenty criminal cases pending in various courts. He decides to stand for election and knows he will win because he will bribe all the fools in his constituency to vote for him. Saris, TVs, cash, liquor, whatever rubbish you give them, they will happily accept and shut their mouths for a few days.'

'This has really happened in Tamil Nadu, sir.'

'It is happening everywhere. Then after he is elected, he can make sure none of his cases ever come to court. And if by chance some even bigger political gangster manages to send him to the lock-up, he will send his son or daughter-in-law or grandson's donkey to take his place at the next election and the whole thing will go on like that.'

'Every criminal politician says he has been framed by his political opponents.'

'Of course. Are we all fools to believe that every single MP is spending his time doctoring video tapes and finding impersonators so that he can fake all the evidence? Even our movie writers can't be as skilled at creating these stories as our *netas*.'

'*Nodi*, sir, India Shining.'
'India Whining.'
'India Pining.'
'Okay, enough. Get the bill.'

The phone had hardly stopped ringing that afternoon. If it was not an irritating press officer trying to elicit a comment, it was an underling from the Superintending Engineer's office seeking a definitive version of the morning's events. Girish, in turn, had asked two members of his team to try to put together an accurate report but they appeared to be floundering in their usual inefficiency.

The only objectively verifiable piece of information was that at about eleven o'clock that morning, a group of unidentified persons had descended on the electricity supply company office at Neelam Layout, an unfortunate South Mysore locality that had only been supplied with sixteen hours of power in the last four days. It was from this very point that accounts began to differ. A manager at the Neelam Layout office stated that an angry mob had torn into the building, smashed windows, ransacked a filing cabinet, damaged computer equipment and stolen the caretaker's bicycle. A bystander, on the other hand, told a news channel that the protestors had simply stood outside the building, chanting and holding placards, until the security guards had begun to taunt and insult their mothers, prompting a lengthy scuffle. One of Girish's colleagues reported that he had received a call from someone who was sure that there had been an attempt to burn down the building.

Girish slammed the phone down, having just informed an officer at the Karnataka Electricity Regulatory Commission that he would revert to her as soon as he was able to ascertain the precise nature and magnitude of the morning's incidents.

'This kind of thing would only happen somewhere like Neelam Layout,' he spat.

'I heard that they were accusing us of purposely not providing them with electricity because it is a Muslim area,' said his colleague Ganesh.

'Such fools. As if we can just disconnect Muslim areas even if we wanted to.'

'When people are angry, they will believe anything.'

'Anyway, they get more than their fair share of electricity. Who asked them all to have four wives and twenty children? Always first to start complaining about anything.'

Ganesh doubted that the consumption of electricity per household in Neelam Layout was higher than in any other fatigued and forsaken part of Mysore but was reluctant to feed Girish's ill temper. It would only result in an afternoon of snide remarks and some petty retribution later in the week.

The story was destined to make it to the front page of the *Mysore Evening Sentinel*. Some of its readers were relieved to note that the accompanying editorial had decided to present the incident as the natural consequence of bureaucratic incompetence and poor governance rather than a clash of divided communities.

'Our state government, in connivance with our electricity companies, has only now decided to close the stable door, by stating it will try to purchase additional power from other states,' lamented the piece. 'Unfortunately for the public, not only has the horse bolted, it has been found, sold off secretly through the good offices of a series of corrupt middlemen and the funds transferred via *hawala* brokers to a *benami* Swiss bank account. Such is the nature of official planning and foresight in Karnataka today.'

With that picturesque image, the editor of the *Mysore Evening Sentinel* managed to capture a number of societal ills in his forceful conclusion. The editorial did little to improve Girish's humour that afternoon.

'Susheelaji? It's Jaydev calling here.'

He always announced himself in a cautious way, as if still undecided as to whether he ought to be calling.

'Hello, one minute, one minute . . . so how are you today?'

'I've just come back from a long walk so feeling very relaxed and refreshed. And you?'

'Oh fine, I've been meaning to visit an old friend for ages now but something keeps coming up. I was just wondering whether I should go today. It's one of my days for the driver, you see.'

'I'm sorry, am I delaying you?'

'No no, not at all. It takes me an hour to get out of the house these days anyway. Making sure everything is locked, switched off, closed, bolted. It's ridiculous.'

'Sometimes I do wonder. Maybe you have things to do and then I call and take up so much of your time.'

'Please Jaydevji, I am not Sunaina, rushing off to meetings every five minutes. I really don't know how she does it. Even the thought of it makes me tired.'

'Well, she's younger, but it's true, so much energy. She reminds me of a person I used to know, my senior at my first job in Calcutta. He was also always running around from one committee to another, pushing bundles of paper into an old *jhola* he used to carry everywhere.'

'This was in Calcutta?'

'Yes, in the fifties. In fact, he even had the same hairstyle as Sunaina.'

'Now you are just being rude.'

'No, really, I promise you. Poor fellow, he must be no more, but if in those days he ever had a tendency to wear saris, he would have looked just like Sunaina. You know, us juniors always used to make fun of him. He had a habit of using long words even when he had no idea of the meaning. He must have just thought that it sounded impressive.'

'I think that is a habit many of us Indians have. Also, why use one word when we can shower you with ten?'

'No, but poor old Mr Mukherjee was really something. He would walk up to you and say: "I have a small piece of work for you. Very interesting. I am sure you will find it highly obstreperous." Or else: "Such terrible weather we are having. Truly sybaritic." After we had lost our initial nervousness in that place, my friend Shailendra and I would keep going up to him and using our own ridiculous words in conversation. I feel bad now; he must have thought we were just two such friendly chaps.'

'You *should* feel bad! Poor old Mr Mukherjee. And I can imagine you and your friend laughing like hyenas the moment his back was turned.'

'I wish I could deny that. But that is exactly what we did.'

'Well, I won't tell Sunaina that she reminds you of some poor man that you all used to laugh at years ago. It reminds me of my uncle who also had a very particular way with words. He was a professor of history at Mysore University. If any of the women in the family had put on weight he would smile and say: "You are looking nice and robust, much better than the last time I saw you. Then you were looking very inadequate." The thing was, he really meant it in a nice way.'

'But he never said it to any of the men?'

'No, but I think the men always looked more than adequate.'

'No doubt. So, what time are you going to see your friend?'

'I don't know. I'm not even sure if she's here or with her daughter. I need to phone and check. I feel very bad for her, you know. She has a very nasty daughter-in-law so she tries to spend as little time in Mysore as possible. But what to do? She has to come from time to time to see her son.'

'The usual *saas-bahu* story?'

'Who knows what exactly goes on? But the daughter-in-law seems to really hate her coming so goes out of her way to make things difficult. Jaya, my friend, doesn't eat brinjal, and she was saying that the last time she stayed there, this girl was making brinjal day and night.'

A swallowed gurgle from Jaydev stopped Susheela.

'It may be funny for you because you are not the one being ill-treated. I hope *your* daughter-in-law treats *you* well.'

'Actually, when I visit she is more considerate than my son, even. But anyway, please continue with your story.'

'Jaya has to use a special foot cream. She used to keep it in the bathroom when she was staying with her son but she is convinced that her daughter-in-law kept hiding it.'

'She was hiding the foot cream?'

'Well, it kept disappearing and who else would take it? So now she has to keep it locked in her suitcase. I mean, is it right, that she has to hide her foot cream in her own son's house?'

'I think the best thing would be for you not to delay seeing her. She needs your support.'

'It really is very upsetting for her. A while back her daughter-in-law dropped a wet grinder and it almost fell on Jaya's foot. She is convinced that it was deliberate.'

'Really?'

'Yes, she mentioned it again yesterday: "Susheela, do you remember when that girl tried to murder me with the wet grinder?" '

'Do *you* think it was deliberate?'

'Well, the girl is most insensitive but I don't think she is a psychopath. Although I suppose it is difficult to tell with young women these days, they all seem so confident.'

'Poor Jaya.'

'Let me tell you one thing, Mr Jaydev: we should be pleased with what we have and not demand too much. My son-in-law may be messy and moody but at least he has never tried to kill me. Anyway, enough for today; I am going now. Just thank God for all your blessings.'

A young doctor emerged from the front of SG Hospital, trailed by a group of nervous, pleading relatives hoping for a second's reassurance before he disappeared behind a closed door again. The doctor walked quickly towards his motorbike and sped off through the gates, his face inscrutable. The hospital was located on a busy road near Tilak Nagar, a squat, desecrated building, once a soft pink, now the colour of wet ash. At the back of the hospital, a series of puddles held their daily consignments of used syringes and soiled bandages.

The reception area was crammed with people. Every seat was taken, weary shapes leant against the walls or squatted on the floor, and a large crush surrounded the receptionists. The room smelt of close bodies, damp cloth and something sulphurous that was making its way in through the open doors. On the wall behind the receptionists, a picture of Mahatma Gandhi hung askew, his eyes decorously avoiding the scene below him.

Uma had not been able to speak to either of the receptionists. She asked a porter to point out the way to the ladies' general wards and followed the direction of his disinterested thumb. The corridor light blinked on and off, sousing the walls with a pale green glow. Through the first open doorway Uma glimpsed the dingy ward, mysterious smears and streaks on the floor, filthy sheets trailing off the beds. A young girl seated at the entrance to the ward stared up at her with enormous eyes. She walked past the girl, looking at the inhabitants of the beds, seeking out Bhargavi. Torpid gazes, inert forms, sapped spirits: Uma took in the desolate parade of patients, trying to draw as little attention to herself as possible, a woman with good health and an upright bearing.

She walked across to the next ward and saw more faces, degraded and decaying, but not the one she was seeking. At the end of the corridor a dark stairway led to the wards on the upper floors. A ghostly form brushed against her legs as she walked up the stairs, making her cry out. In the near darkness she could make out a family of skeletal cats that seemed to have colonised this part of the hospital. She hurried up the stairs, two at a time, not wanting to touch the banister.

The second floor passage was in darkness too. Grimy rubber mats were strewn across the floor and a number of bodies huddled against the walls. Uma shut her eyes for a few seconds to try to accustom herself to the gloom. She turned into the next ward where, unexpectedly, all the fluorescent lights were working. As she stood uncomfortably between the rows of beds, someone grabbed her wrist.

'Uma, isn't it? How did you know she's here?'

It was the distant cousin for whom Bhargavi had found work in Mahalakshmi Gardens, days after starting there herself. Uma had only met her once and had forgotten her name.

'She hasn't been to work for three days and I found out from *amma* that there had been an accident and she was in hospital,' said Uma.

'Accident? Accident, my foot,' said the cousin angrily, still holding on to Uma's wrist. 'Come see what those animals have done to her.'

Uma let herself be pulled along the length of the ward. Bhargavi was in a bed near the far end, her leg in a cast. A bandage covered most of her head and her right eye was a shattered purple bulb.

Uma gasped and covered her mouth with her hand.

'What happened? How did this happen?'

Bhargavi turned her head, her left eye blinking in recognition. She moved her swollen lips laboriously.

'Come sit,' she said, patting the edge of the bed.

Uma drew closer to the bed, her hand still locked over her mouth.

Bhargavi's cousin lowered her voice: 'It was on Thursday night. She had gone to the factory to talk to those girls as usual and a few of them went with her to the bus stand. She spoke to them there for maybe fifteen, twenty minutes and then she walked down to the other stop where she gets her bus.'

Uma listened while keeping her eyes on Bhargavi's crushed face.

The cousin continued: 'Then some woman called out to her and asked her to come with her. She said she was having a problem with the factory owners. Bhargavi had never seen her before but she went with her anyway. You know what she's like.'

The cousin stopped speaking, her teeth biting down hard on her bottom lip. Uma took her hand in hers.

The woman had led Bhargavi through a warren of twisting lanes into a four-storey building that appeared to house another garment factory on its ground floor. They had climbed the stairs, the woman all the while looking nervously behind her as she told Bhargavi that she was desperately in need of help. There was only one vast room on the top floor, empty except for a few crates and bolts of cloth propped up against one wall. A moment later, three men had appeared from one corner of the room, slammed the door shut and set upon Bhargavi. She dropped to the floor. The last thing she remembered before losing consciousness was the strange silence in the room, broken only by the sound of their kicks, like the muffled bounce of fruit falling on grass. A passer-by had heard Bhargavi's groans in an alley later that night and found her under a pile of soggy cardboard boxes.

Bhargavi's left eye blinked again, as if to confirm the story. She tried to speak but winced instead.

'I'll give her this tablet for the pain. It's been a few hours,' said her cousin, reaching into a brown paper bag. 'I have not seen even one doctor on this floor for two days. You have to do everything yourself. Yesterday I had to bribe a nurse thirty rupees to change the bandage.'

'But who was that woman? And those men? Had you seen them before?' asked Uma.

Bhargavi shut her eye and opened it again in response.

Her cousin responded: 'They were definitely people from the factory owner's side. But who can tell where they are or who they are?'

'Did you go to the police?'

'I went to register an FIR day before yesterday. They said they would send someone here to take a statement but no one has come.'

Neither of them mentioned their virtual certainty that no one would come either today or the day after.

Bhargavi managed to whisper: 'I didn't think they would go this far.'

'Don't speak, *akka*, don't speak,' said her cousin, placing a hand on the only corner of Bhargavi's forehead untouched by the bandage.

Uma shook her head slowly, looking from Bhargavi to her cousin.

In the bed opposite them, a woman shifted and turned to face them. Her face was a patchy yellow and drained of all expression. It was clear though that she had turned to better hear their conversation.

'I think I should go. If it starts raining, the buses . . .' said Uma.

'Yes, you should go. It was good that you came,' said Bhargavi, through almost closed lips.

Uma nodded, gently cupped Bhargavi's elbow and then touched her cousin's shoulder. She turned and walked quickly down the corridor, slowing down to negotiate the dark stairs and then quickening her pace again towards the main exit. The rain had started to fall already and a large pool had formed between the exit and the gates. Uma joined the throng at the main doors, all waiting for a short lull in the downpour. Beyond the gates, the fruit and vegetable vendors had pulled sheets of plastic over their carts and were taking shelter in the doorways of shops and in the porch of the nearby Health and Family Welfare Institute building. The rain poured over the roof of Bethesda Church and hammered away on the tops of the tin sheets that covered the rows of cobblers and key-cutters lining Puthli Park Road.

Uma and others at the main doors turned in the direction of a series of shouts and drumbeats. In spite of the torrent, a procession was making its way along Puthli Park Road and approaching the hospital. At the head of the group, a huge Ganesha idol mounted on a tractor rumbled past, its pink and purple hues blazing through the dreary slush. The group was probably on its way to the Shiva temple tank where the idol would be immersed in its dark waters. As the drumming grew louder, the men following the tractor leapt into the air, the heavy showers increasing their abandon.

The charge in the air was infectious. A man standing beside Uma tucked his fingers into his mouth and let out a series of sharp blasts in time to the drumming. Many in the throng began to clap and there were more whistles and shouts. The scenes inside the hospital were forgotten as the frenetic impulses of the procession took over. A couple of young men dashed into the pool of water in front of the hospital and began to kick up a fierce splash. Another burst of applause broke out in the group sheltering from the storm.

A roar went up from the men in the procession. The idol's head was caught in the low-hanging branches of a tamarind tree. The drumbeats grew more urgent as the tractor driver, assisted by another man, tried to scythe away the foliage with a stick. A few more men ran towards the tractor from the hospital to assist in the release of Ganesha's head. Around the tractor the dancing continued as the water beat down. When the idol was finally free, most of the stragglers sheltering by the hospital doors surged forward towards the road. Uma watched as the pounding and yelling managed to drown out even the sound of the rain. The tractor started up again and resumed its imperious progress towards the temple tank.

Mala's phone began to shudder on the bed, the screen lighting up. She broke through the surface of her torpor and picked it up. It was Ambika.

'What happened to you? *Amma* said you're not well.'

'It's nothing. Just a bit of fever.'

'Are you looking after yourself properly? You seem to be falling sick a lot more these days. Have you been for a check-up to see if you're anaemic?'

'I am not anaemic. Must be the weather change or something.'

'You should have a blood test anyway.'

Ambika had begun to believe firmly in her own diagnostic abilities, acquired in the course of managing her husband's nursing home. As her home and professional life prospered, her confidence in her opinions and pronouncements had grown proportionately. She now tended to begin sentences with the phrase: 'I have very often found . . .' A chronicle of Ambika's astute observations would follow, accompanied by instructions to her listener on steps for the future. There had been early signs of these interventions. At the age of twelve, Ambika had discovered that a group of students were operating an examination syndicate, receiving papers leaked by a teacher and selling them on for a sizeable profit. Her alertness led to prompt action by the school authorities, a Good Citizen award from the municipal council in Konnapur and endless recitations of the sequence of events for the benefit of family and friends, while her mother served plate after plate of lentil *vadas*.

As Ambika suggested various therapeutic alternatives, Mala felt a sudden and extreme restlessness swell her skin. She sat up and swung her legs off the bed, desperate for her sister to stop talking.

'I'm fine. Tomorrow I'm going to the office, so there's nothing wrong with me.'

Ambika sounded unconvinced but let the matter rest. Instead, she began to talk about the difficulties she was facing in finding competent staff, despite the generous rates she was willing to pay. Mala looked at the leaden sky through the window, making non-committal sounds at regular intervals. She was annoyed now, her primary impulse being to hurt Ambika in some way, confounding that voice into silence.

'How is Girish?'

Ambika always asked this question as if she knew very well that Girish was exactly the way he always was, pompous and sneering, but she would not be the one to be accused of shirking her duty by not asking after his well-being. His superior attitude was a genuine mystery to Ambika and not one that she pondered in silence. She had observed to Mala more than once that Girish may have read a lot of books but he was still a *babu* in a small office in Mysore, living in that dark, airless house in Sitanagar, while everyone else in India was now ready to lock eyes with the rest of the world.

Ambika's chatter continued. Mala responded with her set of stock responses, another accomplished performance designed to remove any doubts in the minds of her family.

'So, what other news from your side?' asked Ambika.

'Nothing much. We'll be busy the next few weeks, helping Anand and Lavanya when they shift.'

'They are shifting? Where to?'

'A huge house in a new complex. You should see this place. It has everything, two swimming pools, shopping mall, cinema.'

Mala could not remember the precise nature of the other attractions at Terra Blanca and decided to endow it with a few of her own: 'I think there's also a golf course and a waterfall.'

'Have they sold their old house?'

'No, I think they'll keep that too. Why sell if you don't need to, no?'

'Have you seen the new house?'

'Oh yes. It's like a place from some movie. They even have their own school and fire department.'

'Why do they need their own fire department? Who will be setting fire to their house every day?'

'They have made it so that they can live with complete peace of mind.'

There was a pause as Ambika digested this information.

'So how much did they pay for it? Any idea?'

'I don't know the exact amount. But crores. Crores and crores for anything in that complex.'

'Why do they need you to help them shift? They can get some professionals, no?'

'Yes, but they will need help supervising. And we had to offer. Especially since they are taking us to Thailand.'

Mala was enjoying herself now. She mentioned Thailand with a flighty nonchalance, like it was a neighbourhood attraction.

'Thailand? Why?'

'What do you mean why? For a holiday, why else?'

There was a further pause as Ambika tried to make sense of this new revelation.

'But they are *taking* you?'

'For the company, *na*? So generous of them. But they are lucky. God has really blessed them, not like you and me, having to count everything.'

Ambika huffed but made no other comment.

'So how long are you all going for?' she asked a few seconds later.

'Nothing has been fixed yet, but I think three weeks.'

'Three *weeks*?'

Mala searched for further colour that she could add to their holiday plans.

'It's so exciting for me, leaving India for the first time and that too all first-class air fare.'

'But will you be able to be with Lavanya for that long? I mean, it's not easy, no?'

'I have come to know the true side of Lavanya.'

'So arrogant, no? Whenever you see her, sleeveless blouse and cooling glass. Someone should kick her.'

'No no, you're *so* wrong. You just need to get to know her. We have become *very* close after spending so much time together and she really is *such* a wonderful person.'

Ambika became subdued and after a few more minutes discussing Anand and Lavanya's new home she became aware of a few matters that required her immediate attention. In any case, she had only called Mala to find out if she needed anything; she would ring again for a proper chat some other time. Moments after she had ended the call with Mala, she dialled her husband's extension. She intended to find out as soon as possible whether it was really conceivable that there were housing complexes in Mysore with their own fire departments.

The rain had been coming down for a few hours now but the skies still seethed. Shankar was sodden, the water running into his shirt, down his torso and dripping from his jeans. He had peeled off his light windcheater and shoved it under the seat of his motorbike, finding its clammy grip oppressive. He wheeled the motorbike into the shelter of an abandoned lean-to and, tucking a small package under his arm, began to trudge through the mud churned up by the side of the road. He always found these rows difficult to negotiate, with nothing to distinguish them, apart from perhaps a tangle of wire or a damaged bicycle left at the entrance. Today matters were much worse. The rain was sweeping into his eyes and some of the lanes were hidden under a foot of water. He thought of turning back but decided to brave the conditions. It was the last box of sweets and Janaki would be furious if she found out that he had come this far without going on to see Uma.

Janaki had given birth ten days ago. The baby boy had arrived two weeks late, weighing in at eight pounds, with a full head of hair and a breathtaking disdain for his new surroundings. Luckily the birth had not matched the terrifying scenarios that friends had described to him, although he had chosen not to point this out to Janaki. The last few days had been overwhelming: a culmination of ambitions; an indication that dignity and gravitas had finally claimed him. He was now a man.

Shankar needed to finish distributing sweets to friends and family and he had picked the week's most inhospitable day. As he descended into the flooded sprawl below him, he placed his feet on anything that looked solid: a brick embedded in the sludge, a partially submerged plank, the top of a section of pipe. There was hardly anyone around. It was only when he reached the phone box clamped to its pole that he realised the extent of the flooding in the area. The stench of sewage clawed at his nostrils. Three children were splashing hysterically outside their home in the first row, the water reaching their knees. He made his way along the gummy slope to the next row, his feet sinking into the brown ooze. Here too the water was rising. A twist of clothes, some plastic basins, a palm frond and then a curled *chappal* drifted idly along in the current.

Shankar tucked the package into his waistband and rolled his jeans up to his knees. He took off his *chappals* and strode into the water, telling himself he was mad. But his conscience would not allow him to turn back. He knew that Uma lived here alone and he could not simply return home without seeing if she needed any help. His toes sank into the moiling sediment as he pushed against the water, past a drenched mattress propped up against a smoke-stained wall. The doors of most of the rooms were closed but he could see that the water was flowing straight in to Uma's room through the open doorway.

As he approached the room, he caught sight of Uma sitting on the tin trunk, her legs folded beneath her, a framed picture lying face down in her lap. She was completely wet, her hair clinging to the sides of her face and the turquoise from her blouse leaching on to her skin. The trunk was marooned in a fuscous pool, a layer of scum lapping against the back wall of the room where the rain was running down the brickwork. Every particle in the room seemed liquescent, caught in a state of chemical collapse.

Shankar rapped loudly on the open door.

Uma looked across at him in amazement.

'I can't believe it. It's like an ocean in here,' he said, taking a large step into the room.

'In this rain, what are you doing here?'

'I didn't know it was this bad. I came to tell you something. I have some good news.' He heard the incongruous ring of his words and his features creased into an embarrassed smile.

'But first you have to get out of here. You'll get sick and who knows when this rain will stop.'

186

'What good news? Janaki?'

'I'll tell you, but first just come with me.'

'Where?'

'Somewhere dry. Or do you want to sit here in this gutter all night?'

'But where will we go?'

Shankar paused as he looked around the room.

'Look, I'll be back in five minutes. Just wait.'

Uma watched him wade across the room and disappear to the right of the open doors. In front of her, a plastic chair, the only piece of furniture in the room, bobbed about idiotically. The clouds continued in their inexhaustible convulsions, wrapping the room in ribbons of water. Earlier that evening, moisture had begun to seep into the room through the floor, its crevices filling up and foaming malevolently with the liquid disgorged by the saturated ground below. The rain had then begun to pour down the walls as the rising channel outside beat at the door. The rows of rooms had been illegally constructed over a storm water drain at the bottom of the hill leading down from Mysore Junction. Every monsoon they were doused and sluiced, mercilessly beaten for a few weeks by the force of the storms. The torrents had nowhere else to go in that dense maze of battered structures; so they surged onto unmade beds, spouted up around rusting cupboards and spewed over shelves of aluminium pots.

Shankar returned to Uma's room, his head lowered against the lashing blasts, brandishing several sheets of dirty blue plastic.

'Where did you get those?' Uma asked.

Shankar ignored her and stumbled through the water to the back of the room. A smell like curdled milk was everywhere. Tucking the ends of the sheets of plastic into his jeans and grasping the top of the back wall, he hoisted himself up, his caked feet seeking a purchase against the exposed bricks. Leaning one arm against the top of the wall, with his free arm he began to twist the sheets of plastic into tight rolls that he then stuffed into the gap between the roof and the wall. One section completed, he moved further along the wall and rose up again, his feet manically seeking a cleft in which to lodge themselves. As he tried to plug the gap, the room darkened further, the gloom and the dankness meshing into a miasma that swept to the edges of the room.

Shankar jumped back into the water, turned around and shrugged.

'The water's still coming in but it's better. We'll see. Come on, let's go.'

'But where?' she asked.

'It's too far to go to Janaki's mother's house in this rain. We'll go to my house and then I'll take you to Janaki when the rain stops.'

Uma had no desire to go anywhere. She felt like a creature thrown up by the deluge who bore a natural obligation to witness the waters recede. But she also lacked the energy to protest. She slowly lowered her legs into the water, still clasping the picture of Shiva with one arm. Shankar did not offer her his hand. She followed him towards the doorway, taking tiny steps through the turbid pool, as if her feet had been manacled. Shankar waited for her to reach the row outside, his eyes avoiding her face.

'I'll try and close the door and then we can go,' he said.

He tried to pull the door shut with all the strength he could muster but it would not budge against the heft of the water.

'There's no money or jewellery in there?' he asked.

Uma shook her head.

'Then let's leave it and go.'

They worked their way through the flood to the edge of the surrounding slope and then laboriously climbed up to the main road, their feet disappearing into the greedy mire. Every now and then Shankar would turn around to glance down at Uma, catching sight of her outstretched arm as she tried to tramp up the incline without sliding into its swampy creases.

The tides of water continued to drum down. Shankar wiped the mud off his feet on a concrete slab by the edge of the road, slipped his *chappals* on and started the motorbike.

'Why are you standing there? Come on,' he called.

Uma hesitated and then shuffled forward. She sat down behind him, her ankles pressed together in a tense bind, her left hand grasping the rear grab rail, trying to maximise the distance between them. Her other arm pinned the picture of Shiva to her chest.

'Ready?' he asked.

'Yes,' she said, feeling like her legs would abandon her, founder and collapse onto the ground.

Shankar eased the bike through the overflowing ruts, blinking hard to keep the water out of his eyes. The road was deserted as they rode slowly towards the open fields that bordered the highway, the wheels hissing against the wet tarmac. Uma glanced down at the back of the picture of Shiva, now streaked with a web of fuzzy lines. Shankar's back was perfectly straight and his shoulders tight with an inescapable awareness. Six inches of water and wind separated him from Uma and in that space there began to fan out the torturous wings of a new certainty. They brushed against Shankar's vertebrae and paused over the nape of his neck. Uma felt them beat a hot gust against her ribs and cast a shadow over her face. The gap between them was not large but it was enough to accommodate the flailing realisation that, as they headed to Shankar's home in the rain, they would not make it any further that night.

PART THREE

Winter

CHAPTER SEVEN

THE law courts of Mysore were housed in an Indo-Saracenic nugget opposite the faded green of Manuvana Park. The building had gained national prominence when a scene from a super-hit film song of the seventies had been filmed on its front lawn, between rows of flame-hued zinnias. These days the garden was bedraggled and contrite, its flower beds plagued by stray dogs who would collapse in the scanty shade of the frangipani trees like a set of errant commas. Justice, as envisioned by a Scottish sculptor in 1908, sat heavily on a plinth in the court complex. The downturned sword in her right hand looked like a walking aid and the expression on her face appeared to suggest immense relief at having been able to take the weight off her feet. If the artist had intended to create an impression of stately reason, safeguarding truth with a powerful gaze, his facility had failed him. In Mysore, justice took on the guise of an irritated matron who really did not wish to be harangued by the petty squabbles of an ungrateful rabble.

Behind the court car park, a number of shed-like structures housed the more prominent of the city's tireless notaries. This was a prime location: some family feuds over the deserving occupant of a notarial seat here had spilled across generations. The longest serving functionary in this cloister was I P K Rangaraja, a man famed for his probity and his devotion to an ancient tweed suit, worn as a mark of contempt for the Mysore weather. Some years ago he had famously uncovered the participation of a number of his colleagues in a scam involving the submission of falsified land title documents. The unscrupulous notaries were soon attending court in a different capacity and Mr Rangaraja basked in the exaltation that came with successfully guarding a profession from disrepute.

Opposite the seat of the notaries' operations, the shade of a large *sampige* tree acted as a billet for the squadrons of interested parties that gravitated towards any hub concerned with the dispensation of justice. Scribes carrying portable typewriters zealously guarded space on the wooden benches. Ambulance chasers mingled with hotel touts; students at the evening law college shared experiences with sympathetic conmen; journalists killed time by trying to tease out scandals from desperate petitioners. The vexatious litigants could always be identified by their plastic bags full of papers and the lust for substantive advantage that warped their backs.

One gentleman with close-cropped, greying hair in a crisp white *kurta* was a steadfast feature of this juridical bazaar. He arrived on foot every weekday morning at exactly ten o'clock, in his hands a thick folder and a basket containing his lunch *dabba*. His exemplary attendance meant that the scribes even offered him a place on one of the benches. The man spent his time looking through his papers and benignly taking in the day's events. He never solicited conversation but always responded to questions politely, neither enlightening nor offending anyone.

In the past few weeks, security at the court building had been increased, not as a result of threats from terrorists or organised criminals, but due to the increasingly animated conduct of the members of the Mysore Law Congress. The genesis of the strife could be traced back to an incident six months ago when an advocate's motorbike rammed into the back of a judge's car outside the court. There were no casualties but a frenzied row had ensued with the use of vivid language on both sides. Official complaints were made, investigations pursued and the matter would have ended, reaching some forgettable stalemate, were it not for the fact that elections to the post of President of the Mysore Law Congress were imminent. The two main candidates, not confident that caste affiliations and their own distinguished professional histories would deliver victory, had dredged up the incident as a symbol of the disharmony that could disable the Congress's future activities, without strong and dynamic leadership. A bilious brew of local gossip, procedural irregularities, vested interests, caste politics and tutored braggadocio meant that a strike of local lawyers was virtually inevitable. The *Mysore Evening Sentinel* called it an unforgivable perfidy that struck at the heart of the administration of justice. To the congregation under the *sampige* tree, it was simply another inconsequential distraction.

Beyond the parochial concerns of the courts in Mysore, the broader legal community was involved in an intense debate that now engaged many sections of civil society. The subject of the controversy was proposed legislation that could make the declaration of judicial assets mandatory and subject to public scrutiny. The majority of judges, of course, were entirely content that details of their wealth be submitted to the appropriate authorities. In fact, many of them were already providing this information to various bodies who could be trusted to treat it with responsibility and respect.

The contentious issue was whether the particulars ought to be released into the public domain. It was no secret that there were hostile elements who would seize the opportunity to ensnare the judiciary in frivolous litigation and media-fuelled imbroglios, a situation which would neither assist the upholding of fundamental freedoms nor enhance the efficacy of the courts. The Indian legal system had many unfulfilled requirements but a vaudeville centred on the bank balances of judges was certainly not one of them. Campaigners for transparency gave sermons on accountability, institutional integrity and, above all, public confidence. A certain section of the judiciary, however, wanted to emphasise that it too suffered from a lack of confidence in the intentions of the general public.

One pro-information rights commentator stated that what was at stake was the humanity of the judiciary. The response from the editor of a prominent daily was that judges had shown themselves to be all too human. In support of this contention, a former Supreme Court judge was quoted as estimating that twenty per cent of judges in the country were vulnerable to subornation and unlawful inducements. The venerable gentleman, caught between his duty to the nation and loyalty to his old colleagues, had chosen his words carefully, making judicial corruption sound like a highly communicable influenza rearing up in a delicate constituency. In spite of this incrimination, society at large remained optimistic. After all, the conclusion to be drawn was that an awe-inspiring eighty per cent of the judiciary could still be trusted to maintain the rule of law with a humbling display of integrity. In these times of rampant parliamentary and administrative skulduggery, that figure could only be cherished.

In the half-light of the early morning, the loudspeakers set up on the walls of the city's Venkateshwara temple let out a ghostly crepitation. The city was beginning to wake: a rickshaw rolled past the main bus stand, a few labourers sipped their coffee seated on the pavement by Sriram Circle and street sweepers crossed the road towards the front of the temple. A trio of buses, sporting garlands of marigold and jasmine, pulled into the bus stand and eased themselves into a row. A man opened the door of the first bus and jumped down from its steps on to the hard earth below. Three other men followed, their descent a little more hesitant and cautious. They all knew that the slowly brightening day held in store a decisive pronouncement. As they stood uneasily in front of the buses, each light smudge in the sky refracted an ambiguous portent.

The loudspeakers sputtered into the dawn a few more times before releasing the low strains of a devotional song. The singer welcomed the morning, praised the light for its benevolence and gave thanks for the end of night. The men looked down at the spidery trails of *paan* juice on the paved ground, silent and trying not to read any significance into the words of the song. Its sound probably rose up over the temple wall and towards the tops of the coconut trees every morning. There was nothing special about today.

A few minutes later another handful of men arrived at the bus stand, their faces sealed against surprises. They joined the first group, a taut diffidence descending. The men seemed to need a welcoming sign, an indication that they were not simply detritus blown here by an ill wind. One of the men suggested going across the road to the coffee stall and they agreed that it was a good idea. But no one moved.

The driver from one of the buses jumped down and headed towards the back wall of the bus stand compound. The men watched as he stopped by the wall, adjusting his trousers in front of the words 'The Sword of Truth will Safeguard the Voice of Democracy' spray-painted in red. He turned back towards the men and they all instantly looked away.

Just as one of the men pulled out his mobile phone to make a call, a van made its way in to the compound. The door slid open and another group joined those already waiting. As their numbers grew, a buoyant spirit descended over the men and the few women who had joined them. There were jokes, a playful headlock and some theatrical tutting. More people arrived. They came on scooters, by cart and crammed into rickshaws. Eight young men pulled up in a gasping Premier Padmini and three others on a bicycle. A couple in their seventies emerged from a *tonga*, rattled but cheerful. The young man who had first jumped off the bus began a headcount and then abandoned it. He divided the assembly into three sets, one for each bus. It was evident from his manner that from this point no further tomfoolery would be tolerated.

'Vasu, what time are we leaving?' a woman asked him.

'In exactly twenty minutes, whether or not everyone is here,' he said.

In just over three hours they would reach the outskirts of Bangalore and, depending on the traffic, it would be another half hour or so to the High Court. The judgment in the dispute over the government's acquisition of land for the HeritageLand complex was due to be handed down before midday. It had taken years to get to this point and all the parties involved wore their bruises heavily.

The last protest by the theme park farmers in the centre of Mysore had led to a *lathi* charge at KR Circle, futile arrests, avoidable injuries and an abiding sense of failure. A group of community activists led by Vasu had become convinced that focusing on the legal process already underway was the only meaningful option. Rage and venom were easy to reap but the activists firmly held that only a well-placed belief in the legitimacy of their claim could sustain their campaign. It was the type of optimism that could part seas and arrest storms. The alternative was to collapse in the streets around KR Circle as smoke rose into the skies.

A local proverb said that a closed fist could not accommodate righteousness. Vasu said that angry men did not have the cool heads required for effective action. The activists had spent months explaining and reassuring, building up a deep swell that would break on the steps of the High Court, leaving a corpus secure in its ideology and vindicated in its stance.

Vasu's family had lived on the same plot of land for generations, slowly watching the smoggy extremities of Mysore snake up from the horizon. Dowries, debts and disputes had whittled away at the property and now all that remained was an acre and a half of tenacity. When Vasu's father first heard of the land acquisition, he had sensed an intrigue. Although illiterate, he was well informed and he knew that even the most nefarious land-grabbing schemes could come cloaked in official sanction, bearing bouquets of worthless enticements and desiccated promises. Vasu was the only member of the family who had passed his PUC and he was immediately put in charge of getting to the bottom of the rumours and speculation.

Over the last few years Vasu had gathered an abundance of information, made contact with NGOs all over the country, learnt from human rights experts, formed links with other farmers' organisations, consulted environmentalists and visited every village in the affected agricultural belt. It felt like everything he had ever done had been leading up to this day.

Ignoring the acid rawness in his stomach, Vasu began his head-count again.

Behind one of the buses, Ramanna let the *beedi* drop out of his mouth and ground his heel on it until a small pit had formed in the red earth. He pressed at his knuckles languidly, coaxing out a dull crack from each one. He had not expected so many people to be here; certainly not enough to fill three buses. Facing away from most of the others, as usual, he made no attempt to engage anyone in conversation. He was here only because he knew that he had to safeguard his interests. There was little else now to bind him to these people.

Ramanna had no sentimental attachment to his land. In fact, the sight of the rutted path that led to his fields filled him with a stinging revulsion. The land only represented what it was worth in monetary terms: an opportunity to move away from the village and start life somewhere else. The money would perhaps allow him to learn a trade in Mysore. An acquaintance had started a business tending to some of the gardens in Jayalakshmipuram; maybe he could do that for a while. The land was nothing but his route away from the village and its ligatures of antipathy and malice. Ramanna and his family were not served at either of the village's two provision shops. They were ignored at the bus stop and taunted at the post office. Excrement had been left in a torn plastic bag outside their door and broken glass sometimes glinted demonically on the approach to their house. Ramanna had married out of his caste and he had to live by that decision. The inhabitants of the village were well known for their hospitality and good cheer at festivals; what was less well known was the virulent hostility that many of them would direct towards transgressors of ancient codes.

There was nothing Ramanna wanted more than to sell his blighted holding. But he wanted the right price. He would not give up the one thing of any value that he owned for anything less than its proper worth. Now that determination saw him preparing to take a seat on a bus, his face blank, making common cause with some of the people who spat at his children in the street.

Vasu began his headcount for the third time.

The oldest person in the group was Kenchamma; at least, that was the general supposition. Neither she nor any of her female contemporaries knew their exact age. When asked, she would throw her head back and let out one of her soundless laughs, her jaw quivering delicately.

'All the girls in my family grew up like weeds. Who knows the age of weeds?' she would ask.

Kenchamma owned a small parcel of land that lay across the

proposed site for one of the HeritageLand ring roads. She had spent the last fifteen years sitting in the doorway of her house, listening to the smack of her tongue against the roof of her mouth and looking out at the surrounding fields. Her constancy was as much a feature of the landscape as the crackling beds of dried sugar cane leaves or the kites that traced daring arcs with their frozen wings. Her two remaining sons worked the fields and it was their shifting forms that Kenchamma watched. She had lost five children in childbirth, two to measles and one son had been found hanging from a tree at the edge of their smallholding. She had lived on this land for over sixty years, arriving as a girl, already married three years. The land was bordered by a stony ravine, a line of wood-apple trees and the narrow lane that led to the nearest village. These markers traced the physical edges of her experience but their nearness had not blunted her intuition or her foresight. Today she had insisted on making the trip to Bangalore, as the stakes were as high for her as for anyone else.

A woman walked to the front of one of the buses and cracked a coconut on the ground with a deadly swing. A few heads bowed in silent prayer. The elderly had already been allowed to board the buses and make themselves comfortable. Now Vasu began to direct the others towards the bus doors. Two buses had been borrowed from a milk cooperative's local office and the third hired from a tour company. The arrangements had been made, then cancelled and then reconstituted. The angry charge that ran through the community had not helped Vasu in his attempts at planning this journey. But, in the end, he and his colleagues had managed to convince the majority of the importance of a solid presence at the High Court.

The buses moved out of the compound and made their way towards the Bangalore–Mysore highway. The woman who had cracked the coconut took a steel *dabba* out from under the folds of her *pallu* and began to pass around some *prasada*. Her morning prayers had been the culmination of twenty-one days of fasting and the sugary semolina would yield good luck. As the buses gained speed, Kenchamma's reedy voice punctured the chill air. The message was clear. If a woman her age could sing all the way there, no one else had any excuse to brood.

Getting his hair cut had always made Jaydev nervous. Even as a child, every time the barber visited the house to administer to the men and boys in the family Jaydev would steal up the back stairs and seek asylum in one of the unoccupied rooms on the top floor. His elbows piked into his lap, he would endure an anxious spell in a rosewood cupboard that smelt of camphor or behind knobbly sacks of paddy, listening for the sounds of pursuit. All the while, as if in sympathy, a fretful rumble would descend from the pigeons settled in the ancient rafters. The pattern continued throughout his childhood in spite of his mother's exasperated warnings, her fingers twisting his ear into a red ball of flame.

His adult years had meant an inevitable but uneasy accommodation with the monthly ritual. It was not vanity or sloth that brought the unsettling pall. Jaydev felt a disconcerting loss of control at delivering himself up to these silent, sullen men who manipulated his head with brusque gestures and appraised him unabashedly. Trussed in a towel, being goaded by an inconvenient reflection, a handful of waiting men watching his transformation, Jaydev endured his sessions in clenched abeyance. Over the years, habit had brought relief at a shop squeezed into a nook on 5th Cross, its owner as much a creature of routine as Jaydev. The slack hours were predictable, the service rapid and the lights relatively dim. But now, after thirty years, the barber had wound up his business and Jaydev suddenly found himself trying to identify a replacement.

It was not particularly urgent. He could probably go without a haircut for another week or so. But he had thought, in passing, that today might be a good day. It was a Tuesday afternoon and people tended to avoid Tuesdays for haircuts. He had spotted a place that looked passable and he had the time, as long as he could be home by four to have a shower. Susheela was expecting him to pick her up at about half past four. It was the first time he was taking her anywhere and it would not do to be late.

There were a couple of empty chairs outside the shop. Inside, no one was waiting and there was only one customer. He leant back in his chair, eyes closed as the barber dusted off his shoulders with a brush. The barber gestured to Jaydev to take a seat on the bench against the wall. An assistant stood at the end of the room, twisting a button on his shirt, his body popping with neglected energy.

Jaydev sat down, hoping it would not take too long. Seating with no back could turn into a problem. Above his head, a poster of beaming blond men had almost faded into the wall, the images teal with age. He picked up a film magazine and began to turn the pages. He stopped at a story setting out a top star's plans to launch a website dedicated to tackling climate change. The star described in detail the moment he realised that urgent action was necessary during the filming of a chase scene in the jungles of Borneo.

The barber was showing the customer the back of his head in a mirror. Did any man do anything other than nod in buttoned-down approval at this point?

The customer's head bobbed in contentment and he stood up. The barber bowed at Jaydev and indicated the vacant chair.

'My name is Raju, sir. How can I help you today?' he asked.

'I think it needs a good trim. It feels heavy at the back. It might start curling up,' explained Jaydev, sitting down.

'Yes, sir. And the front?'

'The front? Just do something that will go with the back.'

'Not to worry, sir. First time here, sir?'

'Yes, my first time. My usual man left town.'

Raju bowed again, as if in deference to that decision. When he tucked a towel into Jaydev's collar, the skin on his fingers felt cool and grainy. With a flourish, he spread another towel over Jaydev, fussing over its edges. He smoothed out the creases over Jaydev's arms and brushed imaginary fragments off its surface.

The assistant darted forward and asked Raju a question. As he replied, he rested his hands on Jaydev's shoulders, like a friend in the playground making a declaration of solidarity. Jaydev waited for the haircut to begin. He stared at the counter in front of him, not wanting to look in the mirror. This type of lighting played tricks. It made his neck look like it had receded into a cavern and his eyes appear even more deep set, trying to catch the light from their submerged lair. Even Raju looked grey and pinched in the mirror. On the counter there stood small tubs of pomade, hair oils arranged by colour, from amber to mahogany, and muscular bottles of aftershave. An open razor loomed in a jar of milky solution, turning grooming into chemistry. The towel around his neck smelt of talcum powder, which always reminded him of his children, white specks mottling the rubber sheet whenever his wife changed them.

'Sorry sir,' said Raju, speaking louder than was necessary. 'You have to tell these youngsters everything a hundred times.'

The assistant began to move a broom around the clean floor, delivering loud clacks as he manoeuvred it into the tight corners around the chairs.

Raju shot him a look of distaste and then squeezed Jaydev's shoulders.

'Sorry sir, I will start now.'

His hands swept up the nape of Jaydev's neck, bunching the white locks for a quick assessment. He then placed a palm on either side of Jaydev's head and contemplated his face. Satisfied, he picked up a spray and, placing his hand decorously over Jaydev's eyes, he released clouds of fine mist into the air, all the while looking like someone who would really rather not have to intrude in this way.

He put the spray down.

'Sir, machine?'

'No. No machine.'

Raju bowed again. He picked up a pair of scissors and began cutting, blade over fist, the same closeness of clicks that always made Jaydev grind his teeth and look down at his knees.

A man with two young sons walked into the shop and sat down on the bench.

'But last time you said he would cut off my ears,' wailed the smaller of the boys.

'I said if you didn't sit still, he would cut off your ears.'

The prospect of not moving seemed even more terrifying and the boy buried his bushy head in his father's lap.

The assistant tried to engage the older boy in some play involving enthusiastic winking but was roundly ignored.

The white snips were falling like snow on to the floor. Once a glassy black with a noble wave in it, over the years Jaydev's hair had turned into a more tentative sweep, threaded with strands of soft grey, and had eventually settled into a timid, feathery drop, like thoughts made of tulle. Still, at least he had held on to it at his age, more than enough to worry a comb.

Raju picked up a razor and, pulling taut the skin on Jaydev's cheek, began to scrape at his sideburn. The rasping seemed to be coming from inside Jaydev's head and was curiously satisfying, like itchy worries being scratched. The process was repeated on the other side. Jaydev's eyes met his own in the mirror. Everything looked neater, strapped in, kempt. He looked like a boyish old man.

Raju leant forward and said, almost into his ear: 'Sir, head massage?'

'What?'

'Head massage, sir?'

Jaydev had no idea what to say.

So he said: 'Fine.'

He supposed it would be.

His usual barber liked to keep things uncomplicated. There had never been any doubts, ambiguities or massages. Undoubtedly the glitzy salons in town managed to muddy these waters. But Jaydev had never even stepped through their doors. This was why change in these matters was so unsettling.

Raju poured a liquid into his palm, something brown that smelt of forests. Slathering it over his palms, he smiled reassuringly at Jaydev. The fingers that had been like a strip of wet sand were now like warm wax, melding, easing and quelling. The skin on Jaydev's head felt fluid, teeming with spores, as Raju's palms slowly gave up their heat. Jaydev's eyes were screwed shut, the rings and waves of Raju's touch only palpable as an irresistible foreign manipulation. The fingers migrated to his temples, stole on to his crown and then dropped to the back of his head. At the base of his neck, they reasoned and resolved. They fled back up his head in jittery bursts, cool, then hot, then cool again, and spread out over the top of his forehead. It could have been a few minutes or a few hours in that soft-cornered darkness.

'All done, sir.'

Raju ran a comb through Jaydev's hair and smoothed it down with his hand. Silky bristles caressed the back of Jaydev's neck and a cooling wad of cotton dabbed the skin behind his ears. Raju finished the process with a mysterious crack that brought Jaydev back to the grey light of the shop.

Jaydev put money down on the counter, nodded at Raju and the assistant and pushed open the door with more strength than it needed. Outside, he crumpled on to one of the empty chairs. His head and neck smarted from the recent contact. All of a sudden, a great galloping sob rose through him, convulsing his body and placing a chilly finger in the hollow of his throat. He slumped forward, crying tearlessly, long absent tremors billowing out, one after the next. He covered his face with his hands and sat bowed in the chair, until, just as suddenly, the ferment fell away, leaving only complete stillness. It felt like the first moment of the early morning. Slowly, he stood up and stepped off the shop's porch. It had been exactly ten years since anyone had touched his temples, held his head or made much of his neck.

❖   ❖   ❖

Vijaya Road was not the type of thoroughfare featured in brochures or advertisements. It held no interest for the executive board of the Mysore Tourism Authority and could not have been more distant from the frenetic conceptualisation of the organisers of the Lake Utsava. The road was a stubby continuation of the more respectable Acharya Road, squeezed into the concrete jumble behind Sheethal Talkies. A string of bars lined one side of the street with names like Agni, Sagarika and Prithvi, curiously allied to the robust appellations of India's nuclear missiles. The entertainment provided by these establishments varied. At Agni Bar it was a little television, permanently turned on to a sports channel, where everything appeared filtered through orange gauze. At Sagarika Bar, a number of girls in flashy clothes were encouraged to circulate among the patrons, half of them adopting a challenging sauciness and the rest swinging their *dupattas* while staring at the floor. At Prithvi Bar the owner's son, seated on a high stool behind the counter, sang tuneless dirges and was ignored by the clientele.

Opposite the bars stood the nondescript entrance to the

Sangam Continental Lodge. In a previous incarnation the hotel had been the Apsara Lodge, but a police raid and the resulting adverse publicity had necessitated a change of management, a new front door and a different name. The Apsara Lodge had been found to be operating as a brothel, housing a number of Bangladeshi and Nepali girls, all illegal immigrants who were sent to the local women's jail until further notice. The police had discovered a secret staircase leading from the hotel kitchen to a basement room, its entrance concealed behind piles of empty boxes. The room had served to hide evidence of unlawful activities during previous raids, the girls having been herded into the basement following an opportune call from a very obliging local sub-inspector. His eventual transfer meant the end of the Apsara's time on Vijaya Road and what some sanguinely thought would be the break of a new morning.

A few weeks after the raid, the hotel was open for business again. The Sangam Continental Lodge was categorically not a brothel. The new management was either unwilling to shoulder the risks involved in such an enterprise or firmly resolved against the idea on moral grounds. But in death the Apsara succeeded in leaving more than a trace of her distinctive personality on her successor. Currents of wretched desperation continued to drift up the foul staircase and a profound contamination seeped through keyholes and air vents. The hotel guests shuffled past the reception desk in a hurry, seeking only the solace of a closed door. By day the reception desk was staffed by a threadbare woman with a hacking cough; by night a bearded goon sat in the doorway on a wooden crate that tried gamely to contain his colossal rump. Two straight-backed chairs with elaborately carved headrests stood at the bottom of the stairs but no one had ever been spotted sitting there. The kitchen was no longer operational, even as a conduit to a hidden cellar. In the rooms upstairs, a wan intimacy routed alienation for an hour or two before the space had to be vacated and the key returned.

Shankar closed the door of Room 7 on the first floor and walked downstairs. On the landing he nearly ran into a boy who was making a delivery, his arms clasped around six bottles of beer.

'Watch where you're going, sir,' he said, practised and professional. A large patch covered the seat of his baggy shorts.

Shankar continued down the stairs. As he passed the reception desk, the woman called out to him.

'Mister, the key,' she rasped.

'The lady's still in the room. She has the key.'

'What time is she coming down?'

'Just now. Five minutes.'

The woman returned to the prayer book on her lap and Shankar escaped into the street.

Inside Room 7, Uma sat on the corner of the bed. In her hand she held the key, which was attached to a playing card with a hole punched through it: the seven of clubs. The key smelt like the counter at the medical shop, a combination of hot metal and floor cleaner. She turned to pull the sheet straight and then smoothed out the creases on the two thin pillows. There was no window, no picture, no calendar, nothing to look at in the room apart from the fluorescent light's icy glare. A jasmine bud had broken free of her hair and lay on the sheet. She picked it up and ran its pursed nib along her cheek before flicking it into the air.

She skirted around the bed and sat down on Shankar's side, picking at a dog-eared corner of the playing card with the side of her thumb. Someone pulled the chain in the toilet at the end of the corridor and a reluctant gargle made its way through the walls, over her head and down towards the belly of the building.

She guessed that it must be at least ten minutes since Shankar left. She had given him a present for the baby, a bib dotted with a collection of planets. The small square of brown paper lay on his side of the bed: he had either forgotten to take it or had chosen to leave it behind. She stood up and slid the present under one of the pillows. Switching off the light, she opened the door and walked towards the staircase, the key warm in her hand.

The court's decision was handed down in the course of a short hearing. The judgment was unambiguous. There was no doubt that the 'public purpose' test required by the legislation had been clearly satisfied in this case. HeritageLand would provide vast economic benefits, employment opportunities and, with the expected surge in international tourism to Mysore, boost foreign exchange reserves. There could be no clearer formulation of a sound public purpose. It would be inequitable for the court to reject this purpose simply because the conduit for its delivery was private industry. The court was called upon to conduct a delicate balancing exercise and in such cases it was always important to consider the nature of the matter in the round.

Furthermore, the court did not agree with the petitioners' contention that the public benefits brought by the theme park failed to make restitution for the gross inequity of depriving thousands of farmers of their livelihood and the communities in which many had lived for generations. The government had clearly demonstrated that huge developmental gains would be made and the advancement was for all to share. Farmers who owned land were being compensated for the loss of their property and they would have an undeniable stake in the progress of the city and its environs. The government had guaranteed that landless labourers in the area would also benefit from the fruits of the development.

The court further held that the evidence proffered by the petitioners did not decisively support their assertions that compensation had been miscalculated. There was no obvious unfairness. There was evidence to suggest that elements of irregularity had crept into some of the reports submitted by the state's land surveyors and in the provision of notices. This was not, however, a sufficiently egregious violation to warrant the court declaring the entire undertaking perverse, irrational, illegitimate, disproportionate or unlawful for any other reason. The parties were urged to come together to iron out these small differences in the spirit of economic cooperation and national betterment.

The lawyer present at the hearing took Vasu to one side. He was sorry to have kept the group waiting but he had needed some time to look through the judgment. It was a completely unanticipated decision. While they had not expected to prevail on every point raised, the exhaustive rejection of their case was mystifying. But matters could not be allowed to end here. The lawyer and the rest of his team would carefully examine the court's formulations and work out a strategy. Of course, they could not lose hope. There was the Supreme Court. It would take time, effort and money to get there, but it would be worth it in the end. It was precisely for this type of case that the Supreme Court existed.

The lawyer understood that the community would be gravely disappointed. He would come now and explain the decision to those present and, if necessary, would visit one or two of the villages in the next few days. They had to have faith in the legal system. It would be difficult but they would have to be determined and perseverant. They would obtain a stay order on any attempts at encroachment or construction on the land. They would approach the court as many times as was required. If any government or private contractors attempted to defy the orders, they would move the courts again. In the case of harassment or intimidation, the police would be able to assist them. Besides, such conduct would work against their opponents when it fell to judicial scrutiny at the next stage. The lawyer was aware that there had already been reports of the involvement of the Mysore land mafia in certain areas. The important thing was to bring all such incidents to the attention of the relevant authorities.

He could not say how long it might take for an appeal to be heard. He knew that Vasu had witnessed the delays in getting the case to the High Court and so had experience of the complexity of these matters. But the important thing was to emphasise to the community that the fight was not over. They just had to be patient.

Even though it was not a Sunday, the house was steeped in Sunday quiet. Susheela had told the driver not to come. Uma had asked for the day off because she had a wedding to attend. There was no *mali*, no chatter from the students on their way to their tuition classes, no commotion from the Nachappas' garage doors. The morning had evaporated in the gentle heat of newspapers and phone calls, lunch had been perfunctory and now the early afternoon squared up to Susheela like a neighbourhood bully. There were still a couple of hours before Jaydev was due to pick her up. There was no point in having a nap; she did not want to look like someone who had been in bed all afternoon. She walked into the kitchen. Everything was in its place. A piece of netting covered a bowl of custard apples on the counter, beads weighing down its edges. In the pantry she saw that Uma had stacked the month's newspapers and magazines and bound them with twine, ready for collection on Thursday morning. Through the window, she could see that there was nothing on the washing line.

She went back into the sitting room. Her heart lurched when she thought the clock showed a quarter past three but that was just her eyes; it was still a quarter past two. It was ridiculous. What was she doing to herself? It was as if the stiff progress of hands and pendulums in this house had been replaced by the erratic clashing of a monkey's cymbals. She walked into the hallway where the telephone sat next to a vase of gerbera. The truth was that there was no one left to call.

She went upstairs. That morning she had picked out her sari. Nothing that looked too festive or celebratory; a cream chiffon overlaid with sober navy tendrils. Two bottles of perfume stood on her dressing table, almost full. In the drawer, there lay at least another ten bottles, still in their unopened boxes, covered in plastic, the accumulated debris of birthdays and anniversaries. Susheela had never understood these scents, floral gulps with cloying trails that lunged towards the senses. The only smell she really appreciated was the fragile balm of a string of jasmine, practically inferred. But she could hardly emerge from the house to greet Jaydev with long chains of jasmine wound into her hair. The poor man would reverse out of the gates and head straight back home.

She got dressed.

A couple of short hoots sounded. He was here. Susheela picked up her handbag, took a quick look inside and then opened the front door. Jaydev was turning the car around in the road. She locked the door and walked towards the gates. A cordon of dark clouds moved over the garden, momentarily turning the world monochrome. Jaydev stepped out of the car and raised his hand. He looked like he was trying to hail a taxi. Susheela waved back. She thought she must look like a six-year-old at the start of the first day of school. There was no one else in the road.

A strangeness seeped into the scene. They had not seen each other for more than two months but had spoken almost every other day, sometimes for hours. It was a little like listening to her own voice on the answering machine, a startled recognition mingled with a prickly discomfiture. Jaydev appeared a little thinner to Susheela, his face more defined, altogether a more compact person. She lifted the latch, pulled open the gate and then closed it behind her. Jaydev walked around to the passenger side of the car, opened the door and then, perhaps thinking this was too pointed a gesture, left it wide open and returned to the driver's side.

'Right on time,' smiled Susheela, getting into the car quickly.

The inside of the car smelled like an after dinner mint.

'You are looking well,' said Jaydev.

'Thank you; so are you.'

She shut the door, put her seat belt on and settled her handbag in her lap.

'Ready?' he asked, as if they were on a motorbike.

'Ready,' she replied, as if she had settled her arms around his waist.

The car moved silently down 7th Main, the windows closed. At the junction, a stray dog barked at it long after it had gone.

Mini and Mohan Madhavan were celebrating their fifteenth wedding anniversary at the Mysore Regency Hotel. Mini's younger sister Mony had taken charge as party planner and the guest list had spun itself into a healthy gathering of over two hundred and fifty.

'Although in places like Mysore one can never be sure who else will suddenly show up,' Mony had said to her friends in South Bombay.

There had been lengthy discussions about the choice of venue; everyone was agreed that the Regency was not what it used to be. Had anyone been to the Burra Peg on a Friday night recently? Most of the tables seemed to be occupied by men in groups that were a little too large, their laughter a little too loud, their accents a little too earthy. They never ordered gin or wine but managed to put away bottle after bottle of the most expensive imported whiskey. Sometimes they tried to involve you in their conversations about the cost per square foot in Siddhartha Layout or which kebabs to order next. Still, the Lotus Imperial would not be ready till next year and the Regency did have those beautiful gardens sweeping down from the old wing.

Crystal was of course the theme. Mony had outdone herself in sourcing original table centrepieces, seat covers, a dazzling ice sculpture and silk goody bags filled with charming mementos. Guests were encouraged to wear white but neither Mini nor Mohan wished to make it mandatory on the invitation. Mini, of all people, knew that white could be extremely unflattering on some figures.

There had been a little bit of thunder earlier in the evening but the sky seemed to have settled by the time Anand and Girish reached the hotel's side pavilion, their wives a few steps behind. Moments later the power cut out. There was a collective cry from the guests and a nervous few seconds in the near total darkness before the generators swung into action.

The group joined the queue waiting to congratulate Mini and Mohan.

Mala was anxious. She knew that her performance tonight would be feeble, her craft strained and faltering. As she waited, she prayed that she would not see any of her front office colleagues on duty or any of the waiters who knew her by sight. She needed no further reminding that she did not belong here, just as she did not belong at work or at home.

'But where has this tradition come from, recharging your vows?' asked Anand, looking puzzled.

'Renewing, not recharging. It's not a battery,' said Lavanya.

'But what is the point of spending so much money on your wedding if you have to do it all again in a few years?' he persisted.

There was no response. Anand would have to resolve these questions of nuptial husbandry on his own.

Mini looked lovely in a cream and gold sari. Mohan looked drowsy. There were hugs. Gifts exchanged hands. Girish made a witty comment about marriage. Mini seemed to wonder who he was. Lavanya flicked her hair back. Mala looked down. The photographer snapped away.

On the way to their table, there were several asides as Lavanya and Anand saw people that they knew. Mala smiled fiercely every time she was introduced and then stood behind Lavanya. Anand and Venky Gowda bear-hugged each other. Priyadarshini Ramesh, of the Mysstiiqque chain of beauty salons, blew kisses in their direction. The former chairman of the Mysore Regeneration Council galumphed over with a cocktail *dhokla* in each hand. Girish's face gave nothing away but Mala knew he must be bored. She had no idea why he had thought it would be a good idea to come.

A man in a white kaftan put his arm around Anand.

'This man is too much,' he said to Girish and Mala. '*Too* much.'

'Mr Pasha, the theme was white. Not fancy dress,' said Lavanya to him, pretending to look injured.

Ahmed Pasha wagged his finger at Lavanya in delight: 'Naughty, naughty.'

A few minutes after they had sat down at their table, a column of silence settled over them, not heavy enough to spur action, but sufficient to lend a laboured awareness to the evening.

Waiters were handing single white roses to all the ladies under Mony's anxious gaze.

'We don't even know them that well. God knows why they invited us,' said Lavanya at last, clearly wondering why Girish and Mala had been invited.

Mala speculated as to whether she ought to ask about the plans for the new house. It could lead to all kinds of problems. Instead, she asked them when they were next going on holiday.

'Ask this one,' said Lavanya, jerking her head at Anand. 'He is the one who has no time to even scratch his head.'

'Our Thailand trip was not that long ago,' said Anand.

'Yes, and we may as well have stayed here since you spent all your time with your phone. Or looking for other Indians in Bangkok.'

'What rubbish.'

'It's true. The only things that moved him were the sounds of Indians in a public place or when he discovered some word in Thai that had a Sanskrit root. Then he got all excited and stopped looking at his emails for a few seconds.'

Anand smiled to say that it was true, she had just identified his most prominent but loveable weakness.

'Actually, we will also be out of station soon,' said Girish.

Mala looked at him. Something inside her darted out of position.

'Oh? Where?' asked Anand.

'Two weeks in Sri Lanka. I booked it last week,' said Girish, fixing his gaze on Mala.

She looked at his lips, from where the words had come.

'Mala, you never told me,' said Lavanya.

Mala was silent.

Then she said: 'I didn't know.'

'Oh my God, Girish! A surprise holiday; how wonderful! Who would have suspected? You don't really look like the romantic type,' said Lavanya.

Girish, having sought an audience for his grand gesture, began to look embarrassed. He smiled awkwardly at Lavanya and then turned to Mala, perhaps to indicate that it was her turn to reveal the various manifestations of his whimsical nature. Mala looked away. At the next table a boy in a three-piece suit was trying to suck up the remains of his melted ice cream through a straw, puckering his lips and rolling his eyes in a frenzy. Next to him, a girl in pink pearls let out a series of staccato giggles. For the boy it was an early lesson in the addictive power of performance.

'Look, she can't even speak, she's so surprised,' said Lavanya, reaching out and giving Mala a squeeze on the arm.

Mala flinched, her napkin falling on to the grass.

The others all looked at her.

'You've really booked it?' she asked Girish.

'All done,' he announced. 'Thirteen nights. We arrive in Colombo, then the next day we take the train to Galle. One night there, then some time in the jungle at Sinharaja and then they will take us to see some caves. Really ancient, with stalactites and stalagmites and fossils still visible in the cave walls.'

'I think I have heard of this place,' said Anand. 'What is it called?'

'Waulpane cave.' Girish's research had been comprehensive.

'It's meant to be an amazing sight, with a waterfall in the middle of the cave and bats flying all around. After that, we go to Ratnapura, where they have the gems, and then a hill station for two nights. Then to Kandy for another two nights I think, then on to a beach resort and then back.'

'Sounds beautiful,' said Anand. 'Sri Lanka is on our list too, no?'

Lavanya agreed that it was on the list.

'How sweet, he's done all this secret planning. You had no idea?' she asked.

Mala shook her head and smiled in Girish's direction.

'But I have not got my leave sanctioned. What if they refuse?' she asked.

'They can't refuse,' said Girish.

'If you have any problems, let me know. You want me to talk to them?' asked Anand.

'No, please don't do anything like that. Let me ask first. I'm sure it will be fine,' said Mala.

'Well, it is nice to see that romance is not just in the movies,' said Lavanya, clinking her fork on a wine glass.

Anand refused to take the bait.

'You don't have that long to plan, Mala. Any idea what the weather's going to be like there?' Lavanya asked.

Mala did not respond. She stared at the golden orbs that surrounded the swimming pool, growing larger and fainter, as the bats from the Waulpane cave screeched around her head.

Jaydev had given the occasion some thought, while being very careful to appear as if he had done no such thing. The cinema that he suggested was an old single screen in Vishveshvaranagar, respectable enough to be safe, distant enough from Mahalakshmi Gardens to be fortuitous. They seemed to have done little else but talk, so going to the cinema would give them a chance just to be. Sometimes that much was enough. It was not the weekend and there had been a light drizzle every evening for the last few days: there was less of a chance of bumping into anyone they knew. Everything seemed in place.

Under the circumstances, the choice of film seemed almost irrelevant; or it did to him at any rate. Of course it would not do to end up trapped in front of something vulgar or depressing. Luckily the film showing at the Vishveshvaranagar cinema was neither of those things. Faiza Jaleel of the *Mysore Evening Sentinel* had given it three stars, praising the freshness of its young actors and the allure of the Brisbane locales where it had been shot.

The film bore the proofs of its creed. The female lead was a medical student in Brisbane, a firm ambassador of her parents' immigrant values, combining resolute study with stunning expositions of Hindustani music and trays full of *halwa*. When not acting as a totem for multicultural conformity, the heroine would indulge in an afternoon of chaste conversation with an engineering student from Delhi, played with aplomb by the current teen heart-throb. Persuaded by her plain but jovial best friend, she entered the Miss Australia competition and won the title, precipitating a media frenzy and intense interest from a handsome but morally ambiguous Indian entertainment baron, also settled in Brisbane. The unexpected pageant victory also had the happy consequence of sparking an appetite for Punjabi culture across Australia. There followed scenes of *bhangra* classes outside the Sydney Opera House, emerald *lehengas* flaring across the outback and beers across New South Wales being replaced by Patiala pegs. By the interval, there were a number of indications that the engineering student would not give up the girl quietly and a showdown with the entertainment baron on the Story Bridge seemed unavoidable. With a dramatic escalation of strings and piano, the lights came on again.

Jaydev and Susheela turned to each other and smiled awkwardly, as if hating to admit that they were really rather enjoying the film.

'If we can't compete economically, at least on the beauty queen front we have no challengers,' said Jaydev.

'She looks about fourteen,' said Susheela. 'And how is she going to pass her final year exams with all those public appearances she seems to be making?'

'That will be revealed in the second half. Maybe that tycoon is secretly her tutor.'

At least half the balcony seats were empty but who knew what was happening in the rows below. There was certainly enough lewd whistling during the scenes involving the swimsuit competition.

'Excuse me please, I need to visit the Gents,' said Jaydev. 'These days, it's getting ridiculous, every couple of hours.'

Susheela smiled at the back of the seat in front of her.

'Can I get you anything on my way back?'

'No, thank you.'

A moment later she added: 'Good luck,' and then instantly wondered why she had said it.

'I'm sorry?'

'No, nothing.'

'I thought you just wished me luck.'

'Yes, I think I did. Well, you know the toilets are not always very clean.'

'One must stiffen one's resolve.'

'You know, that is one of the saddest things about India.'

'What is?'

'The state of the toilets.'

A strange sound came from Jaydev, something between a snort and a sneeze. His legs grazed against her knees as he walked towards the aisle. Susheela was a little perplexed. She had been entirely serious.

When Uma got off the bus, a long line was slowly filing into the temple premises on the main road.

'What's happening?' she asked a woman.

'Free meals there twice a day for the next two weeks,' she said. 'Some big man has died and his family is making sure he does not rot in hell.'

There was no one she recognised in the queue so Uma stood there, watching the temple authorities maintain order.

The dead man had been widely respected for his philanthropic activities. Every year on Ganesha Habba he organised the distribution of plastic buckets to the needy and during Dasara a mass marriage for poor couples. His sons had chosen to mark his passing in a manner appropriate to his renown, and food was being distributed at a number of temples in the city during the two-week mourning period.

The deceased's colleagues at the Society of Mysore Pawnbrokers had taken a half-page advertisement in the *Mysore Evening Sentinel* to highlight his professional achievements. These included formulating the Society's code of practice and ensuring improved focus on customer service in all member establishments. A full list of his charitable works was also being produced and copies would be bound in his memory at Shivaswamy Printers. A large number of the late gentleman's clients were unable to express much regret, occupied as they were in the daily moil of trying to reclaim their possessions from his shops. But the man's sons were determined to continue the public-spirited traditions, regardless of nod or favour.

The queue was shrinking. A photographer from the *Sentinel* arrived at the temple with one of the man's sons to document the event for the next day's edition. Inside the temple grounds, a speech ended to much applause.

Uma began walking down the slope. The mud had dried, leaving hard ridges of earth that resisted and then cracked under each step. Suddenly she caught sight of Shankar on the main road. He was standing at the edge of the slope, smoking. She understood why he would not call out to her but why was he watching her? She turned and climbed up the slope, her eardrums pounding. As she approached the top, she realised it was not Shankar, not even a man who looked like him. She spun round quickly and hurried back down the hill, looking in both directions. The sun was setting and there were too many phantoms stalking the pitted hillside that evening.

❖   ❖   ❖

As the car headed home through the centre of the city, there was a ferocious show of lightning. An avalanche of blue and silver gave Amba Vilas Palace a fantastical silhouette. Inside the car, the ride felt secure and comfortable. There may have been thunder but they could not hear it over the sounds of the *sarod* that came from the car's speakers.

'Is this okay for you? I thought you had trouble driving at night,' said Susheela.

'Sometimes. There's hardly any traffic now in the opposite direction, so it's fine. It's the oncoming glare that can get difficult.'

None of the traffic lights were working. Jaydev came to a complete stop at each one and then slowly headed forward. This was the hour that the drunks and the reckless chose to take the air of Mysore.

They approached Mahalakshmi Gardens in silence. In front of them the park gates loomed solid and forbidding, locked against tramps and miscreants. The car would be turning into Susheela's road in less than a couple of minutes.

'He is taking me home,' thought Susheela. 'This man is taking me home.'

As if it was the most normal thing in the world.

Slowly Mala lifted her legs off the bed. As she pushed herself up, she prayed that the bed's ancient boards would not creak. Her toes touched the cool floor and she stood up. Her tendons began to uncoil. Girish had shut the windows earlier and drawn the flimsy nylon curtains but the room was not in complete darkness. She made her way into the corridor, leaning against the wall, and crept towards the bathroom, her palm brushing against the fissures and boils in the plaster. Once inside the bathroom, lips pursed, she gently closed the door. Her hand groped for the bolt and gradually began to ease it into place. Without switching the light on, she moved to the washbasin and turned the cold water tap on. She turned to the tap in the wall and turned that on too.

A bruise had formed on her right upper arm like a map of an alien island. There was a clawing burn in her lower abdomen, thrusting up towards her lungs. She moved to the washbasin and rinsed out her mouth. She cupped her hands, repeatedly filled them with water and lowered her face into her palms. Leaving the water to drip down off her face on to her nightie, she switched on the dim light above the mirror but took care to avoid looking at her face.

She then poured water from a bucket into the toilet and brushed the sides of the bowl, making sure it was spotless. Then she flushed the toilet and switched off the light. She turned off the tap in the wall; the water shrank into a steady drip.

She moved to the bathroom door and leant against it. The windows were open and she could feel a breath of cooler air. Outside the cicadas were swallowing the night. She stood by the doors for some minutes. The drip from the tap in the wall was making a low, hollow sound like a distant knock. Beyond the window grill, inky slashes were swaying in the night air. She turned and began to unbolt the doors carefully. It was only then that she realised that her bottom lip was bleeding. She ran her tongue across the split, the metallic sting splicing its way to the back of her throat, wondering if it was Girish's blood she could taste or her own.

She knew she was incapable of going back into the bedroom so she felt her way down the corridor and into the sitting room. Easing the doors shut, she cast about on the sofa for the remote control. She turned the television on, muting the sound.

It was time for a commercial break: sequinned cocktail dresses on long-limbed Eastern European models; salsa dancers striking poses on a yacht; acres of hot bubbling cheese; jet skis leaving a trail of iridescent surf in their wake; confetti raining down in casinos; breakdancing teenagers in fluorescent vests; skateboarders on a suspension bridge; shopping trolleys filled with sunglasses; cricket players brandishing mobile phones in limousines; an electric guitar at the bottom of an aquarium; motor racers on a podium spraying champagne in slow motion; exploding MP3 players; enormous yellow peppers cascading over granite kitchen surfaces; candy-coloured shopping bags gliding by on conveyor belts; rows of empty sunloungers; strings of sapphires poised over shimmering clavicles; pretty girls in belted trench coats stepping on to bullet-nosed trains; a four-wheel drive steadily making its way through a war zone; bolts of crimson silk being hurled off skyscrapers; high heels striding across a luxury hotel lobby; a helicopter landing on a high-rise; a python coiling through tangles of jewellery; polo players signalling to each other; a smiling girl holding up a seashell.

CHAPTER EIGHT

The Promenade by Tejasandra Lake was blocked for general traffic in both directions. The only vehicles being allowed into the area belonged to organisers, performers, contractors or security staff involved in the Lake Utsava and the Mysore International Film Festival. The inspections being carried out at either end of the road added to the air of celebratory exclusivity as ID cards and wristbands were flaunted with enthusiasm. To the officious, the bureaucratic and the socially suspicious, it was a celestial gift.

Once the initial rancour and invective had been overcome, the organisation of the lakeside festivities took on an unfaltering momentum. The selection of the film festival jury had been surprisingly undemanding and the coordination of dates had been effortless. The organisers' strategy of targeting artistic personalities who had not been publicly active for a while had paid rich dividends. The local media were also doing all they could to show their support. The *Mysore Evening Sentinel* was featuring a 'Countdown to Celebration' section, crammed with updates on festival highlights, behind-the-scenes exclusives and a tornado of small advertisements.

The Mysore Tourism Authority had been a model of productivity too. The 'Geneva of the East' campaign had been rolled out across a number of Tier I and Tier II cities, photographs of an inviting Tejasandra Lake, the Promenade twinkling in the distance, appearing in a variety of magazines. Due to budgetary considerations a television campaign had been rejected, but radio spots had been booked on dozens of stations across the country.

The organisers of the Lake Utsava were intent on projecting an image of Mysore as a centre of elite metropolitan accomplishment, able to stand up to scrutiny by global trendsetters. The environs of Tejasandra Lake absolutely had to look the part. A phalanx of sweepers, carpenters, electricians and decorators had been drafted in to bring Geneva to South India. Paving stones were scrubbed, lamp posts were repainted and an exceptional sheen was brought to the barriers rising above the lake's flood defences. A fashionable young artist had been commissioned to produce a mural outside the Museum of Folklore, an avant-garde crypto-tribal conceptualisation of the spirit of Mysore, designed to challenge and energise festivalgoers. The artist was well known for his chronic addiction to a range of illegal substances, and in certain quarters the prospect of his early demise only served to enhance the project's artistic cachet.

A ramp now led up to a giant platform at the central point of the Promenade. Here the vintage cars would ascend to dazzle in the sun. Giant stone torches were being placed at regular intervals along the lakeside; plants and trees had been hired from garden centres and nurseries across the city to infuse greater colour; and the Mysore Archaeology Museum was being painted a warm ecru. The Utsava's dance stage was in place and already being filmed as part of a DVD release marking the grand success of the festival. A media enclosure had been set up opposite the front steps of the Anuraag Kalakshetra and technicians were conducting their final tests on the lighting rig that would illuminate the red carpet. Two outside screens had been erected on either end of the Promenade where, weather permitting, the entries in the 'Panorama: India's Rising Sun' section would be shown.

Not far from the Anuraag Kalakshetra a fountain had been wheeled into place, the water spraying out from the apex of a structure resembling a steel samosa. Although not quite able to match Geneva's Jet d'Eau, according to the Deputy Artistic Director of the Lake Utsava, the fountain added a structural fluidity to the psychology of the urban space.

Not all of the organisers were impressed.

'Even my grandson can piss higher than that,' one board member commented.

If these improvements were settling the costume of Tejasandra Lake, the necessary braids, spangles and flounces were being fastened with similar taste and care. A swathe of banners and logos stretched across the arches outside the museums, fell from the windows of the Galleria and fluttered over the rocks that dropped down to the edge of the water. The sponsors of the Lake Utsava and the film festival were naturally given priority in vantage and visibility in order to ensure optimum brand persuasion among the attendees.

Beyond these concerns, the organisers had entrusted the lakeside to G S Anand and his reputable aptitude at squeezing revenue from every square inch of outdoor space. Mr Anand's company did not disappoint. Everything from plastic cups and paper napkins to the side panels of floats and the huge plasma screens along the Promenade offered up an opportunity to engage in the vibrant commercial hub of India's eleventh fastest growing small city. Designers at Exospace Media had even managed to install in record speed two 'time dilation pods', essentially arcade games enclosed in a plastic sheath, which purported to conduct users on a journey through Mysore thirty years in the future. Those accustomed to G S Anand's sleights of hand would recognise this for what it was: a tour of shimmering towers and sweeping walkways that served as an ideal backdrop for a flood of product placement.

Advertising was also alive in the mind of Venky Gowda, who had dropped in to have a look at the construction of the HeritageLand stand at the Utsava. As far as Venky was concerned, there was no such thing as premature merchandising and he had personally approved the colour of the HeritageLand dental floss that would be on sale at the festival, along with an exciting array of other HeritageLand products.

The festival organisers were all too aware that the security arrangements would need to be beyond reproach. Senior police personnel had authorised the relevant sub-divisional officers to round up known miscreants, rowdy-sheeters and other objectionable elements in anticipatory custody. A specially trained unit would be responsible for crowd control and the maintenance of law and order on the lake shore. Metal detectors had been installed at all the entry points to the Promenade and CCTV cameras would cover the majority of proceedings. City officials had also enlisted the assistance of the police in conducting background checks on those who had sought licences for stalls at the Utsava handicrafts bazaar. The question of who would bear the cost of the extra policing had yet to be finalised but the police department, commercial sponsors, festival organisers and civic authorities were each quietly confident that it would not be them.

There were only a few days of preparation left. The giant staff of anticipation drummed away steadily, marking time, focusing minds, making reputations. For those involved in the event, the world had shrunk to the size of a strip of asphalt that glittered across a few hundred metres at the edge of the dimpled waters of incomparable Tejasandra Lake.

They were to set off early. The dawn fog was still smothering the garden with its attentions, the lawn a murky opal and the giant bougainvillea smeared into obscurity. Susheela had suggested delaying their departure until the visibility improved but Jaydev had insisted that there would not be a problem. He was right. In less than a quarter of an hour a sluggish sun began to burn through the fog, creating clear channels around the waxen forms of the familiar surroundings. Bamboo Corner was silent, now only a banister of heavy mist curling up around the trees. The corner house shaped like a violin emerged into the morning like a surrealist's fantasy and the shapes on Gulmohar Road became distinct, walkers making their way home from the Gardens.

The trip had been Susheela's idea. The drive would be easy except for perhaps the last fifteen kilometres up through the hills; there she knew Jaydev would take the bends slowly. At the summit there existed a place simply called Viewpoint. There was no temple, no market, no monument; only a handful of benches at the edge of a copse, facing the slope that led back down to the rumpled rug of paddy fields below. At times, on one side of the path that led up to Viewpoint, an old man sat next to a pile of tender coconuts. There was never any sign of how he had managed to get there with his stock or of how he proposed to leave; only his mirage-like presence in front of the eucalyptus trees.

Before dawn Susheela had packed some sandwiches and made a flask of coffee. She had put some extra sachets of sweetener into her handbag. In the basket there went a pack of paper napkins, two plastic cups and stirrers, two apples and a packet of butter biscuits. Jaydev no longer sounded the horn at Susheela's gates. He preferred to call her mobile and let it ring a couple of times. It was yet another adjustment to the structure of unspoken arrangements that governed their meetings. The rather casual enquiries as to the presence of maids and drivers; the knowing references to crowded places that simply got on one's nerves; the pointed avoidance of their own neighbourhoods; the search for distant entertainments that would satisfy their apparent craving for a change from the staid routines of their social set. There had been further visits to cinemas in unfamiliar localities. One overcast afternoon they had had coffee at the canteen in the Akaash Astronomical Observatory, a place frequented only by the occasional foreign tourist or visiting academic. Perhaps the oddest rendezvous had been a sudden late-night trip to the twenty-four-hour pharmacy at the J S Desai Hospital.

Jaydev had called Susheela just as the ten o'clock bulletin was ending.

'Did I disturb you? I'm sorry, I only just realised how late it is.'

'Not at all. I'm still downstairs.'

'You will think I'm mad but I wanted to ask you something.'

'Yes?'

'I need to go to the medical shop. I've run out of some pills that I need to take in the morning.'

'You're going there now?'

'The all-night one at J S Desai. And I was wondering, if it's not too late for you, if you felt like coming on the drive.'

'What, *now*?'

'No, of course you're right. Please, I'm so sorry. I don't know what comes into my head sometimes.'

'No, wait. I'll come. Can you leave in maybe ten minutes?'

'You'll come?'

'Yes. Why not? Just give me a missed call when you get here.'

'Of course. I'll do that.'

They had driven through the silent streets of Mysore, the only other movement being silver dogs streaking into the shadows. The lights had been dim at eye level: a pale yellow bulb hanging over the entrance to a government building; the waning neon sign over a shuttered supermarket; a hint of lustre as the car turned at a junction, its lights reflected in a shop window. But far above their heads the hoardings glowed like gems. White teeth, gleaming car bonnets and gold screens lit up the sky, sending shapeless searchlights into the heart of the city.

'Is this what it has come to for us? A drive to the medical shop is now an outing?' Susheela had asked.

'Aren't you excited about your sudden tour of Mysore by night? When was the last time you saw the roads this quiet?'

'Probably that day. The day we first met.'

'We had met before that day. You just don't remember.'

'No, I don't. Which is a surprise to me. I am normally very good at remembering things like that.'

In the hospital car park, while Jaydev was at the pharmacy, Susheela had looked up at the building's dark windows. This was the place where Sridhar had spent his last days, endless hours when she had waited, sometimes with her daughters, sometimes alone. The heel had come off her sandal when walking up the entrance ramp that last morning. She had given a ward boy some money to go and find her daughter on the fourth floor. A few hours later her husband had died. But when Jaydev returned to the car, of course, there had been no need to bring all that up.

This morning they were on a proper outing. Susheela opened her window just a fraction and, her crimson shawl tucked snugly around her, narrowed her eyes against the whip of wind on her face. In recent years she had only worn the shawl once. It was what she would normally have termed a bold choice for a woman of her age. But Susheela's nerve seemed to be firming up these days in matters beyond the merely sartorial.

In less than two hours Jaydev was shifting gears as they negotiated the steep rise to Viewpoint. There were no cars impatiently tailing them and nothing hurtling down in the opposite direction.

The road ended at the top of the hill, in a clearing marked by a faded white line. Jaydev got out of the car and walked around to Susheela's side. He held the door open for her, the expression on his face deliberately purposeless. As Susheela stood up, the wind picked up, ruckling her sari and sending a plastic bag careening through the trees and over the edge.

'See, in any beauty spot, even if there is not a soul about, you will still find some filth,' she said. 'That is what people here do.'

Jaydev shut the door, took the basket from Susheela and looked around. There was no sign of the coconut seller. The only other vehicle was a dirty motorbike a few feet away.

'Which way?' he asked.

'If we go down this small path, there are some benches that face the valley.'

Susheela walked into the shade of the copse, where the light dimmed to the green of old bottles and the chill escaped out of the grooves in the bark. The path led through clumps of sweet violets and dense bushes of angel's trumpets, hanging their heads in some unknowable shame. The ground was uneven so she stepped carefully, hearing the similarly cautious tread of Jaydev behind her. Above their heads there was an occasional whisper, caught only by the woody shoots on the highest boughs. Neither of them spoke until the trees had thinned out and they were back on the open hilltop, the sun bold again. In front of them five benches stood in an arc facing the glorious drop.

On one of them a young man sat with his back to them.

They both stood still.

At last, Jaydev said: 'How about the one at the end?'

'Yes, that's fine.'

Susheela loosened her shawl and let it hang slackly from her shoulders before sitting down. Jaydev placed the basket between them and smoothed down his hair.

The young man did not look up. He was in his late twenties, the angled planes of his face making him look like he had been hewn out of a single piece of stone. The frames of his glasses were thick and black, widening his long face. He held his hands locked in his lap.

Rather than gazing at the view, in spite of themselves Susheela and Jaydev found themselves studying their neighbour. Every now and then the wind would puff out the front of his papery shirt. The man remained immobile.

'There's an unusually grave young man,' said Jaydev in a low voice.

'He looks very sad, no? Like he is caught in a great dilemma. And so thin.'

'What do you think is bothering him?'

'God only knows. Maybe he is suffering the pangs of a deep and unrequited love.'

Jaydev laughed.

'You can do better than that.'

'Okay, maybe he has lost his job, he has fought with his entire family, he has no idea what to do with the rest of his life and he has not got a single friend in the world. Happy?'

'*Arre*, why would that make me happy?'

'You know we should not be sitting here speculating like this on that poor boy's problems.'

'Maybe we are wrong and he does not have any problems. Maybe he just looks like that.'

'Oh my God, do you think he is here to jump?' asked Susheela.

'No need for such drama. He is probably just enjoying the view. Mind you, the poor fellow probably will jump if we don't stop staring at him.'

In the background a line of bush quail let out a series of long whistles, peaking in an alarmed tremolo. Then the low of the wind pressed back in. The young man and the possible reasons for his malaise were forgotten as the sun warmed the backs of their necks. Below them, the valley was totally still, in that moment sealed off from the world's intervention. The wind hummed on.

'Why don't you come for dinner next week?' Susheela asked.

'Dinner?'

'Yes, my place.'

'At your place?'

'Yes.'

'Are you sure?'

Susheela forgot the strictures of politeness and paused to think about whether she was sure.

'Yes, I am sure. It won't be anything elaborate of course. Something simple.'

'Well, then I won't come.'

'Fine, don't come then. You should be happy an old man like you even gets an invitation anywhere.'

'I should be happy about the insults too?'

'Yes, that too.'

The silences between them were now rich with contentment, the pleasure that could be gained only through an intimate civility. Susheela no longer spent these pauses reflecting on the nuances of her comportment. As the fancy took it, her mind swooped through flurries, plunged into craters or simply lay motionless in a luminous shoal.

'I spoke to Priyanka yesterday,' said Susheela.

'She is the elder one?'

'Yes.'

'How is she?'

'Fine. But I don't know how. She seems to lead such a busy life that it makes my head spin just hearing about it.'

'We also once had those lives.'

'I never had the kind of life she seems to have, where every hour of every day is audited, planned, disposed of.'

'And your other daughter?'

'Well she is the opposite. I won't hear from her for a while and there will be weeks unaccounted for. But to me that seems more normal.'

'I think we all have parts of our life which are unaccounted for. They simply don't appear in our conversations with other people.'

Susheela threw one end of her shawl over her shoulder. The sun had disappeared behind a long boat-shaped cloud. At their feet, silver grasses banded together before beginning their procession over the lip of the hill. There they plunged headlong over the edge, dashing towards the velvet shadows of the jackfruit trees that stood further down. The air itself was contemplation.

'Is it too early to have a sandwich?' asked Jaydev.

Susheela smiled.

'Not at all.'

Mr Tanveer's printer jolted into action, making a sound like an angry goat. Mala looked across at Shipra who now spelt her name Shiiprraa. She had consulted a numerologist a few weeks ago and had been advised that some minor alterations to the spelling of her name would enhance her destiny number and provide for better numerological vibrations. Shipra became Shiiprraa and an email was duly sent out to inform her family, friends and colleagues.

Mala had made no progress with the figures she had been asked to reconcile. Her head was bent, shoulders rigid, eyes narrowed, body suspended in an arc of concentration. But her efforts were directed at trying to regulate her breathing and dull the panic rising inside. They were due to leave for Colombo in two weeks. She had told Girish that her leave had been approved even though she had not dared bring the subject up with Mr Tanveer. She glanced at him. He was staring anxiously at his screen with what appeared to be chalk marks around his mouth.

Over the course of a couple of evenings, Mala had feigned great interest in the trip. She had followed the itinerary and had asked about clothing, food and history. She had looked over his shoulder as he showed her image after image on his new laptop. But the efforts had cost her the stupefying enervation of sleepless nights, long hours spent making out shapes behind her eyelids and listening for sounds of morning.

From Mala's seat she could see what Shiiprraa was working on when there was no glare from the window. Shiiprraa's screen saver showed a beach, a hammock slung between palm trees, a hummingbird and a sea that was an impossible blue. Would the sea in Sri Lanka look like that? Girish had said five nights at a beach resort. He would take her hand and they would walk along the shore in the early evening, their fingers laced tightly. There would be a hard warmth from his hand and a soft warmth from the breeze. He would point things out to her: a fishing boat, a crab that staggered into a hole in the sand, and across the water, India.

'Coming along?' asked Mr Tanveer.

She nodded weakly and reached for a file on her desk.

There were thirteen nights, he had said, filled with jungles, ruins, temples, wildlife, churches, train stations, tea gardens, museums and those walks along the beach. She would wake to his soft snoring in a hotel room with sealed windows and the bedspread neatly folded on the luggage rack, preparing her first words of the day. She would have to anticipate what he thought of someone they met on the tour bus and whether that was an acquaintance that needed to be nurtured. On an afternoon when he had not spoken for over two hours she would anxiously wonder whether or not to suggest something delicate and diverting for the evening, affordable and appropriate. She would need to pay attention and understand and, all the time, listen, judge, gauge, while knots of desperation tightened around her lungs.

The piercing ring of the phone on Mr Tanveer's desk broke into her thoughts.

'Accounts. Tanveer here.'

He stood up.

'Of course, sir. You don't worry, sir. For what reason am I here? Consider it already done.'

He replaced the receiver and then sat down.

The words and numerals on the paper in front of her shifted in blocks, like a child's puzzle. Both her colleagues seemed to be engrossed in whatever they were doing but Mala still did not feel it was safe to look up. She worried that if she caught Mr Tanveer's eye at this point she would simply have to leave the room and never return.

Seconds or perhaps minutes went by and the image of the beach returned to Shiiprraa's screen.

Another vision flashed through Mala's head. She and Girish were in the sea, she near the shore, the water rising up around her thighs and he, a distant head, floating away from her, his arms slicing cruelly into the sunless water.

The figures on the page came back into focus. She now inhabited a place where it was impossible to separate the real from the imagined, like the needle pricks that she could feel on her palms and the chunks of ice that rattled around in her heart.

There seemed to her to be only two options. She would have to tell Girish that they could not go on holiday and face the likely consequences. Or she would have to go to Sri Lanka and then return to work, the penalty of her unauthorised absence drawing down dimly over her. Unless the terror engendered by either scenario forced her into a third option.

Uma had just put the last scoop of rice into her mouth when she heard the scrunch of gravel. She saw the *mali* slowly straighten his body, drop the sack he was holding and walk towards the gates. She had a sense that she had seen him perform exactly the same action half an hour ago, but no one had come to the gates then. The day had been imbued with strange shifts in the progression of events. Susheela had asked her to come to work early and then left as soon as she arrived, wrapped in a new red shawl. She had got into a strange car, the driver's identity hidden by blades of mist.

After that Uma had been alone in the house. As she swept and dusted, the silence had been heavy and exacting after the early morning turmoil. She had spent the previous night at the Sangam Continental Lodge, at first light rushed back home in a rickshaw for fresh clothes and then arrived at Susheela's at the agreed hour. There had been a brief argument with Shankar when he had insisted on giving her money for the rickshaw. She had finally accepted it but by then their tight voices seemed to be disagreeing about something else altogether. He had ended the conversation with a joke about her hair, which had been even more riotous than usual that morning. As she got into the rickshaw, she had felt his hand gently press the dip between her shoulder blades.

It was the disorientation of metamorphosis. The entry of kindness, pleasure, subterfuge and uncertainty, where before there had been only a wary monotony. The encounters at the lodge were hardly flecked with the glitter of romance or promises foretold. Yet they carried the weight of fascination. There was the knowledge of a secret, lodged deep within. There was the solicitude of a generous regard. There were flights of fantasy, realised in the harsh light of the Sangam's first-floor rooms.

Shankar's single act of sympathy on the day of the floods had brought forth from her the only possible response in gratitude. He had accepted that gratitude with a humility she had never known. The palisade around her had fallen away, stake by stake, as the hours of her days reorganised themselves into new blocks of longing. Until recently, she had warded off new experiences for this very reason. Her encounters with Shankar had deposited a patchy lamina of expectation over her life that now obscured her vision and made everything that had been familiar seem somehow unsettled.

When she heard the key in the lock, Uma rose at once. She hurriedly rinsed her plate at the back sink, as if trying to erase the shame of sustenance.

'Uma?' called Susheela, who had just come in through the front door.

Uma walked back through the house.

'Had your lunch?' asked Susheela.

Uma nodded.

'Here, for washing,' Susheela said, handing her a basket with a flask and a lunchbox in it.

Uma took the basket and then said: 'I need to leave a little early.'

'Yes, that's fine. You came early.'

Uma nodded again and slipped out of the back door.

Susheela sat down in an armchair and shut her eyes, her face in absolute repose.

A few minutes later, when Uma walked past her to go upstairs, Susheela was fast asleep.

Twenty years ago, the Central Lending Library – not to be confused with the City Central Library – occupied the entire ground and first floors of 34 Mirza Road, a three-storey building supported by sturdy pillars the colour of earth. Registration was free, members were allowed to borrow up to six books at a time and there was a special Reference Room for rare or delicate collections. The Chief Librarian had his own office adjacent to the Main Reading Room, and the noticeboard in the veranda usually advertised a variety of English literary events. Particularly well attended in those days were the Mysore Literary Society's Great Masters discussion evenings and the talks and readings arranged by the University of Mysore's Department of English.

In the late nineties, the library was confronted by a deadly combination of drastically diminished allocations from the state's consolidated libraries' fund and shrinking interest from the residents of Mysore. In spite of the heroic efforts of the then Chief Librarian, the library was compelled to reduce its active lending stock and take up residence on the first floor of the building. The prestigious ground floor was quickly occupied by the offices of the Mineral Concessions Directorate, the Reading Rooms were lost forever and, along with the fustiness of old paper and threadbare armchairs, the astringent odour of loss pervaded the upper rooms.

Continued financial adversity meant further deterioration in the core collection and the imposition of a registration fee and refundable deposit. Little enterprising flourishes like the intro- duction of a home delivery service and a single computer for public Internet access did not improve matters; the library was forced to cede some of its first-floor space to the insatiable appetite of the Mineral Concessions Directorate.

Girish had accompanied the library through its lengthy travails, a frequent visitor to the Reading Rooms as a student and still a loyal member. Of course these days he purchased books online, at the regular book expos and in the seductive bookstores at the malls; but he still periodically negotiated the uneven stairs leading up to the first floor of 34 Mirza Road.

The current Chief Librarian at the Central Lending Library was a retired academic, a man who once held considerable influence at the Department of History at the University of Mysore. Traces of his former standing remained in his puckered lips and the haughty look of enquiry he directed at the strays who wandered up to the first floor. How he reconciled his current circumstances with the significance of his legacy at Mysore's leading institution of further education was a perplexing question, as imponderable as what he did to occupy himself during the course of his barren days on Mirza Road. A thin, carefully groomed moustache and a promontory of dyed hair made him look like an unlikely hybrid of Clark Gable and Dev Anand. Naturally, Girish's dislike for the man was intense. They behaved in each other's presence rather like the first and second wife of a lascivious seignior. Having lost pride of place to the more comely third wife, all that remained was for them to belittle each other in the course of meaningless battles.

Today their discussion touched on the precise meaning and origin of various Latin phrases but it was clear that neither of them could muster up much enthusiasm to ambush the other. After a while, Girish drifted back through the room's dark aisles, casually running his finger along the rough cloth spines of the older reference volumes. Daylight had faded and the dim lights above the shelves only served to emphasise the hopelessness of any search. He had come to the library with the half-hearted intention of picking up something interesting and improving for Mala to take on holiday. Very soon after his marriage, his natural didacticism had trained itself on his young wife, a blank slate, ready to receive his painstaking inscriptions. His instruction was absorbed but seemed to have little impact on Mala's desires and enthusiasms. But Girish persevered.

He remembered once having watched a Bengali film set in a period before independence. A cultured landowner, equally comfortable with Keats and Kalidasa, had been forced, or perhaps had blundered, into marriage with a traditional wife whose ambitions had only swept as far as the elaborate palanquin in which she had arrived at her new home. The landowner had quickly made amends. He had engaged an English tutoress, a woman of steel and scholarship, who would endow his new wife with all the important attributes of classical cultivation and learning. The young wife had spent hours closeted with the gracious lady, exploring music, literature and history. Scales had been sung, dates memorised and quotations relished like plums sucked dry of every last drop of juice. Girish could not remember what happened in the rest of the film but he had begun to recall with increasing regularity those first images where a woman, in spite of herself, was lifted on to the same plane as her husband.

That was all he asked for, he said to himself: a consort who could be his equal, a truly companionate wife. He had suffered the occasional doubt but he had never thought it would be impossible to achieve with Mala. He sometimes felt the need to overwhelm her with good things, with the care and the direction that she needed. He had to protect her, guide her and warn her. Girish was not a man so lacking in self-awareness that he could claim complete ignorance to the effects of his little slips of self-control. But he viewed them as the unfortunate adjuncts of his zeal, the collateral damage precipitated in trying to bring equilibrium to their relationship. As he stopped in front of a shelf crammed with dusty classics, he told himself that they would have the time and the space on this holiday to forget each other's transgressions, her infuriating dispassion, his occasional irascibility. They would explore and discover, returning home refreshed and renewed.

Twenty kilometres from the self-regarding bluster at Tejasandra Lake, the light was dim in Vasu's house. Resting his back against the cool wall, he could just about make out the outline of the rolled up bedding on the floor and the bicycle leaning in the corner. The two windows were shut. A wispy curtain hung over the doorway leading outside, its uneven hem sighing in time with the breeze on the porch. Around the edges of the curtain, the day was a spotted gold, an ugly, grimy compound spreading over the sunlight itself. His father was in the inside room, lying down on the wooden bed whose boards screamed in rage every time they were disturbed. His sister had returned to her husband's house. He had a good idea where his two brothers were. The whole morning they had spoken of fire and missiles, revolt and combat, action and engagement, damage and disorder. Then they had disappeared without saying a word to him.

The disappointment at the High Court had been overwhelming. There had been the long journey back to Mysore, the three buses caught in dense traffic most of the way. The recriminations had begun even before they had left Bangalore, accusations of manipulation and fraud levelled not only at the establishment but also at him and his colleagues. The meeting called by the *gram panchayat* the next day had turned into a jostling, snarling affair and had to be postponed. The next meeting fared no better. Those who had always maintained that the courts would never come to the villagers' assistance paraded their furious affirmation from house to house in the dusty lanes.

Just as suddenly as Vasu's efforts had collapsed, the rumours had sprouted and burst into the village's every nook. There was talk that Vasu had always known that this would be the outcome; he was in the pay of the state authorities, the real estate developers, the land grabbers; his only intention had been to distract them while the merciless reality unfolded behind their backs. He had been seen having secret meetings; there had always been something shifty about him; how could they not all have known?

There was other talk too. It was said that the victory at the High Court had only hardened the government's position further. The minister in charge had been heard saying that he would ensure that the farmers would be punished for their intransigence and temerity. Bureaucratic obstacles would be put in place to make certain that they would never see even the small compensation that was owed to them. There were reports of other harassment. Funds that had already been earmarked for expenditure in these *taluks* would be diverted elsewhere and any future projects would bypass them entirely.

There were specific examples so the conjecture had to be true. One farmer had it on good authority that the distribution of subsidised fertiliser to these areas was soon going to develop an inexplicable bottleneck. Another had heard that power load-shedding would increase dramatically in the coming months, paralysing pumps and delivering a string of hardships designed for debasement. Apparently local *babus* had been made to understand that complaints against them would not be referred to superior officers; police officials had heard that they were to have even more of a free rein in controlling any unacceptable law and order situations.

At first Vasu had been moved to react angrily. He had demanded proof from his accusers; he had waved documents in their faces, the evidence of months of toil; he had stabbed his finger at his own stupidity for trying to give these ungrateful wretches a legitimate voice. But even his storm needed sustenance and the latent heat had simply dissipated.

One evening he had walked into an informal meeting at the house of a village elder. His intention had been to admit his mistakes and appeal to the reason of the community. He had meant to wrap his anaemic confidence around the platitudes of the lawyers and present it to the men as a fresh start. Every road had obstacles; they could not say it was over until all options had been exhausted; they needed to have faith. The words had turned brittle and acrid even in his own mouth.

When he had slipped off his *chappals* and walked into the house, a weary hostility had descended. Insects buzzed around a hurricane lamp placed at the centre of the group of men and the *lotas* of coffee scattered at their feet. Vasu had stood awkwardly at the door, not having been invited to sit. The men's goodwill was as impenetrable as the fug of *beedi* smoke.

'With what face have you come here?' one man had asked, his voice deadened by failure.

Vasu had looked at him and the others whose eyes held the same whetted flint. Without answering he had turned around and returned home. He did not know with what face he had gone there.

Like every morning, Susheela slipped the key into the letter box on the gate and pulled open its door. Out of the chaos of restaurant menus, sari sale flyers and magazine subscription offers, Susheela pulled out the programme for the Mysore International Film Festival, the logos of its proud sponsors prominently displayed on the cover.

On the inside page Jaydev had written: 'What do you think? Warm regards, Jaydev.'

It was the first time that she had seen his handwriting and it made her smile. What clues to his character lay in those finely pointed Ws and the vertical tails of the Ys? Susheela had once picked up a guide to handwriting analysis at Great Expectations. The one thing from the book that had stuck in her memory was that the greater the rightward slant of the writing, the more emotionally expressive the person. She smiled again, picturing Jaydev's reaction to her confident assertions regarding his personality, based on the straight lines and sharp edges that dominated his seven-word missive.

Mala sat on the corner of the bed, her mind registering and processing the morning's sounds. It was before half past eight as the old man next door had not turned on his radio. The regular slap of wet sheets against stone by the tap outside meant that Gayathri had not finished the washing yet. In the bathroom, the drumming of water continued. Girish had not emerged. But he would soon and if she had not spoken to Gayathri by then, she would have to just let it go. It was important to Mala that she did not let it go.

She walked to the back door and peered at Gayathri's hunched form through the gap between the hinges. Her right leg was extended behind her at a curious angle, as if she were about to break into a run. Mala felt a tickle in her throat and retreated into the kitchen, her heart thumping. She could sense the blood flowing up through her neck, around her jaws and towards the sides of her head. She looked at her watch. It was half past eight. The old man turned his radio on.

She returned to the bedroom. Girish's clothes for the day were laid out on the bed, a familiar form that seemed to want to grab at her but lacked the flesh or bones to support its desire. The blue and white striped shirt with its collar stiff and primed, the navy trousers with their legs flowing off the edge of the bed, the tan belt laid across the waistband in a single loop, the white handkerchief placed to the right of the shirt, and the brown patterned socks folded into a careful peak. Where were the shoes? The blood surged back into her head as she tried to remember where she had put the shoes. She hurriedly opened the cupboard doors and looked inside. Then she knelt down on the floor to see if they had slipped under the bed. She rushed to the front door to see if Girish had left them outside. As she was hurrying back to the bedroom, she remembered that she had polished them the previous evening. So they had to be somewhere near the back door. In the kitchen, she unclenched her hand as she glimpsed them, gleaming at the top of the back steps.

Gayathri was wringing out the sheets, cheerfully throttling the coils with her strong arms and then unwinding them to hang out to dry. It looked like she had nearly finished. Girish was still in the bathroom. Mala dared not think she had already succeeded but it was beginning to look like it was possible. She did not want to walk to the washing area to talk to Gayathri: the sounds of Girish coming out of the bathroom would not reach her there. She thought that at best she only had a few more minutes.

There were about thirty hours left before they were due to catch the bus that would take them to the airport. A few hours later, they would be on a direct flight to Colombo. Before boarding, they would browse the duty-free shops and have a coffee at one of the cafés. On the plane, Girish might fall asleep, his head nudging Mala's shoulder. He would probably engage the cabin crew in conversation. Mala would smile. They would land and then clear immigration. There would be urgent tasks, looking out for bags, changing money, checking vouchers. Girish would probe, explain and hurry. Or he would be silent and casual. They would be in Colombo at the start of two weeks of exoticism, the threat of tectonic displacement vibrating under her feet.

She began to count the lies she had told to get her to this point. She had lied to Girish about booking her leave, paying all the bills before they left and setting aside the clothes she was packing. She had lied to her parents about when they were returning. She had lied to Ambika about the reason for the trip, a supposed promotion for Girish at work. She had lied to Lavanya and Anand about her excitement, trilling over the sights in store. She had lied to Mr Tanveer and Shiiprraa, not even having mentioned the trip. There was only so much enumeration that she could undertake before her predicament broke over her head like a breached dam. Her eyelids felt like massive weights had been placed on them. She went to the kitchen sink, splashed some water over her face and wiped it off with her hands.

Gayathri walked into the kitchen, tucking a stray pleat in under her stomach.

Mala said: 'Come with me one second.'

She led her into the sitting room. The bathroom door was still closed.

'You remember, we will not be here for two weeks from tomorrow?' she asked, turning to Gayathri.

'From tomorrow, is it? I knew but good thing you reminded me. My brain is turning into batter.'

In the background there was a shift in the sounds coming from the old man's radio. Perhaps he had switched stations.

'Here, hold out your hand,' said Mala.

Gayathri looked at her suspiciously.

'Why?'

'Just do it.'

Gayathri pushed her hand out and then, with a chuckle, shut her eyes too.

When she felt the cold weight on her palm, she opened her eyes and took a step back.

A gold chain lay coiled in hard mounds in her hand.

'What is this for?'

'It's for you.'

'For me? But why?'

'Please, just take it.'

'I can't take something so expensive for no reason.'

Gayathri stretched out her hand to give the chain back to Mala. It was Mala's turn to take a step back.

'It's for you. So just take it.'

'No no, I can't do that.'

'You should never tell Lakshmi to go away. She may never return.'

'But I don't understand.'

'You will.'

Gayathri looked at Mala for a few seconds and then at the chain in her hand. Nodding, she tucked it deep into her blouse. She picked up a plastic bag that she had left on the table.

'God bless you,' she said softly.

Mala managed a smile.

At the door, without turning around, Gayathri said loudly: 'So in two weeks is it then?'

Mala nodded: 'Yes, see you in two weeks.'

The door shut, the gate bolt screeched across the paving stone in the yard and then Gayathri was gone.

What happened could probably be blamed on the uncurling of a tiny fist. It was that single movement that wrenched Shankar's heart out of place and set in motion a perfectly avoidable set of events. He had seen his infant son reach out hundreds of times before, pummelling the air and then pulling at invisible filaments in total absorption. A familiar dimple formed in the side of his fist and then creased into a fat fold of baby flesh. The outstretching of a helpless arm was nothing new. But this time, as his son slowly unfurled his fingers, Shankar felt the knowledge of his infidelity smash down on his chest.

Staring at the coloured rings that hung over his son's crib, he spoke.

Janaki's interrogation was forensic and emotionless. She desired as much detail as Shankar could be compelled to provide. She tried to pin occasions down to the nearest day; she followed up on instances, durations and locations; she demanded full descriptions, always repeating the same question in a voice like a thick blade until Shankar provided a response. She compiled the grim catalogue as if she had developed an addiction to that hot stab of revelation. At one point when the baby started to cry, she coddled him in the folds of her sari and, mechanically rocking his head against her knee, continued the questioning. Her need was avid and she scythed through Shankar's shame till she had gathered up every last kernel of information. Then she put the baby back in his crib and left the room, shutting herself in the bedroom for an hour or so.

Shankar sat at the table, glancing occasionally at the bedroom door but not daring to look at his sleeping son. Apart from the scales of traffic, rising and falling beyond the open windows, the afternoon was imbued with stillness, like grief, like death. The long period of questioning seemed to have removed all the oxygen from the air. Breathing now involved only stolen gasps of waste vapour, thin and foul.

When Janaki emerged from the bedroom, she picked up the baby's kit bag and methodically began to fill it: nappies, bottles, clothes, formula, a blanket, squeaky toys and a rattle. She checked the contents of her handbag. Briefly she stepped back into the bedroom and then returned, holding her phone charger and a purse. She picked up her own keys from the hook on the wall and also the keys to her mother's house. Then, lifting the baby out of his crib, she settled his head into the soft dale of her neck. She picked up the bags with her free hand and let herself out of the house.

Shankar watched her movements like a condemned man replaying in his head the pronouncement of his judgment. When she had gone, he put his forehead down on the table, the plastic surface sticky against his skin. He had imagined this scene many times over the last few weeks. The surprising thing was that her departure had unfolded exactly as he had visualised it, no better, no worse. He was left with the stinging thought that no matter how badly he had misjudged himself, he had judged Janaki perfectly.

The lane outside the house had not woken from its afternoon slumber. It had been hours since the last vegetable vendor had rolled past, the shutters of the provision store on the corner were down and the toddlers at home were probably still napping. But clearly not everything was asleep. The smell of fresh dung rose into the air like a blast of scorched raisins.

Mala closed the gate behind her, lips pursed, placing the latch back on its rest with precision. She walked as quickly as she could to the end of the lane, looking straight ahead, trying to ignore the way the strap of the bag was cutting into her shoulder. There were no rickshaws at the corner. She would have to walk to the main road. Or she could wait here for a few minutes. On any other day perhaps, but not like this, not today with her bags.

On the other side of the junction, the last few children were getting off a minibus impatient to leave, its engine growling urgently. Two teachers conducted a hasty count of the checked pinafores and the pairs of grey shorts. A moment later, two of the boys decided that the time was right to move on and ran across the road towards Mala. Before the teachers had time to react, the rest of the group began to follow them. In no time, Mala was buffeted by a surge of small heads, clammy palms pushing at elbows, all around her hot breaths and stifled yelps. One child's chin ended up in Mala's hand, both looking at each other in amazement at this sudden contact. In a solitary world, bereft of clear signs, the slightest irregularity had to be interpreted as a lodestar, bright with significance. So what did it mean that she found herself so trapped that she could not even make it across to the main road, stranded in a pool of chattering children?

'Stop!' shouted one teacher from the other side of the road. 'Not another step!'

She came running across, stumbling over her *dupatta*, furious and terrified. The children froze.

The teacher grabbed hold of the arm of the first offender and smacked his leg.

'What did I tell you? What have I been telling you all day? What is wrong with you? This is your last warning. Do you hear me? If you do anything like this again, I will tie you to a coconut tree and leave you there all night for the rats and scorpions,' she shouted.

The boy's eyes grew marginally wider.

'Say sorry to Auntie. All of you, say sorry now,' she commanded.

'Sorry Auntie . . .' filled the air, dragged out into an undulating chorus.

'It's okay,' Mala managed to mumble.

'I am also very sorry, madam,' said the teacher. 'They are just impossible to control.'

'It's nothing.'

'Truly, I am sorry. Do you know what the time is please? Because of one of these apes, I broke my watch yesterday.'

'Yes, it's nearly four.'

The panic in Mala began to rise again.

'Thank you, madam. Okay everyone, in a line, two by two. Now!'

The children scrabbled to one side and began to order themselves.

'One more day is over and I am still alive. What else is there to say?' said the teacher as the group began to move off.

A few moments after they had gone, Mala replied: 'Nothing. Nothing more to say.'

Perhaps that was the sign.

She picked up her bags, crossed over towards the main road and hailed a passing rickshaw.

At the bottom of the slope leading down from Mysore Junction, a pipe had burst and water was spraying upwards, arcs of joy in the afterglow. A teenaged boy had wasted no time in taking advantage of this fortuitous state of events. As Janaki came down the slope, he stood with his back to her in his underwear, his hands soaping his back, lost in his lathery abstraction. There was something compelling about his insouciant pleasure that made her slow down to look at him as she walked past. He turned slightly and she could only just make out his face in the lilac light. His eyes were firmly shut and his cheeks sucked in as he let the jets hit his body, the soap running down into the ground in patchy streaks. Just as Janaki passed him, the boy opened his eyes. The expression in them changed. His lip curled up lewdly.

'What are you staring at? Want to join me, Auntie?' he asked.

Janaki stopped walking, her face devoid of intent.

'Yes, I'll join you. And then I'll cut your filthy tongue out of your mouth and put it in your hand.'

The boy's adolescent bravado shrivelled in the rime of Janaki's flat tone. Suddenly he was just an almost naked boy in a puddle of waste water. He looked down at his wet feet and then, almost as an afterthought, turned his back to Janaki again.

She continued walking and turned into the dense grid of tiny rooms. Curious glances bounced off her as she purposefully picked out her route. An occasional visitor to the area would not normally have been able to negotiate the rows with such ease. But Janaki's fury provided her with an adrenalin-fuelled clarity that brought to mind all the markers she needed to find Uma's room: the collapsed section of chain-link fence, the perennial stack of corrugated iron sheets and the yellow telephone box clamped to its pole.

Curls of smoke rose through the gaps between the walls and the roofs of several rooms; there was the punch of curry leaves and wafts of kerosene; a girl walked past carrying two eggs. Janaki had timed her visit carefully. She was sure Uma would be home by now. In another life, this had been the fabric of her friendly conversations with Uma, questions about her routine, her work, her life.

The industrial clatter from Mysore Junction rolled down the hill and melded in with the sound of an impromptu cricket match at the edge of the rubbish dump.

'Catch, catch, catch, catch, catch,' went up the chant.

There was a loud roar as the ball was caught.

Janaki turned into Uma's row. She was sure this was the one. In the first doorway, a woman was combing out her daughter's waist-length hair, winding a section around her fist and then determinedly dragging the teeth through the taut strands. The girl endured the ministrations with a scowl. The mother paused as Janaki stepped over the girl's outstretched legs and continued to walk down the row. The girl twisted around enquiringly to face her mother who simply shrugged and pushed her daughter's head back into position. There was a job to be done.

Janaki reached Uma's door and looked at the peeling blue paint. There was no lock on the outside latch. She listened for sounds of movement or conversation but could only hear the distant commotion of the train station and the shouts of the boys playing cricket. A baby began to cry in the neighbouring room.

Janaki knocked loudly on Uma's door. It was the rap of authority and onslaught. She waited but there was no answer. For a moment she thought she heard a draught of deeper silence emanate from the room, a breath held, a beat skipped. But she could not be sure.

She knocked again, even louder. Again there was a sense of a frozen instant on the other side of the door, a suspension of will.

Janaki knew that her rage was too much for an assessment of something so subtle.

'Open this door. *Dagaar munde*, I know you're there,' she shouted, her fist hammering against the wood.

She waited a moment.

'I said, open it.' Her voice broke.

Uma's neighbour Parvathi came out of the next room, her face pinched with apprehension, a baby almost slipping through her weak grasp.

'What's the matter?' she asked.

'Where is she?' Janaki asked. Her knocking did not stop.

Parvathi looked at the door anxiously.

'She is inside. She must be, there's no padlock here. And the door's locked from the inside. See?' Janaki gave the door a violent kick. She seemed to be talking to herself now.

A few heads had begun to peer through open doorways. A group of boys edged forward from the other end of the row, keeping their distance, but within earshot.

'I know you're there. Open this door.' Each of Janaki's words was accompanied by a smash.

An elderly man emerged from the room on the other side.

'What is going on?'

Janaki seized the hasp and began to shake it, slamming it against its staple.

'You must stop that, my child. What has happened?' asked the man, stepping forward.

Janaki looked at him. Sweat was stinging the corners of her eyes and running down her neck.

'She won't open the door. But she is inside. It's obvious that she's inside.'

'Why don't you come back tomorrow? Are you a relative?' he asked soothingly.

'No,' she hissed. 'I am nothing. She needs to open the door now.'

She gave the door another kick.

'No, no, please, this is not the way,' said the man, reaching out to stop her.

Janaki shrugged off his arm and pressed her whole body against the door, heaving at it with her hip. The veins in the wood shuddered, the jamb creaked, the whole frame shook, but the door remained locked.

A group had begun to form outside Uma's door, leaving just enough space around Janaki for the heat of her rage to tear into the ground.

'Is the woman inside sick? Has she fainted?' someone asked.

'Should we call a doctor?'

'I think it's this lunatic at the door that needs the doctor.'

Word had made its way to the owner of Uma's room, who lived a short distance away. There was a commotion, someone was trying to break into the room, there might be damage, a police case, a whole month of unnecessary hassle.

The landlord pushed through the group.

'What is this, madam? Why are you trying to break this door?' he demanded.

'What has it got to do with you?' Janaki asked.

'It is *my* door, it is *my* room, it is *my* business. Will your grandfather pay for the damage?' he shouted, primed for battle.

'Get out of the way,' she spat.

'Why do you need to get inside so urgently anyway?' asked the older man, trying to intercede.

'I need to speak to that whore inside and I will speak to her today no matter who tries to stop me,' she said.

'But why? What has she done?'

'When she has finished fucking your son, you can come and ask me what she has done,' said Janaki, wild-eyed.

'This woman is crazy. Someone take her away,' went up a cry.

'Don't you dare touch me,' screamed Janaki.

The crowd closed in and soon a whistle pierced through. A police constable was on his way.

'Let her taste the policeman's *lathi*. She'll remember her way home,' said a smirking boy.

Janaki managed to get a few more kicks at the door before she was edged away by the crowd towards the entrance of the row. There were more jeers, more appeals for calm. It was another half an hour or so before the constable managed to convince her to leave the area.

To those who had gathered outside, each blow on the door had seemed heavier than the last. To someone on the inside, each impact might have sounded like the head of an axe cleaving the wooden frame, a hinge shattering into fragments and the thud of thousands of splinters embedding themselves in every part of the room's walls and floor. It might even have sounded like the deafening blast of demolition, a structure being ripped from its foundations, setting off a series of seismic currents. Or maybe to someone on the inside it had all been curiously noiseless; maybe all that could really be heard was the sound of the deep hush that lay thick at the heart of any betrayal.

As Girish approached home, the muezzin's call to prayer echoed through the evening air. It was an invisible kite wavering on the breath of faith, a sound no longer heard so much as simply absorbed every evening. His footsteps were heavy, kicking up a little dust as he moved up the lane. He lifted the bolt, walked through the gate and noticed that no lights were on. Could Mala be asleep at this hour? He rang the bell, its fierce jangle alerting only him. He rang again, this time holding the button down. Irritation swamped him like a sudden rash, unseen welts of annoyance rising up. Where had she gone at this time when she should be packing? He fumbled in his jacket pocket for his keys, let himself into the darkness of the house and slipped off his shoes.

'Mala?' he called, turning on the light in the hallway.

'Mala?'

He walked into the bedroom and then the kitchen, still holding his shoes. He walked back into the bedroom, pressed the light switch and then opened the cupboard door. As he flung his shoes down, the other cupboard door swung open. Moving to close it, he stopped. It was nearly empty. Most of the clothes were gone. Had she packed already?

He looked up above the cupboards and saw that the smaller case was missing. So she had packed. But where had she gone? He looked for the case in the bedroom and then in the corridor and the sitting room. He walked back to Mala's cupboard and began to pull open the drawers. Most of them were bare.

There was a rush of comprehension.

He grabbed his keys and opened the locker at the back of the cupboard. As far as he could tell, the cash was undisturbed but Mala's jewellery was gone. He shut the locker door and returned to the sitting room.

The light from the hallway threw a pale arc across the floor, lending a spot of colour to the objects in the room: the collection of Air India Maharajas, the ceramic frogs in the glass-fronted cabinet, the waxy sofa. It was only when Girish turned towards the front door that he noticed the television. The screen was smashed all the way across, two almost parallel lines racing from one corner to another. In between these cracked tributaries, a black void took the form of a visceral wound, reflected minutely in his own dark iris.

CHAPTER NINE

When Mala arrived in Konnapur, it was late. Only the most wretched residents of the temple town were to be seen outside at that hour, along with one or two disorientated travellers. She managed to share a rickshaw with an elderly gentleman who was going her way. After she had paid her share, the rickshaw rumbled away, leaving her in the road with her bags. The moon was nearly new and there were no streetlights. The outline of her parents' house seemed to have been cut into the night's dark pelt.

She was worn out from the journey. The leisurely pace of the bus had made her restless but she had also dreaded arriving at her destination. At the halfway point there had been a halt and everyone but her had got off the bus to stretch their legs. Through the dust-coated window she had caught glimpses of a young girl feeding an infant on an upturned crate and a chicken being chased by an angry woman. The wait had seemed endless. Vendor after vendor pushed trays of fried snacks up at her window, making her move across to the aisle seat. A boy selling musical pens had boarded the bus and persisted in trying to make her buy one until the conductor returned. The driver had turned the engine on, the frame of the ancient bus shuddering with intent, and then just as suddenly turned it off again. Finally they had resumed their journey, a group of girls on the back seat singing '*Sare Jahan Se Achcha*' over and over again.

Their dissonant voices still rang in her head as she prepared herself to knock at the door, the chorus scratching at her tongue. The only other sounds she could hear were the hymns of the cicadas melded in with her own uneven breathing.

It was only after her second set of knocks that a light appeared in the front window. Minutes later Babu appeared at the door, his eyes puffy, the neck of his vest sagging indecently.

'Mala? At this time? What has happened?' he asked.

'I'm sorry I woke you up,' she said softly.

Babu caught sight of the bags and stared at them, as if they were more likely than his daughter to provide a sensible answer to his questions. Rukmini had also emerged into the dim light of the hall, her hair standing up in a series of fearful crests.

'Can we please talk in the morning? I promise I will tell you everything,' said Mala, her voice nearly severed with exhaustion.

The house returned to darkness and they all went to bed.

'She can't come running here every time they have a quarrel,' grumbled Babu, settling his hip into the familiar dip in the mattress, 'I'll tell her tomorrow.'

'You don't tell her anything, at least until we have found out what has happened,' snapped Rukmini, finding an outlet for the anxiety that had begun to well up in her breast.

'What is a life without compromise?' asked Babu, turning over to face the wall, and falling asleep immediately.

Rukmini shot him a dark look and locked her hands over her belly. She knew that the combination of worry and annoyance would keep her up for most of the night.

The next morning the three of them moved around the house like strangers at the scene of a calamity. Rukmini and Mala were excessively polite, smothered in a flurry of banal enquiries and reassurances. Babu remained silent, but his wordlessness had the quality of glue, oppressing the other two as it oozed over their efforts at normalcy. Just as Mala had steeled herself to begin some kind of a genuine conversation with her parents, there was a knock on the door. One of Babu's ex-colleagues and his wife were delivering invitations to their son's wedding. They were surprised, they said, and delighted that Mala was there too. Babu and Rukmini would have to ensure that she came with them to the wedding, if she planned to be in Konnapur. Rukmini laughed. Mala's plans changed all the time. How had she given birth to two such disorganised daughters?

After the visitors had left, the three sat down at the table. Before Mala said anything of significance she asked them for one thing only, that she be granted the concession of being allowed to tell them the whole truth. Once her account was given, she was prepared to collude in whatever connivance was required to placate the outside world. She had after all become an expert at dissimulation and deviation over the past few years. Whether what was required was an artful silence or a cunning pantomime, she was willing to participate, as long as her parents would grant her the grace of hearing what she had to say.

It was a festival day in Konnapur. Reedy drifts of *nadaswara* accompanied by solid drumbeats were approaching the temple, less than a couple of kilometres away. As Mala spoke, she had to stop from time to time as the noise engulfed her words. The procession was getting closer. A celebratory rattle descended around the figure of the deity, hoisted on the shoulders of several young men. Rukmini closed the windows and returned to the table. Babu continued to look at his hands, placed flat on the table's surface, as if to show that he too had nothing to hide. The barrage touched the walls of the house as it passed by. It forced its way into the room and tried to wolf down Mala's testimony. Finally, it moved away, sweeping its rhythm and quake to the foot of the temple's soaring tower.

❖   ❖   ❖

Those in charge of the beautification of the area around Tejasandra Lake had unspoken aims far greater than the mere spectacle of a festival. They were setting down a template for aspiration, new rules to govern public spaces, perhaps even changing the fabric of modern urban mores. In the name of the common good, the crude and the coarse had to be conquered and a ruthless grandeur imposed. The benefits would be self-evident to all the faithful who witnessed the celebrations at the edge of the lake. To the rest, invisibility would be graciously bequeathed.

The theme park farmers had been effaced from the public's consciousness with a brisk stroke. The news of the High Court decision had made front page news and all the major bulletins, of course. But then a membrane had seemed to knit over the wound even before it began to heal. The farmers were back on their land, the old fears flourishing again, as if they had never been assured of any kind of victory in the first place. Meanwhile the drone of topicality had settled over the latest corporate scam, cricketing disappointments and renewed party factionalism before inevitably moving on again. All over the country the curators of public interest knew that attention spans were short but appetites ravenous.

The pressure on the farmers was beginning to mount. Acres of sugar cane abutting the proposed HeritageLand site were found blazing mysteriously. Irrigation equipment was damaged in the middle of the night. A number of farmers were arrested on the basis of incomprehensible charges and refused bail. Intimidating representatives of a prominent land developer began to pay visits to some of the houses in the affected areas. A group of former activists were badly assaulted and abandoned in a gully. Wells were poisoned. Four young men who had set out on a pilgrimage, praying to see an end to the villages' troubles, never returned.

At the same time, a new movement had taken form. The definitive failure of Vasu and his colleagues meant the rise of something far more hostile, a combative ardour that moved around the periphery of the city like a silent cyclone. The aim of these farmers was to reclaim their visibility and retrace their faded outlines by taking their grievances, not to the palaces of justice, but to the boulevards of culture.

The eyes of the world would soon be on Mysore. They were determined that along with the dazzle of celebrity and the sheen of art, the world would be blinded by the flame of their protests along Tejasandra Lake.

This time they had taken close charge of all preparations. There would be no advance notice to the authorities and no opportunity for pre-emptive action. They would arrive in Mysore in batches, separate groups making their way to the Promenade at designated times for maximum impact. They knew what to carry and where to hide. Two vests, a thick flannel undershirt and wadded up plastic bags would provide a few layers of protection when the *lathis* began to strike. Chilli powder flung into the air as policemen approached would release a few seconds of valuable time. Scarves and monkey caps were essential to avoid identification on CCTV. Breathing through a wet cloth tied around the nose and mouth would help temper the violent sting of tear gas. Rubbing a rag soaked in vegetable oil on skin could help alleviate any burning sensation. Tear gas canisters were extremely hot and could only be picked up if hands were protected. If trying to escape pursuit, nails and sharp fragments of brick scattered in the road could puncture the tyres of police jeeps and motorbikes.

Vasu's brothers would return late at night in the week before the Lake Utsava, their hoarse whispers dying down as they un-rolled their bedding in the front room. In hardly any time their breathing would be heavy and even, filling every corner of the house. Facing away from them on the far side of the room, Vasu would be awake until the early hours, marking the passage of night with the beat of his right foot against the floor. He was not allowed to be privy to the preparations around him, but they were breaking his heart.

Mala's tale was different from other tales. Some of it was told that first morning but its full heft could only be conveyed in the refuge of long silences and the nuance of truths only partially exposed. Its substance came from her gradual disclosures and her irregular recollections. Rukmini was a patient woman and did not push Mala into giving her an immediate and complete account. Her questions were never unprompted and her observations fell gently into their laps, like down. She did, however, watch Mala constantly. As she prepared lunch, sinking her knuckles into the roll of dough, she would glance across at her daughter's moving shadow. When they knotted up plastic bags of vegetables from the market to put into the fridge, her gaze would settle on Mala's silent profile. In the evenings she would make sure she could hold Mala, reading on the back steps, steadily in her sight. She was not sure if Mala was aware of this vigil; she was barely aware of it herself. But at this time, it was all she could do.

Mala found herself once again in the room she used to share with her sister. Time dislocated itself. The crystal vase stood in the same corner of the windowsill, still waiting for fresh flowers to grace its narrow mouth. There was still a checked sheet on the bed, yellow and blue, or red and blue, tucked severely under the hard pillows. Some of Mala's old accounting textbooks were wrapped in plastic and laid on the bottom shelf of the cupboard. She had told her mother that she would not need them again but Rukmini had always been cautious. Time's fragments rushed at Mala. The temptation was intense: to step back through the glass, to reclaim her place in those settled images, to regress into the girl of whom nothing much had been expected. But she now knew far too much to return.

In the sitting room, the framed poster of Shakespearean quotes still hung above the television. She remembered the day the television had arrived. There had been countless adjustments of the antenna cable; even the polystyrene blocks had been discarded with the utmost care; in the first flush of ownership Rukmini had embroidered the letters 'TV' on the cloth that would keep the screen free of Konnapur's redoubtable dust clouds. The television had continued to be given its due respect and, in return, it played its part in the maintenance of propriety in the house, remaining decorously hidden under the cloth until six every evening. Rukmini considered the watching of television during daylight hours a slovenly and reckless pursuit, the province of alcoholics and slatterns.

In private, Rukmini and Babu turned Mala's situation over in their heads until they fell back, exhausted with heartache.

'We should tell the police,' said Babu to Rukmini.

'What is the point of telling the police now?' she asked.

'That bastard should be in jail.'

'How will that help her? And who will put Anand's brother in jail? Tell me that first of all.'

'Why didn't she tell us sooner? That is the thing I don't understand.'

'Me too. Something we did or said made her feel that she could not come to us. We can't even ask her what.'

Babu put his hand on her arm: 'But she is here now.'

Babu's powerlessness in the face of his daughter's experiences gradually ground down his spirit. He grew taciturn and his perennial ribbing of Rukmini ceased. He began to spend more and more time lying on his side in the bedroom, complaining of a series of aches. When he emerged from the room he would sometimes smile sadly at Mala, a plea for forgiveness perhaps.

'Is it because I am here? A married daughter back in her parents' house,' she asked Rukmini.

Rukmini raised her hand, a whisper away from her daughter's shoulder.

'No, it is because all this time we could not see your unhappiness. We were blind to what was happening to you. It's not because you are here. He has been changing over the last few years anyway, nothing to do with you or me. Maybe just age.'

Mala had noticed the change too. Babu had always been an instinctive raconteur, a man who could command an audience, who had a fine feeling for the pace and punch of his stories. Their veracity was irrelevant; the pleasure lay in their intoxicating rhythm as characters were cut down to size, myths expounded or absurdities laid bare. The chronicles seemed to have dried up now. The few traces that remained of his volubility centred on a very specific narrative: narrow, repetitive tales involving thwarted ambitions and intimate disappointments, a record of where his life had ended up. Mala could not help but be worried and looked to her mother for reassurance. Rukmini would merely sniff. She was not one to indulge such introspection; as far as she was concerned, he simply had too much time on his hands. The real worries were elsewhere.

One morning Mala sat on the back steps again, as she had done so many times cramming resolutely for each set of examinations. Even the early mist in this town seemed to be imbued with dust, the drifting palls taking on a tincture of the packed earth. It was all out in the open now. Her words, baked hard by utterance, had freed her. What had seemed impossible was suddenly all around her, at her feet, in her core. She had been married, she had spent three years with her husband and she had returned home. It was still so surprising to her: the menace of chance, the intensity of misery, the velocity of collapse, the wonder of egress.

She waited for the shame but it did not come. Her only concern now was to make sure that her parents did not torment themselves. To that end, she was prepared to go to any length. She knew Rukmini had been watching her constantly. Even now, she felt her mother's presence somewhere in the kitchen behind her. Mala would keep an eye on them too. She would step into any breach. She knew now that she could.

She smelt coffee and stood up to go inside. It was warming up and she took off her cardigan.

She would never see Girish again. It seemed incredible.

Susheela walked over to the fence separating her garden from the Bhaskars' side patio. Bhargavi was bent low with a broom in her hand, neat mounds of leaves swept up in various corners.

'Bhargavi, can you come here one second?' Susheela called over the fence.

'*Amma?*'

'This is the third day that Uma has not come to work. Do you know what has happened to her?'

'No, *amma*. I only know as much as you. Maybe she is sick.'

'But I have asked her to always phone, or ask one of the neighbours to phone, if something like that happens. And she has always done that in the past.'

'I was going to go over to her place today anyway. I will find out.'

'You know where she lives?'

'Yes, I have been there before.'

'Something must have happened. People don't just disappear like that. I simply don't understand it.'

'Don't worry, *amma*. I will find out today.'

'Oh, one more thing. Can you come and do a couple of hours for me after lunch? I have spoken to Mrs Bhaskar and she does not mind. This is the third day Uma has not come, you see.'

'Shall I check again inside?'

'I have already spoken to her but you can if you want. Can you come at two?'

'I can.'

'What a relief. I have told the *mali*; he'll let you in.'

Susheela returned to the house through the back door and surveyed the scene in the kitchen. She had done what she could over the last couple of days but the place was looking decidedly distressed. These things always happened at the most inconvenient times. Jaydev was coming over for dinner that night, and no doubt would find her weeping and dishevelled, presiding over pandemonium.

'Enough drama,' she said to herself aloud and began to go over her mental checklist.

The bone china crockery had not been used for a while so it would all have to be washed. The current whereabouts of the linen napkins was a mystery. She had most of the cooking still left to do and would have to go over her lists of ingredients again. Uma's continued absence had mangled all Susheela's systems.

The fairly absurd thing was that the peripheral details had all been accomplished in good time. The boy from the dry-cleaners had come yesterday with the curtains and had put them up. A handyman had been summoned to fix a listing shelf in the kitchen. She had asked him also to polish all the woodwork and get some-one to clean the downstairs windows. Then she had reorganised the photographs on the dresser and brought out a silver and coral Nepalese urn that had been languishing in the spare room. That morning she had cleared the magazine rack of weeks of detritus and replaced some of the cushion covers.

As she surveyed the room on her way back to the kitchen, she was acutely aware that they had never been inside each other's homes. He had no idea what hung on her walls, lined her shelves, lay on her coffee table. The idea that this evening would be one more modest step in their discovery of each other released a train of glee in her mind, a fact that would remain buried. There had been no sign of it when she had called Jaydev the day before to confirm the time and to enquire whether there was anything that he did not eat. Apparently he did not care much for beetroot but everything else was fine.

She had been brisk and businesslike: 'That's perfect then; see you tomorrow at eight.'

'You sound like you are inviting me for an interview,' he had responded.

'Mr Jaydev, I cannot help how I sound. Now if you don't mind, some of us have work to do.'

What he had not been able to see was her giddy smile.

As Susheela began to slice through some tomatoes, the doorbell rang.

'Not today,' Susheela muttered, walking to the door, her mind whipping through the possible identities of uninvited guests destined to introduce more turmoil into her day.

She leant into the spyhole and sighed. The distorted countenance of Vaidehi Ramachandra stared back at her, its rippled surface hardened against any alibis.

Susheela opened the door, easing a smile on to her face.

'Vaidehi, come in. What a surprise.'

Vaidehi wagged her finger. 'You may have forgotten your friends but your friends have not forgotten you.'

'Now, there's no need for all that,' said Susheela, wagging her finger back, desperately trying to predict how long this visit would last. The woman was too tiresome for words and the sight of her sari border, as always an unseemly two inches above her bloated ankles, only served to irritate Susheela further.

'I was in the area visiting my sister-in-law and it occurred to me that it has been so long since I even caught sight of you,' Vaidehi announced. She settled herself in the armchair, her gaze wandering about the room.

'So lovely, your place,' she said, with the tone of someone who had emerged after several years in a dank cave.

Susheela stared modestly down at the carpet.

'And how are *you?*' Vaidehi continued, still smiling. 'You seem well.'

'I am well,' said Susheela. 'Nothing to complain about.'

'Really?' asked Vaidehi, a little too quickly it seemed to Susheela. 'Well, if one can say that then what else does one need in life?'

Susheela was already beginning to tire of the oblique pronouncements. She neither knew nor cared why Vaidehi was here, although she suspected that it had something to do with that ridiculous pamphlet from all those months ago. She needed to chivvy along the proceedings.

'You'll have some coffee?' she asked.

'I'll never say no to your coffee,' said Vaidehi. Her eyebrows were raised in a delighted conspiracy.

Susheela could not bring herself to smile. She stood up.

'I'll just be two minutes,' she said, standing up and walking to the kitchen.

Vaidehi immediately followed her.

'Something smells delicious,' she said. Her voice had turned into a poisonous cant with an obvious intention to provoke. Susheela did not respond, spooning coffee into the filter.

Vaidehi walked over to the hob and peered into the pan.

'*Halwa,*' she crowed, as if a significant clue had fallen into her lap.

Susheela reached into the fridge for the milk.

'Special occasion?' asked Vaidehi. 'Sweets, all this preparation in the kitchen?'

'I just decided to make some *halwa*. My neighbours love it so I'm going to send some over later,' said Susheela, her voice tight with impatience. 'Come, let's go back and sit down. The coffee will be ready in a couple of minutes.'

'That's so thoughtful of you. I always say, we have to look out for each other because no one else will.'

Susheela was not sure whom Vaidehi counted in her team of responsible protectors. Her thoughts drifted to the tasks she had to finish before Bhargavi was due to arrive to clean the kitchen.

'So, I want to hear all your news,' said Vaidehi.

'Well, I don't really have much news,' said Susheela with a quick laugh. 'Children are both fine, I am fine, everything is going well. I think the coffee is done.'

Susheela went into the kitchen and emerged with one cup. In spite of her instincts for hospitality, she had decided not to risk cake or biscuits.

'You're not having any?' Vaidehi asked.

'No, I have just had some.'

Vaidehi took the cup and carefully lowered her top lip into it.

'Delicious, as always,' she said, her mouth a dangerous pantomime.

A silence settled over the pair. Vaidehi took another sip of coffee, still looking keenly at Susheela. Through the open windows they could hear the mid-morning birdsong nipping at the air.

Vaidehi put her coffee down and leant forward.

'The truth is, Susheela, I have come here to help you. To warn you.'

Susheela dragged her gaze to Vaidehi's merciless face.

'I don't understand. Warn me about what?'

'First of all, you must promise me that you will not think badly of me. I have come here with only good intentions. It is not easy for me to talk about this either.'

Susheela looked blank.

'So do you promise?'

Susheela nodded mechanically.

'People are talking,' said Vaidehi and leant back again, as if she did not intend to say anything more.

'Talking about what?'

Vaidehi lunged at the question.

'Talking about *you*. And your, I don't know what to say, your *friend* Mr Jaydev. They are saying all kinds of things. You are going everywhere together, behaving like senseless youngsters, these are the kinds of things.'

Susheela stared at Vaidehi.

'Like I said, I have come here as a friend because I think you should know these things, what they are saying. I have tried to defend you but you know how people think. The thing no one can understand is this: why *you* of all people should stoop to such things.'

Vaidehi paused as if she expected an answer but then continued.

'See here, of course it is not easy being a widow, everyone knows that. But you are from a good family, your husband has left you comfortably off, you have children with good jobs, you don't need to go chasing after a man with money. What will you do with more money?'

Susheela had grown pale but stayed silent.

'You have not gone mad, suddenly thinking you are eighteen again. So why should you be running around after an old man like this, making a fool of yourself? So what if he has that big Yadavagiri house? That is what everyone is asking, Susheela.'

Vaidehi picked up her cup and noisily swallowed the rest of the coffee.

'I am sorry to be the one to tell you this my dear, but you have become a laughing stock in this city.'

Vaidehi put the cup down squarely on the coaster.

'Yes,' she said, 'a laughing stock.'

The editor of the *Mysore Evening Sentinel* was adding the finishing touches to his comment for the next day's edition. When he completed an item that he found particularly insightful, his hooded eyes seemed to retreat further into his face. He read through the column one more time so that the conclusions would resound in his head as he drove home. The piece was intended as a wake-up call on climate change to the residents of Mysore. There was an urgent need to change lifestyles, adapt processes and harness new technologies. This would all take time, so in the interim readers were urged to purchase more eco-friendly products and reduce reliance on air conditioning when the weather began to change in a few weeks.

He emailed the final copy and prepared to leave the office. He would be home in time to have a rest, change into a smart suit and then make his way to the Anuraag Kalakshetra for the opening gala of the Mysore International Film Festival. Not only was it important for him to be seen at such events, this time he had a reserved second-row seat at the premiere. He had also just received news that one of the national dailies was looking for a deputy editor, a literary craftsman with a wealth of reporting experience and exposure to the frenetic tumult of major news stories. It had been a good year and, without a doubt, his time had come.

After Vaidehi had left, Susheela returned to the straight-backed chair where she had been sitting. The cup was where Vaidehi had left it, an ugly brown blot marking the side where it had made contact with her mouth.

She remained immobile for some time. At lunchtime the vegetable vendor went past, the familiar shout failing to penetrate her consciousness. Across the road, the Nachappa boy left the house on his motorbike and returned an hour later. The *mali*, sensing that he would not be found out, decided to take a nap in the shed.

The doorbell rang just as the downstairs clock struck three. Susheela knew it would be Bhargavi.

When she opened the door, she said, 'Sorry Bhargavi, there has been a change. Can you come tomorrow instead? I'll speak to Mrs Bhaskar later. Don't worry, I'll still pay you for today.'

'No, *amma*, you don't have to do that,' said Bhargavi and walked back towards the gates.

Susheela returned to her chair and watched her leave, before sitting quietly as before. Her gaze seemed to be following the border of the carpet, parallel lines of gold and brown, dusted with motes.

Eventually she stood up and went to the kitchen. Reaching for two plastic bags in the pantry, she lined one with the other. She then lifted the heavy pan off the hob, biting her lip with the effort, and emptied its contents into the plastic bags. The *halwa* made a sad slithering noise as it slipped over the sides of the pan. Susheela meticulously scraped the pan clean before soaking it in the sink. Tying the bags up in a double knot, she opened the back door and walked to the outside bin. She lifted its lid and dropped the bags inside. The *halwa* hit the bottom with a muffled blow, bloodless and final.

'Mr Jaydev? It's Susheela.'

'Yes, tell me.'

'I am so sorry to tell you this but I will have to cancel for tonight.'

'Oh no. Why, is everything all right?'

'I am so sorry for the short notice.'

'Has something happened?'

'Nothing has happened exactly but I really need to cancel. I hope that you will not be offended. I am so sorry.'

'But I am not following you, Susheelaji. I mean, all of a sudden?'

'Jaydevji, I don't know how to explain it to you but please try to understand. Sometimes events just overtake us and we have no control over such things. And then everything has to change.'

'But *what* has happened? You are just talking in riddles now.'

'Please Jaydevji.'

'Are you not feeling well?'

'You are not trying to understand me. Please, these matters are beyond our control. Surely you must be able to see that.'

A pause began to grow, the kind of dead air that could never be filled by breath or static.

'Well, as long as you are all right and there is no bad news.'

'No, there is no bad news.'

Another silence threatened to descend.

'Goodbye.'

Susheela hung up.

The opening gala of the first Mysore International Film Festival was a sensation. The Promenade had been transformed into the cynosure of contemporary culture. Not only had representatives of the national press descended on Tejasandra Lake, the festival had managed to attract some international media attention too. The beacons that had turned the Anuraag Kalakshetra into a dazzling alcázar were matched only by the celebrity wattage on the red carpet. Beyond the organisers' most outlandish prayers, stars from Bollywood, Tollywood, Kollywood, Mollywood and Sandalwood had made an appearance at the event, their respective entourages managing to overwhelm the local dignitaries, press corps and gathered fans. There were enchanting vignettes of previous junkets to Mysore, passionate endorsements of the treasures of the Lake Utsava and a general adoration of the circumstances that had brought them all together at last.

The members of the festival jury appeared delighted to be in each other's presence and were more than generous with their time and perspectives. The press were most keen to engage with the president of the jury, a director of heavy-handed comedies of errors who had been involved in a couple of infamous casting couch scandals in the eighties. Equally popular was his fellow judge, a cine queen of yesteryear who looked ravishing in an ivory lace confection. Her fans had eagerly followed her much publicised victory over an addiction to gin and prescription painkillers, and were now keen to see her in the flesh.

'Madam, you are a vision of beauty and grace!' shouted a photographer.

'Young man, I hope your girlfriend is not here,' she replied, her voice husky with her new medication.

The president of the jury made a charming speech on what could be achieved when disparate communities came together in an urban setting to build a cultural edifice that the rest of the world could only look on in envy. Faiza Jaleel emailed the first part of her report to the sub-editor in the office within minutes.

Representatives from the main sponsors were also keen to take advantage of the unique promotional opportunities. Their business cards were discreetly handed to photographers to ensure that their names and designations were noted correctly. As the constellations gazed benignly down on the lakeside proceedings, a number of quaint friendships were formed in the media glare: starlets and city corporation officials, minor socialites and the board members of the Mysore Tourism Authority, local captains of industry and the Chief Officer of Mysore Central Jail, Nuclear Thimma and everyone.

With the frenzied distractions on the red carpet and the blitz of jubilation on the Promenade, it was hardly surprising that the merits of the film that was screened that evening remained something of a mystery. Indeed, reports appeared on a couple of news channels setting out observations on two entirely different features. The organisers of the film festival, however, had their own yardstick by which to measure the gala's success, and by those norms, the opening was declared a triumph. It was the perfect launch pad for the inauguration of the Lake Utsava the following day.

Bhargavi looked at the string of mango leaves hanging across the door and the scattering of marigold petals on the ground. Someone else had definitely moved into the room. The door was padlocked.

She knocked on the neighbour's open door. Parvathi emerged from the room, wiping her hands on the front of her sari.

'Yes?'

'I was looking for Uma, your neighbour.'

'She has gone.'

'You mean, she has left this place?'

'Yes, gone completely. Some new couple is there now. They moved in yesterday.'

Parvathi turned to go back inside her room.

'One minute, one minute,' said Bhargavi. 'Do you know where she went?'

'Look, no one knows where she has gone. She just disappeared like a thief in the middle of the night. Didn't even tell the landlord. He had to break open the lock the next day and then saw that most of her things weren't there. What was left, I think he took.'

Parvathi's eyes narrowed as she looked at Bhargavi.

'Are you a relative?'

'No, I just needed to speak to her about something.'

Parvathi laughed weakly.

'Other women have been coming here to speak to her too.'

'But why did she just disappear like that?' asked Bhargavi. 'It makes no sense.'

'You really don't know?'

'No.'

A fight between children broke out in the room behind Parvathi.

'Look, I can't stand here and talk to you all day but ask anyone here and you will soon find out why.'

She disappeared into the darkness of the room.

Bhargavi looked again at the shreds of marigold lying on the damp earth, before moving away. She still walked with a slight limp even though it had been a few months since she had left hospital. It took her a few minutes to get to the next row where she knew some people. She had always been adept at soliciting information and this was an area where tales would be recounted all too readily.

Before long, she had to deal with a fairly full picture. There were accounts of endless trysts, numerous men visiting the room late at night, money that had changed hands, husbands lured to their ruin, furious wives hammering at the door, bottomless depravity, wrecked lives. Bhargavi knew that somewhere in the folds of the toxic hearsay there lay a seam of truth. It would take her one or two more days before she could run her fingers along its ragged joint.

The morning of the Lake Utsava saw a great deal of activity on the Promenade, even in the darkness of the early hours. Areas of scaffolding were removed at the last minute, some of the smaller stages were wheeled into place and loudspeaker systems were given a final test. Gate officials and festival stewards were instructed on the conduct of proceedings while sweepers moved around them in a prearranged formation. Lengths of cable maundered below stands and displays, eventually making their way towards banks of generators ranged in the roads that led off the Promenade. A few railings that had been forgotten were being painted in the dull glow of the streetlight above them.

The Lake Utsava was due to be formally opened by the Minister for Tourism at a short ceremony later that morning. The organisers had spent unconscionable hours poring over the precise seating arrangements in the inauguration marquee, anxiously appraising the relative importance of, among others, the Deputy Assistant Director of Mysore Zoo and the Acting Mayor's daughters. Chains of chrysanthemums would shortly be wound around any offending utilitarian space. The red carpet that had endured the media's coruscating affections the previous night had been moved to the VVIP section of the marquee. Venky Gowda's seat had been specially brought in from Bangalore.

By the time the sun's first beams began to lick at the waters of the lake, a sense of exhausted achievement had settled over the length of the Promenade. Authorised stallholders were now free to set up the expositions and the organisers were conducting their final checks in the festival zone. In a few hours the dignitaries would be garlanded, the ribbon cut, the plaque unveiled and eager arms raised in elation. The morning's frosted light bounced off the steel and glass lattice that covered the Museum of Folklore and tumbled over the miles of silver bunting that stretched out in every direction. The scene was set for the city's most high-profile public celebrations in recent memory.

They had run out of most of the daily specials at the Vishram Coffee House. The waiters, through habit, reeled off the lunchtime treats and stood by the tables, practically daring the patrons to attempt to order one of them. Even though the peak rush had come and gone, the din was intense. A table for two was quickly swabbed with a wet rag and the two bank officials sat down, both sighing heavily.

'For what reason do they bother to tell you about these damn lunchtime specials if they never have them in the first place?' complained the senior bank official.

His junior colleague was sympathetic.

'It is typical behaviour, sir. That is why the country is in this state,' he said sadly.

The two men put in their order and stared for a moment at the frenzied loops left on the table by the wet rag.

'Sir, did you watch that programme last night?' asked the junior official.

'Which programme?'

'About the Chinese.'

'Which Chinese?'

'Sir, it was a programme about these Chinese people in China. They are running schools where small, small children are learning Hindi. So nicely they were speaking, sir, even better than children here.'

'Chinese children learning Hindi?'

'I promise, sir, you will not believe. They were having conversations, so clear it was. Standing in a line, all smart and very good discipline. But one thing I could not follow, sir, for what reason Hindi? English, Spanish or German, I can understand. But Hindi, sir?'

'It is because by the time they invade us, these children will have grown up and then they will be able to order us around in Hindi.'

'Sir, they must know we don't all speak Hindi, no?'

'What difference does it make to clean their shoes, whether they tell us in Hindi or Chinese or Kannada?'

'That is true, sir. We need to be very careful but our government is doing nothing about this danger. One day they will just walk across the border and we will all be sitting here waiting.'

'As usual.'

'Sir, you know, the Chinese language is called Mandarin.'

'You duffer. The Chinese language is called Chinese. Mandarin is the capital of some province. In the south, I think.'

Their lunches arrived, the food so hot that the junior official's glasses steamed up. Conversation was minimal while the two men ate, their concentration all-consuming. A beggar who had made his way into the restaurant was chased out and given a stern warning by the owner. At the adjacent table, a man let out a long, satisfied belch, his crash helmet still in his lap.

The bank officials had just finished eating when a tall man knocked against their table, on his way out. The senior bank official knew him so they exchanged a few pleasantries before the man left.

'Sir, who was that?'

'Just someone I know through my cousin. Can't even remember his name. What is happening to my memory?'

'Sir, I have always felt you have an excellent memory.'

'Anyway, he is G S Anand's brother.'

'The advertising man?'

'Yes.'

'If he is G S Anand's brother, why is he eating here, sir?'

'How should I know? Do you think G S Anand has nothing better to do than to feed all his family members every day?'

'Sorry, sir.'

'This fellow, it's a sad story. He is separated from his wife.'

'Sir, this separation is becoming very common now, even in our culture.'

'They say the girl's family cheated him into the marriage. She had lots of mental problems, which they managed to hide and then dumped her on to him. He only came to know after the marriage. One day she started to behave very weirdly.'

'Really, sir? What was she doing?'

'I don't know the details but they say she was very disturbed. I think she was smashing all the furniture and the TV at one point.'

'*Ayyo, howda*, sir? Who told you this?'

'My cousin is known to his family. They told him just the other day. So this Girish, that is his name, tried to manage the situation for quite some time but it was too much. He had to send her back to her family. How can he look after a mental patient?'

'It is too much, sir, the kind of cheating that goes on these days.'

'That's what. Poor fellow, you just never know sometimes what can happen.'

The man at the next table stood up and looked around the restaurant.

'Hey, is that TV not working?' he asked one of the waiters.

'If you want to watch TV, sir, you better stay at home.'

'No, no,' said the man looking irritated, 'there is something happening at the lake, some trouble, the police have arrested lots of people.'

'What's happened?' asked someone else.

The questions became louder and more insistent in the Vishram Coffee House as news of violence at the Promenade spread. Conjecture and fabrication were pumped into the stale air of the room as diners called up friends and listened to the waiters bringing news from the street. The man from the next table had rushed off to find out more, leaving behind the helmet he had so carefully tended over the course of his meal.

The two officials paid the bill and left the restaurant. It was time for them to head back to work, but their walk down the street was unhurried. They peered into shop windows and the interiors of restaurants, looking for a television. On a day like this, it would not hurt to be a little late.

Rukmini's visitors stared at the ground. It was one of many lulls in the conversation. They had looked at Mala once during the entire period and given her a frozen smile, a single accusation at its heart. They had come there as if nothing had happened. But they had also decided that they already knew about what had happened.

Rukmini raged under her composed exterior. If they would only say something, she would counter it. She would smash her hands against her temples and say it was not her daughter's fault. Dragging them to where Mala was sitting, she would describe, with great care, every single brutalising experience of which she had knowledge. She would demand that they imagine all the others that had remained sequestered. She would rip each imputation from their guts and tear it to shreds in her lap.

The lull continued. Gazes shifted, there was a dry cough, a hand beat time lightly against a cushion. Then they stood up to leave, and after that they were gone.

Rukmini's jaws were set tightly together as she picked up the used coffee *lotas*.

Babu emerged from the bedroom where he had been waiting for the visitors to leave.

'I just heard on the radio,' he said, 'there have been riots in Mysore.'

'What?' she asked, straightening up.

'Mala, turn the TV on,' he said.

Rukmini's daytime prohibition was overturned and the room was filled with the noise of gunfire and sirens.

The *ayah* was frantic. Her sister had called her to ask her if she had heard about the trouble at the festival. Not knowing what to do, she had turned on the television, a liberty she would never have allowed herself under normal circumstances. The first sight she saw was a man being helped to a makeshift shelter under a sheet of tarpaulin. His head seemed to have split at the top, his hands helplessly trying to stop the blood flowing into his eyes. The *ayah* made sure Shruthi was upstairs playing and then called Lavanya's mobile. It rang but there was no answer. She then called Anand. A message told her that the network was busy and asked her to try again a short while later.

She knew that Anand and Lavanya had been at the opening ceremony of the festival. Lavanya had called her for a quick check just as they were being seated for the inauguration speech. That was four, maybe five hours ago. She tried both numbers again but she could not get through. The words 'Riots at Mysore Festival' flashed repeatedly on the screen. The reporter managed to convey the sense of panic and chaos at the scene but provided no information on what had actually happened.

She called her sister, who passed on some more news from a friend who had managed to return from one of the roads near the lake. Apparently, one of the buildings on the Promenade was ablaze, possibly the big shopping centre. She did not know if there had been a bomb blast but there was definitely a fire in the area.

The *ayah* went upstairs again to check on Shruthi. When she came back downstairs, the screen showed a clear shot of the northern end of the Promenade. Fumes were drifting across the road, over the rocks at the water's edge and blowing out over the lake The ashen sweep made it difficult to see where the wings of smoke ended and where the water began. She switched off the television in case Shruthi wandered down for some reason. In a couple of minutes she would try the phones again.

All three televisions were on at the Bhaskars' home, each tuned in to a different news channel. Bhargavi stood in the hallway looking at the huge screen in the sitting room. Mr Bhaskar was standing to one side, eyebrows angrily knitted. The camera seemed to be focusing on a deserted building while a male voice exclaimed in the background. She could not make out his words and did not understand the significance of the office block. It did not even look like it was anywhere near the lake.

She crept upstairs and stood outside the older son's room. On his television a reporter was pointing to a police barricade where uniformed guards were milling around a jeep. In a few moments, a distinguished looking officer began to speak to the press, his tone grave and deliberate. He would not pretend that the crisis was completely under control, but the law enforcement authorities were taking all necessary steps to prevent an escalation of the situation. It was important that members of the public were made aware that the violence was attributable only to a few senseless individuals who were determined to indulge in criminal and anti-national activities in order to undermine Mysore's reputation for peace and harmony. They would be dealt with swiftly, in accordance with the law, to ensure that the city returned to normal as soon as possible. The officer turned his back on the ensuing volley of questions and walked quickly towards a waiting car.

Bhargavi watched as the camera returned to the Promenade, displaying the bleakly prosaic configuration of defiance. Rocks and bricks curved through the air on their implacable trajectory. A fire blazed in the distance. The contours of the retreating protestors shifted as the arrangement of helmets, shields and body armour moved forward in a sudden spurt. The scene shook violently and then returned to the placid surface of the lake again.

Bhargavi sat down on the floor, her eyes pinched in concentration. The images she was seeing did not fully accord with the haunting presence in her head, the repeated appearance of a dark woman in a yellow sari, her unruly hair twisted into a braid, holding all her belongings as she navigated her way through a city of smoke and screams.

At the Mysore Regency Hotel an emergency meeting of the Contingency Plan Committee was drawing to a close. It had been decided that security would be increased all around the perimeter of the hotel grounds and that extra precautions would be taken at the gates. Text messages would be sent to all hotel guests informing them of the trouble in the city and advising them to stay in the hotel. Hospitality managers would also be in charge of providing periodic updates on the situation to everyone at the hotel. Extra supplies of food, bottled water and diesel were being delivered and the stockpile of emergency torches and blankets would be checked immediately. Senior members of staff were briefed on their roles in case of every eventuality, from a bomb blast in the hotel vicinity to an armed attack by insurgents. The liaison officers in charge of communication with all relevant emergency services also swung into action. Personnel trained in first-aid procedures were dispatched to report on the status of medical supplies. Floor plans of the hotel were photocopied but would not be distributed yet. There was a delicate balance that needed to be maintained between precaution and panic.

Susheela called her younger daughter.

'Prema, it's me.'

'Hi *amma*, how come you're calling at this time? Everything all right?'

'Yes, everything's fine. Actually, not everything. I'm fine but I thought you might have seen online or something that there has been a lot of trouble in Mysore.'

'Really? No, I didn't know. What's been happening?'

'There have been riots by the lake and explosions and God only knows what.'

'What?'

'On the TV they are saying that it is those farmers again, although no one is sure about anything. They went there to ruin that lake festival and the police responded and now things are just terrible. They say some people have died. And there are flames coming from some of the buildings on the Promenade.'

'Are you serious?'

'It's all they are showing on every channel. It's truly terrible. I don't know what is happening to this city. Such strange things seem to be going on. First, Uma disappears without a trace. There's been no news from her. Just like that, she has left town, it seems, without even a word. These people, after all you do for them, sometimes it really makes you wonder. And then, well, then this happens.'

'*Amma*, one second, this will get very expensive for you. I'll just call you back.'

Susheela continued to describe the bewildering images that flashed and froze on screen. There was nothing new to say after a while but they stayed on the phone, both knowing the precise nature of the comfort that was needed.

'Okay, I'd better leave you now,' said Susheela.

'No, it's fine. I am not doing anything anyway.'

'But this call will be costing you a lot.'

'No, it won't. There's no need for you to go anywhere if you don't want to.'

Susheela asked Prema a couple of half-hearted questions about her teaching before a curious tremor crept into her voice.

'*Amma*, is there something else wrong?'

'No, no. I think it's just when you see all this destruction and madness in your city, it's very shocking, you know.'

'Yes, but you're sure there's nothing else, no?'

Susheela experienced a desperate desire to unburden herself, a vigorous jolt to her carefully maintained hoard of experiences and impulses. The quiet concern in Prema's voice had in a moment bored through the hard surfaces of that private vault.

'I don't really know how to tell you.'

'Is it something serious?'

'No. That's the stupid thing. It's not serious at all. But it's the only thing I have been able to think about.'

Susheela's anxieties were ripe for revelation. Her account unfolded slowly, full but measured. She mentioned the day that she had been stranded in the city, an incident she had never discussed; she spoke of the unexpected meeting at the Erskine Club and the dinner by the lake; she revealed the sudden pleasure of the lengthy phone calls that surfaced in her life by stealth; she told the story of the first time they had ventured out, feeling audacious in the quiet streets of Mysore; she acknowledged the significance of each subsequent encounter; she explained that she had woken up to the possibilities of a new friendship. She told it all. Finally, she described Vaidehi's visit and her own reaction to it.

'Oh my God. I don't know what to say,' said Prema.

'Maybe it was not fair of me, to tell you this all of a sudden.'

'Of course you should tell me. I am glad you told me. So, after that woman came to your house, you didn't tell him about what happened?'

'No. How could I? It was too awful.'

'But have you spoken to him since the day he was supposed to come over for dinner?'

Susheela paused.

'No. I did call him once more but I was very relieved that he was not there. There was only his answering machine. I left him a message saying that we could not meet again as it was very difficult and I hoped that he understood.'

'That's all?'

'I don't know. What more can you say to a machine?'

'You didn't even try to talk to him after that?'

'No. I know that it was very bad of me but I just reacted to what was happening.'

Neither of them spoke for a few seconds.

'You have no idea, living abroad, what it's like for someone like me here,' said Susheela, her voice becoming louder. 'What people are like here, the judgments they make, what they think, what they say. You have no idea.'

'I know what it was like when she came to see you and I can understand that you were in shock. But you must at least talk to him and explain what happened. How hurt must he be feeling, *amma*? Beyond that, I am not going to tell you what I think you should do. If you can't continue this friendship and ignore vicious people like that Vaidehi, that is up to you. You are the one who has to live there. But you must at least talk to him once more to explain. Don't you think so?'

'Yes,' said Susheela, 'you're right. You are more than right. That is what I need to do.'

It was difficult to form an accurate judgment of the gravity of the disruption at the lake shore and the scale of the state's response.

Teams of riot police were witnessed streaming into the area but unconfirmed reports stated that Karnataka State Reserve Police personnel had also been mobilised to bring the situation under control. There was talk of special counter-insurgency battalions, Central Reserve Police Force commandos and even the National Security Guard. A well-connected source told one news channel that COBRA units were on their way to Mysore. The airwaves were overloaded with the lethal sparks sent out by special militias, auxiliary paramilitary forces and elite combat squads.

Accounts of the perpetrators of the violence varied enormously too. It was by turns called a terrorist operation, a Naxalite uprising, a Maoist insurrection, a separatist agitation and a communal riot. Fingers were pointed at al-Qaeda, home-grown terror cells, the ISI, hostile neighbours, fanatics, anarchists, radicals, militants and fundamentalists. Borders had not been secured, intelligence had not been collated, leads had not been followed, signs had not been read, lessons had simply not been learnt.

To eyes hardened by the relentless images of the information age, the scene at the Promenade bore the banality of catastrophe. Armed guards stood at all the approach roads, the skeletons of destroyed cars framing the scene. The entire area was sealed off and a curfew in place. Shattered glass was strewn across the steps of buildings and over the wide pavement opposite the lake. Blood streaked the wall and railings that formed part of the flood defences. Hundreds of shoes and *chappals* covered the newly tarred road in both directions. Smouldering tyres blocked some of the side roads. Half a mile away, the shell of an incinerated bus directed its macabre gaze towards what was left of a giant hoarding for the Lake Utsava. The silver bunting had been torched and had drifted to the ground as fine, feathery ash.

The Tejasandra Galleria had not, as reported, been set ablaze. The smoke that had turned the sky above the lake into a dark, distended belly had come from the unprotected stocks of diesel, struck by a flaming missile. But the Galleria had not escaped unharmed. Every ground floor window was smashed; rubber bullets and tear gas canisters had found their way into the atrium and art gallery; a police barrier had been hurled at the glass lift; there was blood on the moulded pillars that soared towards the upper loggia. Fittings had been ripped from carefully papered walls and furniture smashed against the floor of the marble foyer. Merchandise was ruined, trailing in dirt or wrapped around marquee poles and lamp posts. Undressed mannequins had been flung over the lake wall: a few lay mutilated on the rocks, more floated in the water, arms raised towards the heavens, their humiliation complete.

The Museum of Folklore was shrouded in soot. Inside the Anuraag Kalakshetra, axes and machetes lay at the foot of the winding staircase. Debris covered the stage in the auditorium and the seats had been systematically slashed, their innards weeping onto the floor. Opposite the entrance to the building, the frame of the specially commissioned fountain was dented and shamed, its basin filled with rocks and broken bottles. Further along the Promenade, at the foot of the ramp designed for the vintage car display, there lay ten dead bodies, their necks impossibly twisted, a final tribute to the city's special day.

Susheela's thoughts had not strayed far from her conversation with Prema. It was definitely the right thing to do. She called Jaydev.

A strange voice answered the phone.

'Is Mr Jaydev there?'

'No madam, he has gone out of station.'

'All of a sudden?'

'He went yesterday only.'

'And you are?'

'Caretaker, madam.'

'Can you tell me, where has he gone?'

'To America, his son's place, madam.'

There was a pause.

'Madam?'

'Do you have any idea when he will be back?'

'He said he was going for about three months, madam. Maybe four, but he will phone to let me know.'

'I see. Thank you.'

'I can give you his son's phone number in America, madam, if it is urgent.'

'No, thank you, it is not urgent.'

'Okay then, any other message madam?'

'No, no message.'

Susheela hung up and tried to work out a few dates. But her mind did not seem to be functioning properly. She kept starting all over again on this simple calculation. The man had said that Jaydev would be back in three or four months. She supposed it could be longer than that. There really was no way of telling.

She turned and walked towards the windows. The shadows were lengthening across the lawn, long bodies with eerie heads stretching towards the house. The dahlias, stubbornly blooming beyond their season, seemed strange and forbidding in that half-light, their faces purple with venom. On the other side of the lawn, creatures seemed to be moving in the upper reaches of the jackfruit tree, alert to the workings of her mind. The world outside was united in judgment: the bougainvillea glowered at her through the kinks in its boughs; a dark nebula descended over the garden, angrily screening off the coral sky; the rose bushes looked bitter and defeated. The windows were still open and the dusk's chilly breath began to invade the room. Susheela continued to stand motionless, watching the night draw in completely. The shift did not take long. It was what she imagined the final vestiges of sight to be, as it faded into blindness.

EPILOGUE

Mala and Rukmini sat in front of the television, neither of them paying any attention to it. On screen the anchor for a talent show took off his jacket and began to dance in front of the judges, keen to show that despite his training at one of the country's best drama schools, he was still grounded enough to participate in the rough and tumble of popular entertainment. Rukmini was in a state of near slumber, her head gently swaying and her glasses marooned over her forehead, stranded in the course of a half-performed intention to go to bed. Mala was putting together Babu's medication for the next day, his tablets for hypertension, diabetes and cholesterol placed in rows on her lap. He was getting ready to go to bed, stating that he had a stomach ache.

'It didn't seem to affect your appetite at dinner,' Rukmini commented, with a glance at Mala.

'It won't help my stomach if I starve to death,' he responded crossly, before leaving the room. There the cupboard door was noisily opened and closed a couple of times and a pillow shaken against the mattress. This was followed by an overwrought coughing fit.

'Every month he becomes more and more like a child,' Rukmini said, with a sigh. 'I thought after bringing you two up my work was done, but look, it's started all over again.'

The bedroom door was now firmly closed. Mala looked at Rukmini and smiled. Her mother's mouth had lolled open and her eyes were rolling back into her head. She now looked like an old souse, after a particularly lively night out.

Mala gently shook her awake.

'You had better go to bed. You are starting to look like someone who has had too much *arrack*,' she said.

'*Chee*,' said Rukmini, sliding her glasses back on to her nose.

The talent show had come to an end. A special programme began on the need for civilian activism on social and environmental issues. There was going to be a panel discussion on how communities could come together to ensure better urban governance, taking into account all strata of society. The panel guests were introduced: the state's Minister for Law, Justice, Human Rights, Parliamentary Affairs, Municipal Strategy and Social Welfare; a spokesperson for the opposition; a renowned cultural commentator; an eminent print journalist and Mr G S Anand, CEO of Exospace Media Ltd and head of the recently formed Taskforce for Civic Harmony.

Anand's face looked wider on television, his teeth whiter, his skin paler. He smiled with authority and ease, a man who dealt out charming sound bites like cards falling from the hands of a casino croupier. Rukmini threw an anxious glance at Mala who was looking at the screen, her face inscrutable. Suddenly Rukmini was struck by how very young she looked, in spite of everything.

'You cannot stand in the way of progress and expect not to be crushed,' said Anand, in response to a question from the show's host. 'The smart thing to do is to stop obstructing the vehicle and get on board.'

Mala watched Anand's hands fan out as he emphasised his key points. She was astounded that she was related to this man; she had been in the habit of visiting his house two or three times a month; she had listened to his wife talk about her household arrangements on scores of occasions; she knew what was in their dining room dresser, where their bread came from and how often they had back massages. It was through his good offices that she had secured a job and on his wife's advice that she had begun to experiment with make-up. Tonight she was watching Anand interact with learned experts, as she sat on the cane sofa in her parents' tiny house, a row of her father's tablets still in her lap. At first, there may have been an altered cadence in one of the chambers of her heart; her head may have felt slightly lighter; she may have felt a hurried breath at the back of her neck. But there was nothing more than that now. She could concentrate again on what they were saying, as if she had spent the last few years watching the programme every week, seated here with her mother.

'I would like Mr Anand to explain how he expects people to support policies that take away their livelihood in exchange for empty promises,' said the opposition spokesman.

'And I would like the honourable gentleman to explain why he supports criminal upheaval, wilful destruction of property and savage attacks on law-abiding citizens in the name of some romantic notion of rural idealism,' shot back Anand, his face still comfortable, still charming.

He was gazing candidly at the camera now, directly at Mala, straight into the heart of her home. Looking into his eyes was like seeing a once familiar hillside denuded and devoured, trans- formed into a sweep of concrete and glass, bearing only a fleeting impression of what was once known.

'I didn't know he appears on TV,' said Rukmini, still anxious.

'I didn't know either,' said Mala.

Rukmini stole another look at her daughter.

'Enough of this,' she complained. 'These people only know how to talk. As if braying on TV like a donkey will solve anything. Why don't you change the channel?'

Mala switched to a nature programme that showed a boat gliding over the waters of a dark river, penetrating into the depths of a jungle.

'Ambika told me that you had said that you were all going on a trip to Thailand, paid for by Anand,' said Rukmini, her eyes on the boat as it coasted past dense undergrowth.

'I just said that. It wasn't true.'

'I know.'

They turned to look at each other, both smiling.

'She has been grumbling to me that you won't talk to her about any of this,' said Rukmini.

'So what did you say?'

'I said that she should stop pestering you and that you will talk about it when you want to.'

Mala did not respond. She put Babu's pills into an envelope and placed it on the coffee table.

Rukmini leant forward and gripped Mala's hand, covering it with both of hers: a hot, tight embrace that tried to seal off the past. Neither of them spoke.

As suddenly as Rukmini had taken her hand, she let it drop.

'I must go to bed now,' she said.

She stretched, yawning loudly.

'Look at me, sitting here till God knows what time, as if I haven't got to wake up in the morning. You'll switch everything off?'

Mala nodded.

'And don't forget to lock the front door.'

Mala nodded again. Rukmini took off her glasses, gathered up the folds of her wayward sari and walked slowly to the bedroom. The door shut quietly.

Mala turned the volume down and continued to look at the screen. A man's hand was holding up a tiny insect, its glossy shell like a precious stone cut out of the centre of the earth. Its spindly legs waved and glinted in the background, as it tried to climb up the man's smooth palm.

Behind her a window banged against its pane, and a few seconds later, she thought she could hear rain. She turned off the television, walked to the front door and pulled it open. The gabbling in the darkness was layered over the silence of night in a small town. The temple's tower rose up in the distance, its edges streaked with snatches of moonlight. Lifting her head towards the sky, she held out her arm. There were no actual droplets. She could make out the loamy smell of rain and hear its rush building somewhere over the trembling rooftops. The world twisted into the shape of a teardrop, its gasps seeming ever closer. But still nothing fell from the skies. Perhaps it was just the wind changing direction.

ACKNOWLEDGEMENTS

My thanks to the many friends and well-wishers who have been so generous with their support right from the start.

I am particularly grateful to Richard L MacDonald for reading the first draft and for support that goes back a very long time; to Jeri O'Donnell and Asha Rao who read and commented on an early draft; to Shashikiran Kolar for crucial website and photographic assistance; to Michael McMullen for unwavering encouragement; and to Arshia Sattar for many kindnesses, including her comments on parts of the manuscript.

I am grateful to Tara Gladden for her careful editing, Antony Gray for the typesetting, Jacqui Lewis for proofreading the text, Jon Gray for designing the perfect cover, Angela Martin for publicising the novel and Karen Maine at Daunt Books for all her editorial assistance.

All my thanks to my agent and friend Priya Doraswamy for her helpful advice and her faith in the book.

A special thank you to Natasha Lee for coming to the rescue when it was most required.

I am indebted to Laura Macaulay at Daunt Books for giving the book a home and for opening so many doors. Her careful work on the manuscript has been invaluable.

I owe an immeasurable debt to K J Orr for words, edits, counsel, insight, laughs and so much more.

And finally, my deep gratitude to my parents and my sister Mamta for a lifetime's love and support.